SECRET SPARK

VECTOR CITY SUPERS
BOOK 1

KELLY FARMER

For all the other weirdos who watch superhero movies and worry about what happens to the people and businesses that get destroyed during those big action fight scenes.
I wrote this book for us.

CONTENT NOTES

This is a fun, fairly lighthearted story with on-page sex. There is a nonviolent kidnapping, a lot of lying, references to family estrangement (not related to sexuality or gender), and people with superpowers mostly using them against each other, but occasionally on regular humans. One of them does mind control. Please read with care, and enjoy!

CHAPTER 1

Sadie readjusted her bouncy red ponytail to prep for closing time cleaning. Another few minutes and she could politely inform the woman and man typing away at a corner table that Vector City Coffee closed at ten.

Her feet hurt, which wasn't her fault. These cute purple Mary Janes had insoles from the drugstore down the street. Pounding concrete sidewalks on her commute and standing all day behind the counter was simply a tiring thing to do. Blaming cute shoes was like arguing with that vindictive pigeon who pooped on her apartment balcony every day: a big waste of time.

Besides, the shoes went perfectly with her bright blue cigarette pants and matching sleeveless top. It would've been a disservice to the outfit *not* to wear them, even though said outfit was covered by her drab gray work apron.

The energy of a warm summer night permeated the coffee shop. Most of the drinks she'd made that day had been iced, which was fine. It was a good lazy Sunday for iced coffee or tea. It just didn't allow her to craft fun designs on top of a hot cappuccino.

The open, airy vibe of Vector City Coffee and white-and-gray décor telegraphed cold drinks, cold sandwiches, muffins that were not fresh from the oven. The moody indie music and stiff metal chairs made you feel more like sitting at attention than relaxing.

All things Sadie would change.

Her heartbeat doubled as visions of her dream café played about her head. Warm, cozy, inviting. Wooden tables, comfortable chairs, a couch or two. And color. And a jukebox if she could find (and afford) one. It'd be stocked with oldies and real old oldies and random pop songs from the past few decades. Whatever struck her fancy, because it'd be *hers*.

She slid the glass door on the back of the display case to start gathering the unsold pastries. A boom sounded outside. Then a second one, louder and closer. A huge burst of unnatural wind stirred dust and garbage along Bromley Street.

The intensity picked up. Several bolts of small, contained lightning flashed across the street.

"Not again," Sadie groaned, shielding her eyes.

One of the wide front windows shattered as a large lump of a man crashed through it. The coffeehouse vibrated from the impact.

He sat up fairly quickly. Brushed bits of glass off his skintight black spandex. His face was masked other than eyeholes and a space for his nose and mouth.

He stood, stamping more glass off his massive frame. No mistaking which Superhero with that body. It was Lunk. Tremendous strength packed every bulging muscle.

Amit came running out of the back, untied apron flapping around him. Utter disbelief made the manager's brown eyes grow comically huge.

Lunk looked around, met Sadie's gaze, then gave a small shrug. "Sorry," he said in a deep timbre.

"Aw, come on!" Amit all but shrieked.

A lithe figure in black and crimson ran past the newly created hole, laughing loudly. Her long, dark hair bounced with every step. Oh, no. *Spark.*

Two more Villains quickly crossed the street—Ice in his black getup striped with dark blue, Breeze in his charcoal-gray outfit. Ice shot a spray of snow at Lunk's face on his way by.

Lunk frowned, then charged through the broken glass and back out to protect the citizens of Vector City.

Catch dropped to the sidewalk from above. Hooray! Catch was here! Looking commanding and protective in head-to-toe navy blue. She followed in hot pursuit.

Sadie's heart soared as she leaned over the counter to catch one last glimpse of her Superhero crush. "Go get 'em, Catch."

"I don't believe this." Amit stomped over to the accident site. "That's the third time this year. What are these dumbasses doing?"

"Last time, it was one of the bad guys," Sadie said.

"Yeah, who got thrown through the door by Flight." Her boss kicked at a large chunk of glass.

Sadie picked up the cordless phone. It'd been smart to add the twenty-four-hour emergency board-up company to their speed dial.

The man and woman at the corner table went back to typing.

Amit grumbled and groused as he snagged the phone from her. "Why couldn't it have been one of the others? Why'd it have to be the biggest frickin' Super the city's ever had?"

Sadie nodded in agreement.

"Flight crashes through tall buildings, since he flies around. Race is too fast to get caught."

"Catch absorbs energy, so she doesn't cause too much damage," Sadie pointed out.

"Yes, she does." Amit shook his head. "They all do."

She bit back a retort in defense of her heroes. Particularly Catch. "It's not the Supers we have to worry about. It's the Villains. The ones who shoot fire and ice and mess with your head."

Amit harrumphed and got on the phone. Sadie headed to the utility closet. There had been wind and electricity outside—most likely the work of Breeze and Volt. Which meant Hide could be lurking about. Hard to tell with someone who got all invisible. The Villains loved sneaky diversions.

Then again, they were led by Trick, a dude who did mind control. One guy she hoped to never cross paths with. Liars were the worst. Manipulative liars were the worst of the worst. A fact she knew all too well.

Sadie carried two brooms and dustpans over to the mess. She'd only have to do a thorough cleaning of three tables and a few chairs. Their tempered glass shattered mostly downward in compliance with city building regulations. At least staying late would mean extra money in her savings account.

A twentysomething white guy stopped in front of the gaping hole to snap a photo, then went on his way.

The bank across the street had probably been the target. It was one of those "private banks" that catered to a select clientele. Her meager savings account didn't meet their minimum requirements, so at least her money was safe.

Amit ended his phone call with the board-up company. He grabbed a nearby garbage can and dragged it over. "There's a reason we don't have tables along this wall. Can you imagine how much our liability insurance would go up if someone got hurt by these jerks?"

"It could've been worse," Sadie said.

"'Protectors of the city,' my ass. What'd be nice is if they weren't destroying the city they're supposed to be protecting. Why don't they protect our insurance rates by watching where they're going?"

"We can file a claim through the SuperWatch app."

"Why bother? Nobody ever sees a payout."

"Villains don't care what they destroy," Sadie said. "The Supers have to meet them where they're at."

"Can we do an exchange program with a different city? We get their Supers while they take ours?"

"Every city has similar problems."

"My brother lives in Oceanview," said Amit. "They don't have nearly as many mishaps. Their Supers take it to the sky and over the water."

"They're coastal," Sadie reminded him. "We've only got the river, and it's lined with skyscrapers."

"Over in Destine, they set up a fund to help with repair costs."

"That was after the big robotic sidekick fiasco. And their taxes went sky high."

Amit went on about dreading his phone call with Vector City Coffee's owner. Sadie tipped a chair to the side. Bits of glass tinkled off the seat. What if something like this happened to the comfy couches in her dream café? Would the insurance rates be better if she leased space in a smaller building in a more residential area?

Reality sank low in her gut. One of the major obstacles to opening her café was insurance rates. They were cost-prohibitive. And what if disaster struck and she didn't have a financial cushion for those couch cushions? And the paperwork involved, and having the proper building materials…

Superheroes and Supervillains played out their good guy/bad guy battles while regular people tried to do their jobs and go about their lives.

Still, the tradeoff was having crooked criminals running rampant through the city. High premiums and replacing the occasional window were better than the bad guys winning.

Another fact she knew all too well.

It was after midnight by the time Sadie got home. She swiped her keycard at her building's main entrance. The blue-accented lobby was empty and quiet. She plodded on weary feet to the alcove of mailboxes. Okay, maybe it *was* the shoes, though she hated blaming them.

Her slim mailbox held a coupon for a nearby Mexican restaurant. Ooh, good junk mail for a change. She double-checked in case there was a newsletter from one of her favorite animal rescue groups hiding in the back. Or on the extremely unlikely off-chance one of the several exes who were "totally gonna pay her back" had made good on an empty promise with cash or an old-school check. That would probably bounce.

She headed out toward the elevators. A voluminous yawn overtook her face, which she didn't bother covering. Her eyes got all squinty and she squeaked out a whoosh of breath.

Then she blinked and noticed someone waiting for an elevator.

A gorgeous white woman watching Sadie with amusement toying at her lips.

She stopped short, instantly embarrassed. The woman's dark brown hair was pulled into a little bun, showing off an undercut. Her buttoned-up, short-sleeved seersucker shirt and olive-green pants didn't disguise the cut of finely sculpted muscles.

Sadie reflexively smoothed her rounded bangs. Good thing she'd had a recent color touch-up so they were a brilliant auburn.

"Late night?" the stranger said.

"Yeah," Sadie said. She cleared her throat and found the ability to walk again.

"Doing something fun, I hope."

"Working, so not really."

"That's too bad." The woman held a large gym bag in one hand. The lighting around the elevators was dimmed in the evening, but it did sort of look like she might have recently worked out. That glow of physical activity.

Sadie pointed at the bag. "Getting home from a workout?"

Pleasantly Glowing Person glanced down at it. "Sort of. I was at work, too."

"Are you a trainer?"

"I work at a gym."

Before Sadie could ask which one (not that she knew about local workout places), the elevator doors in front of them opened.

They stepped in. Sadie pushed the button for the seventh floor. "Which floor?" she asked.

"Same one."

"Really? What apartment are you in?"

"Seven fourteen."

Elation twirled up her chest. "I live across the hall in 709. We're neighbors."

"Cool. I just moved in."

"I've lived here for two years. Let me know if you have any questions about anything."

"I will." A citrusy ginger aroma wafted from Pleasantly Glowing Person.

"I'm Sadie Eagan, by the way." She giggled at how weird that sounded. "Wow, that was sure formal. *Sadie Eagan.*"

Her new neighbor laughed, too. "Joan Malone. Since we're being so formal."

They shook hands firmly, almost professionally. The warmth in Joan Malone's hand was definitely friendly. As was her languid smile that hinted at good times for its lucky recipient.

The elevator binged and delivered them to their floor. They walked into the bright hallway light. Joan's strong jawline was more pronounced, and—

Whoa. Her eyes. Their color. Amber and golden and brown. A swirl of shades Sadie had never seen before.

"What do you do for work, Sadie Eagan?" Joan asked, her voice low and unhurried.

Sadie forced her gaze from those eyes. "I'm a barista at Vector City Coffee."

Joan switched her nylon gym bag to her opposite hand. "Oh yeah?"

"It's over on Bromley, near the corner." With a snort (ugh, so embarrassing!), Sadie added, "The storefront with a giant hole in it."

Joan blinked. "Really?"

"One of our windows got blown out by Lunk tonight."

"You don't say."

Nodding, Sadie said, "Third time this year we've had an incident."

"By the Supers?"

"Twice it was the Supers, though I guess technically the other time was, too. One of the Villains got tossed out of the air and crashed through our front door."

"Out of the air, huh?" Joan said, squinting curiously.

"Yeah. I watched it happen. Flight was doing his thing up high, and then got sprayed with frozen pellets by Ice, so he threw Ice down, and…"

"Ice crashed through your door."

"Yeah." Sadie made a circle with her arms. "He left a huge puddle. We had to squeegee it out with mops and brooms."

Joan's lips twitched. "I've heard it can be messy when all his ice melts."

"Can confirm, it is."

Her new neighbor glanced down the hall. "I think sometimes…" Joan scratched at an ear. "I mean, I've heard people talk about it. They don't mean to. I don't think they're trying to damage anything. It just happens."

"The Supers? No, of course they don't. They have to do what's necessary to protect the city."

"Right." Her rather lovely mouth flattened into a thin line. "The cost of doing business in Vector City."

"Well, the cost keeps going up."

"Is that why you're clutching that coupon like it might blow away?"

Glancing at the mailer for the Mexican restaurant, Sadie joked, "You never know when there'll be a taco emergency."

Joan tilted her head. "Nothing worse than a taco emergency."

Sadie opened her mouth to agree, only… *Taco emergency?* "Uhh…"

Her cheeks burned with a deepening blush.

Joan's eyes lit up with humor. Maybe a little interest, too. They were utterly captivating. It was hard not to stare at them. To stare at all of Joan. She was hot. Like, really hot in a chiseled Greek statue way. She was only a few inches taller but commanded twice as much space with her energy.

Hot New Neighbor Joan saved Sadie from further humiliation by walking toward their apartments. Sadie fell in step with her. Self-conscious warmth settled into her skin, or maybe it was excess exercise endorphins radiating from Joan.

"Sorry your workplace got hit again," Joan said. "Vector City Coffee, right? On Bromley Street?"

"Yep." Sadie gave her a smile. "Feel free to stop by."

"Sure," Joan said. "My schedule can be unpredictable, so I might miss you."

"Then you'll just have to try and try again."

"If at first I don't succeed."

Her grin widened at Joan getting the joke. Sadie slowed to a stop in front of her door. The multicolored crepe paper flower wreath added a pop of happiness to it. "It was nice meeting you," she said.

"Nice to meet you, too," Joan said.

"Just knock if you need to borrow a cup of sugar or something."

"That's mighty neighborly of you."

"It's important for new residents to feel welcome." Sadie tipped her head to the side, conveying that Joan was a very welcome addition to the building.

Joan continued to her apartment. She paused and gave Sadie a devastatingly sexy look over one shoulder. "Goodnight, Sadie Eagan," she said quietly.

"Goodnight, Joan Malone."

Good night, indeed.

Sadie peeked into the hallway as she leisurely closed her door. Joan stood at her door for a moment. Was she listening? For what? A pet, maybe. Or with Sadie's luck, a spouse. Though Joan had said *I just moved in,* not *We* or *My equally hot partner and I just moved in.*

Joan unlocked her door and slipped inside, closing it just as fast.

Sadie flicked the lights on in her small, open-concept kitchen. It was pretty late. She'd probably have a hard time winding down and going to sleep. Not just from the ordeal at work, but from meeting a gorgeous, flirty new neighbor who lived steps away and was possibly available.

Without Lunk, she might not have met Joan tonight. The Supers had done it again. Bringing good things to the residents of Vector City whether they knew it or not.

Thanks, Lunk.

CHAPTER 2

Joan yawned as she slumped onto the laminate tabletop. She propped her head up in one hand and shook her iced coffee with the other. Wrong move—the ice would melt. She used the straw to stir it instead.

Monday afternoon sunlight filtered through the cracks around the thick curtains inside the warehouse. Kind of a metaphor for her life: glimpsing bits of light wherever she could.

Mark picked up his coffee mug and sighed. He set it next to Joan. "Can you...?"

She tilted her head to give her twin brother a look. He made a pathetic face in return.

"It's cold," he whined.

She reached over and touched a finger just inside the maroon ceramic mug. His more-oat-milk-than-coffee began to steam.

"*Thank you,*" Mark drawled.

"Learn to embrace iced coffee."

"Yeah, when you embrace a steaming bowl of chili."

The thought would make her shiver. If she could shiver.

Joan shifted in her plastic chair with a groan. Just because it was their secret lair didn't mean it had to be so...secret lair. A nondescript workshop that could be for a mechanic or a wood-worker. Or a group of Villains staying on the down-low. The fridge hummed louder than a buzzsaw, and the faucet in their makeshift kitchen rattled every time a truck drove by. A hand-written sign above the sink declared *"Keep Our Lair Beautiful! Wash your damn dishes. That means you Irving."*

Mark sipped his coffee, careful to use the mug's handle. Like how Joan tried to only drink from a straw. Beverages were the worst when it came to temperature regulation.

"You'd think we'd have figured this out by now," Mark said. "Spark and Ice, world-renowned Supervillains—"

"Are we?"

"—can conquer any daring feat of villainy, but can't drink coffee without it turning into room-temperature sludge."

"The norms have the advantage there," Joan said.

Mark reclined in his chair, lacing his fingers behind his head. His blond hair was in its usual polished perfection. As were his pink short-sleeved polo and tan chinos. Like he'd gotten a full night's rest compared to Joan's wet mess of hair, jeans and Vector City Vultures baseball shirt.

Her outfit said they'd had a tiring evening evading the Supers. But then she'd run into her cute neighbor.

"Speaking of norms, I met one of my neighbors last night," she said with a smile.

Mark returned her grin. "And I'm guessing by you telling me, she was attractive and female."

"She was indeed. She lives across the hall."

"What's she like?"

"Pretty adorable. Very colorful. She was wearing purple shoes. Her hair's red and curled under, like you'd see on an old-time movie star."

"Cute."

"Her name's Sadie." *Sadie Eagan.* She grinned at the memory of Sadie saying her name so properly. "She made a joke about a taco emergency. I'm pretty sure it wasn't meant to be dirty, but it could've been construed as very suggestive."

Mark snickered. "Of course you'd take a joke about a taco emergency that way."

"I have taco emergencies. They aren't usually taken care of by women with normal lives. Which reminds me," she said before her brother could wind up with a retort. "The coffee shop that got hit last night is where she works. I think you got tossed into it by Flight a few months back."

Mark screwed his eyes up to the ceiling. "Oh, yeah. He knocked me off that sweet ice pyre I built in front of the jeweler."

"You can't build a pyre out of ice," Joan told him for not the first time.

"My *ice pyre*," he continued, unbothered. "It was beautiful. Thick and high…"

Joan snorted.

"I like my pyres thick and high, like how you like your tacos to be emergencies."

She shot a finger gun at him.

"And then Otis had to be all heroic and fly through it to break it up. I gave him a hell of a snow shower."

"We should take care of the café," Joan said.

Mark nodded. "God knows Otis and Company won't."

The Supers never paid for the damage they created. Otis—well, Flight, as the norms called him—relished all the glory and took the free shit people gave him. Even though he and his crew cost the city more than the supposed Villains ever had.

"So did you ask Cute Neighbor Sadie on this thing the kids call a date?" Mark asked.

"I don't think the kids call it a date anymore."

"If she has a funky, old-school vibe, she'd like to be asked on a date."

"I might," Joan said.

Sadie seemed nice. Friendly, chatty, open. The sort of woman

Joan had always wanted to hang out with. But it was hard to date anyone not into villainy. The women who understood her were part of the criminal element, or else fans of the criminal element who thought it'd be cool to get with Spark. Which meant she had to wear her Spark getup with the facemask and long, dark wig. Which was kind of weird.

She wanted someone to like her for boring old Joanie, not for Spark.

Hmm. Sadie wanted her to stop by Vector City Coffee. Today might be a good day to inspect the damage while also seeing Sadie's bright smile. Would she be wearing another fitted top that highlighted her ample chest? Dare one dream for a V-neck? Could a lonely lesbian get a little peek of cleavage?

Hell yes, please and thank you flickered through her lower abs.

Perry finally came out of the bathroom. He was dressed for a corporate business meeting in a sharp navy-blue suit that complemented his tan skin and sandy light-brown curls. He took these meetings way too seriously. He took everything way too seriously.

The newspaper tucked under his arm made Joan tease, "You're really living up to the whole Breeze moniker with how much wind you just broke in there."

"Joanie, you've been making jokes like that since you were sixteen." Perry looked to Mark. "You two need new material."

Mark grinned. "Like we've matured in the past nineteen years?"

The fluorescent light above the table reflected off Perry's glasses. He noticed their doodles on three fast-food napkins. A logo idea for Hot and Cold, a proposed menu for the food truck, a badly drawn sketch of a food truck with stick figure Mark and Joan smiling big.

"That again?" Perry shook his head.

Tempting though it was to cover them up, Joan left them in place. "You know it's our dream," she said.

"It's a pipe dream," Mark said.

"All your dreams are pipe dreams."

"Thick and high."

"I don't know why this appeals to you," Perry said. "Serving the community that's shunned you your whole lives."

"It's something different," Mark said.

Joan touched the menu ideas. "You know we love to cook."

Perry sighed. "I know, but—"

"It'd give us the chance to go legit. Do something good for once."

"You've tried, Joanie. It's always the same. Your place is here."

She rolled her eyes and stuck her tongue out. Mark made fart sounds with his mouth.

"Just because *you* love the life and have never wanted to do anything else..." Joan tried not to smirk at how much that'd bug the shit out of Perry.

He narrowed his eyes at her.

"No, Joanie." Mark got all dramatic. "Péricles Barbosa, the Brazilian Brain himself, earned an MBA and had the perfect career lined up at the most prestigious art gallery in Vector City. Only to have it all thwarted because, *oh*, such a powerful being cannot exist in normal society."

"Let's get to the agenda." Perry sat across from them and pulled his all-important weekly agenda from his jacket pocket. "Item One. Any problems last night? I think everything went well other than the Supers giving us a headache at the end."

Joan shook her head while sipping her iced coffee. They could do bank heists in their sleep. "I can't believe all those old savings bonds were just sitting there."

"Equal split of the cash," Mark added. "Not a bad night."

"Lunk broke that coffeehouse window. They've had multiple incidents. Can we slide them some cash to cover this time and the other times?"

"Ten grand?" Perry said.

"Sounds good," said Joan. Mark shrugged his hands, not caring one way or the other.

It sucked that Sadie's workplace had been hit so many times. The money would help with repairs and lost revenue. And guilt. Mom-and-pop businesses were just trying to get by, like them.

Perry scribbled a note. "Damn Kade. You'd think he could hold his own body weight. I didn't push him with that strong of a gust."

Mark plopped his chin in his hand. "Ah, Lunk. So beautiful. So clueless."

"So straight," Joan reminded her twin. "And *such* a Super."

"I remain optimistic."

"You don't even know what he looks like under his mask."

"With an ass like that, I don't need to."

Perry slid his pen down the agenda. "Item Two. Who keeps taking tools out of here and not bringing them back?"

"Joanie," Mark said without hesitation.

"Way to throw me under the bus." Joan told Perry, "I grabbed a few things to put my new shelving unit together."

"It's been going on for weeks. I needed a crowbar last night to get into that safe deposit box. Volt had to zap it open."

"I'll bring them back when things are set up at my place."

Mark's face crinkled in confusion. "Why did you need a crowbar to put together a shelf?"

"I used the crowbar to make sure my alarm system's working," Joan said.

"This is what happens when you move so far away from me."

"I moved five minutes from you."

"*Seven* minutes," Mark stated. "And do you know how long it takes to get up to your fancy high-rise apartment?"

Joan flattened her palms on the table. "I know you both aren't happy I moved into a heavily populated building. But seriously, what better cover than to hide in plain sight?"

"Just bring the tools back," Perry said. "And maybe get your own."

"Joanie has a whole boxful of tools." Mark ducked as she took a swipe at him. "It's under her bed and—"

She flicked a tiny fireball at him.

Mark snatched it and fizzled it out. "And it has a *big, thick* rainbow heart sticker on top."

Joan shot several little fireballs at him that he neutralized mid-air with a burst of snow.

Perry crossed his arms. "Are you done?"

"Yes," Joan said, then muttered to her younger-by-eight-minutes brother, "I won't tell him what you've got under *your* bed."

"If you need help settings things up, you can call me."

"I know, Per." Joan gave him a smile. "You don't have to worry about me."

"I'm always gonna worry about you two," Perry said. "You're my exhausting almost-children who I've tolerated for too many years."

Mark made heart hands. "We love you too, Per."

Joan copied his heart hands. "Thanks for raising us to be the upstanding citizens we are."

They owed everything to Perry. Even though he was barely fifteen years older than them, he'd taken them in when their actual parents decided it'd be better for the twins in the city rather than destroying various parts of their hometown.

Breeze might be a hard-nosed Villain to everyone in Vector City, but he was also just Perry, who whooshed the first guy to break Mark's heart into the river while the douche was on a date with someone else. He was the one who'd told them the Heroes' real first names, which he'd learned over the years. He'd taught the twins the importance of balance. That a family could be made out of Supervillains. He'd shown them how to survive when everyone else had turned their backs on them.

"Next item." Perry glanced up from the agenda. "Trick's proposition."

Joan and Mark groaned. *Speaking of family I only want to see at Christmas...*

"I know you don't want to discuss it, but we have to make a decision."

"I decide we ignore him like usual," Joan said.

"I second that." Mark raised his mug in a toast.

Perry quirked an eyebrow. "Trick wants us to—"

"—stop calling him Melvin," said Joan.

"Well, yes, but—"

"Put a curse on his parents for naming him Melvin," Mark said.

Perry sent them a weary glare. "Will you take this seriously for once?"

"Have we ever taken anything seriously?" Mark said.

"This time it's different. Trick's doing a lot of bad stuff, and he wants us to join him. Establish dominance over Vector City. Use scare tactics to make people submit. If we don't want to be associated with him—"

"We don't," Joan and Mark chorused.

"Then we have to tell him no. Let people know we're not trying to take over the world or hurt anyone."

Joan scratched her nose. "The three of us haven't been connected to some of the worst things he's done. Even the Supers can attest to our refusal to harm people. Not that they would."

"We have principles," Mark said. "No knocking off small businesses, only taking from heavily insured corporations…"

"I agree with you, but it's not going to be easy with Mel's whole…" Perry gestured to his head. "If we go against what he wants, he'll manipulate the norms around us until we give in. That only creates more chaos."

Thank god Trick's mind control didn't work on Supers. The altered DNA they were born with that gave them powers also gave them immunity from him. It drove him nuts. As long as there were people he couldn't control, he'd never be able to completely take over.

Some Supervillains had grand visions of world domination, while others were more or less petty crooks. Crooks who could burn through bank vaults with a flick of the wrist, but still… A girl had to do what a girl had to do to survive.

"Eh, don't worry about Mel," Joan said. "He's still got his henchmen."

"Hench-people." Mark *tsk*ed at her. "Don't disrespect Ethel like that."

"Sorry. His hench-persons Volt and Hide."

"Thank you."

"Boring Ethel and stinky Irving," Joan muttered, to which her brother laughed.

Perry jotted a note on his agenda. "Which one of you wants to tell him?"

"You're the Man, Per," Mark said. "You can speak for us."

"Does that make you my hench-people?"

"No, that makes you our democratically elected representative."

"I'll do it," Joan said. She was not afraid of Melvin.

"Do it soon," Perry said, and scribbled another note. "He'll keep bugging me otherwise."

She sipped her disappointingly bland home-brewed iced coffee. According to the clock on the wall, it was 3:15. Sadie might be at work. She could hook Joan up with something sweet.

"Anything else?" she asked. "I'd like to stop by Vector City Coffee to assess the damage."

"That's not why you're going." Mark waggled his eyebrows. "A cute woman works there."

Perry gave Joan the stern look she'd been on the receiving end of more times than she could count. "You can't go near there. We were seen."

"It's not like I'm gonna swing by in my Spark suit," she pointed out.

"We have to stay low profile. Especially if we're trying to disassociate from Trick."

"Ah crap, that's right." Mark made an exaggerated frown. "You'll have to run into Cute Neighbor Sadie at home."

"Wait, she's your neighbor?" Perry said, voice pitching higher in alarm.

Joan held her palms up. "It's fine. She thinks I work at a gym."

"Does she know where you live?"

"It's literally across the hall."

"Joanie—"

"Everything's cool. Relax."

Perry rubbed at his temples and muttered in Portuguese. "Nothing makes me worry more than when the two of you tell me everything's cool."

"Everything *is* cool, Per," Joan said.

"Don't go near that café. You know better than that."

Mark looked at her. They shared the same thought in unspoken twin-speak: *He hates it when we try to be normal.*

Perry had worried when Mark tried culinary school. Worried when Joan had that brief series of office jobs in her twenties. Worried when she'd announced she was moving out of the same building as them to get a little breathing room. No matter how hard the Malone twins tried to live among the norms, it never lasted long.

Mark's phone vibrated with an incoming text. "Ooh, I'm getting a hot tip that there's gonna be a shipment of gold bars arriving from Australia on Wednesday."

That would be a sweet score. The sort of thing they could use toward opening a food truck.

Perry perked up. "Get me the details. Let's keep this one to ourselves."

"Like I'd ever share with Melvin and Company unless they already knew about it." Mark made a face.

Joan touched the napkin with her childlike rendering of her and Mark in front of their Hot and Cold food truck. It really was a pipe dream.

Damn it. They had to avoid Bromley Street until things cooled down. It'd be crawling with cops, and the Supers would be sniffing around. Which meant not seeing Sadie unless they happened upon one another at home.

She should probably steer clear of Sadie anyway, for her cute neighbor's own good. Getting tangled up in villainy wasn't something norms should do. Especially not someone unknowingly getting involved.

Joan sighed and slurped her lukewarm coffee.

CHAPTER 3

Sadie held the glass door open for her coworkers. Amit and Nyah passed through the front entrance. They all preferred it over walking through the alley behind Vector City Coffee at ten-thirty at night.

She tugged on the door to make sure it was locked. Then she joined Amit and Nyah on the sidewalk. "Hump Day done," she said, taking her hair out of its ponytail.

Amit grimaced at the still boarded-up window. Work on Allegria Tower was tying up a lot of resources and manpower. The top corner had been taken out by Breeze and Flight a month or two back. A bit ironic, since the building housed the corporate head-quarters for Allegria Insurance.

"It'll get fixed," Nyah said. She zipped up her carnation-pink hoodie. The bright color made her rich brown skin glow in the streetlight.

"And we have the money to fix it," Sadie said.

Amit snorted. "Guilt money."

"Who cares?" Nyah checked her phone. "Mysterious money shows up in our bank account with a note saying 'For the window.' Probably from Lunk. He paid for what he broke."

"I don't care who it's from. It's the bare minimum for what they should be doing."

"I'm sure Lunk feels bad for what happened," Sadie said.

How thoughtful of him to help pay for repairs. She didn't expect Lunk to take credit or make a big deal out of it. The Supers enjoyed a good photo op, but this blunder wasn't something they would want to draw attention to.

Amit typed a quick text, then tucked his phone in his jeans pocket. "Get home safely," he said.

Sadie thanked him while Nyah said, "Enjoy your day off. Let me know if you figure out how to get out of the abandoned factory."

Her coworkers moaned about their latest videogame obsession and where they'd both gotten stuck. Sadie stooped to retie the lace on her white canvas sneaker.

"Let me know if the repair company calls," Amit said.

"We will," Sadie said.

He headed to the right. Sadie fell in step with Nyah in the opposite direction. There was never much traffic—foot or car—in the business district at this time of night. The quiet city glow was one of her favorite things about living here. Being out and about while the rest of Vector City was tucked inside.

"I hope the window does get fixed this week," Sadie said. "Then I can tell my mom it's been taken care of."

"Is she still being paranoid about your unsafe work environment?" Nyah asked.

"Oh yeah. She's called every day."

"Yeesh."

"I guess I can't blame her. It's a bit ridiculous for us to have had so many incidents."

Ny slid her thick elastic headband down around her neck. She patted at her two curly high puffs. "My mom thinks I should move back to Oceanview because it's safer there."

"My mom thinks living in any city is a dangerous gamble. If it's not incidental damage, it's all the *crime*." Sadie widened her eyes the way her mom did when she acted like bad things didn't happen in small towns or the suburbs.

A familiar *whoosh* echoed in the sky. Flight had been watching the area more lately. Probably from the recent bank break-in.

"Speaking of." Sadie pointed up.

Flight zoomed over a few low rooftops, his bright red cape flapping behind him. He studied the ground for any signs of trouble.

"Big help he is now," Nyah muttered. "A few days ago would've been nice."

"The Supers can't be everywhere," Sadie said.

"The Villains aren't fools. They'll avoid this area. It's pointless to patrol here."

"I don't mind. It makes me feel safe."

Nyah studied her, a smirk playing about her lips. "You are so loyal to them. Like the Supers can do no wrong."

"I can't help it," Sadie said. "Ever since I saw Race and Catch save that school bus full of children. It was stuck on the train tracks. Catch stopped the train with her bare hands." She stretched out her arms to demonstrate. "Literally slowed it to a crawl."

"And then Race pushed the bus off the tracks in the nick of time," Ny said. Then she grinned. "You love to tell this story."

"So? It was frightening and amazing to watch."

"And is the reason you have a marginally unhealthy obsession with Catch."

Warmth seeped into Sadie's cheeks, but she didn't care. "Catch is the best."

"Nah. Give me Lunk and all that weight pressing down on me." Nyah gestured at her voluptuous figure. "He could handle all this."

"He'd be lucky to handle all that."

"Damn right."

Sadie's phone buzzed a couple of times in her back pocket. Maybe the SuperWatch app with new Hero or Villain sightings.

Nope. Her stomach clenched at three texts from Ferret Guy.

Hey I know its last minute but can u watch my
babies for a week or two

Tomoro

Prob not longer than two weeks

"Unbelievable," Sadie muttered.

"What?"

She showed Nyah the texts. "Remember the guy who asked me to pet-sit his three ferrets for a week and it ended up being a month? While he went on vacation with another woman right after we stopped seeing each other?"

"The ferrets who shit all over your apartment?"

"And got into literally *everything*."

"Oh hell no." Nyah shook her head.

"Yeah, hard no." Sadie swiped on her screen. "Delete."

"Don't give in when he asks again. Which he will."

"Uh, considering he still owes me for the carpet cleaning he was 'totally gonna pay for'?" She jammed her phone in her pocket. "I know I'm a pushover, but I don't forget easily. Especially when I have to shell out money I don't really have for something like that."

He'd fooled her once with buttering her up about watching the ferrets that were admittedly cute. When he'd posted photos on the beach with some tall brunette hottie *for a month* and then conveniently never returned texts about paying for the carpet cleaning, it was shame on Sadie.

Ugh. Why did people have to suck?

Flight circled overhead, then continued east toward the river. "You know what would be a great superpower to have?" Sadie mused. "The ability to tell when someone's lying."

"That'd be a blessing and a curse," Nyah said.

"The positives would totally outweigh the negatives. It'd save a lot of time and energy if I could weed out the liars."

"That's the superpower you'd want the most?"

"I think so. Flying looks pretty cool, though."

Ny pulled her hood over her head and held it against her cheeks. "I'd want invisibility. I could creep around, play tricks on people, listen in on everyone's conversations."

"You want to be Hide?" Sadie made a face.

"I wouldn't go full Supervillain. Just sneak up on people for fun."

"I bet he sneaks up on everyone."

Nyah looked around, then raised her eyebrows. "Maybe he's here right now."

"Stop," Sadie said, and shivered. "That's scary to think about."

"It's probably another blessing and a curse. I'd learn shit I don't want to know."

"True."

A plump young white guy in glasses chugged past them, looking up and down from his phone. Kind of a strange thing to be doing in dress clothes, but to each their own.

They reached the bus stop where Nyah would catch her ride home. "Don't stay up too late trying to get out of the factory," Sadie teased.

"You know I will," Ny said.

They laughed and waved goodbye. Sadie hastened her steps, settling into her Single Woman at Night pace. Not because she felt unsafe. Flight was nearby, or could be if she needed him. It was just the reality of being a woman.

She passed one of the old buildings original to Vector City, its cornerstone stating its completion in 1903. About the same time people with unusual abilities began to be reported across the globe. Many theories had been posed as to why, but the overall consensus was some humans had simply evolved. Sadie supposed this was why a lot of people distrusted the superpowered. Not all human beings had evolved to embrace differences rather than fear them.

The storefront that used to be a mattress store was still available for lease. It wasn't the right fit for a café. At least not her dream café. The location was okay, but she didn't get a *Yes!* vibe from it. It didn't feel like the right time, anyway. She didn't have enough money saved up.

Her phone buzzed again. Another text from Ferret Guy.

Ill pay you ok?

Ugh. She didn't need money that badly. Was it any wonder why someone would be more into Superheroes than regular joes? They saved busloads of kids and upheld truth and honesty and made her feel protected. People like Ferret Guy…did not.

She had to reply, if only to get him off her back. She typed *Will you also pay me the money you promised last time*, but deleted it. That made it sound like she'd be up for it. Better to be more direct, less wishy-washy.

Sorry, not available.

She almost added something like *Good luck finding someone* or *Have a good vacation*. "Don't do it," she told herself. Saying *sorry* was bad enough, but she didn't want to be mean. Even though she had a right to.

She sent the text and put her phone on Do Not Disturb before he wore her down. She'd ignore any more texts from him. Should probably delete his number, only seeing *Ferret Guy* reminded her that she'd changed his contact name to remember what he'd done. And similar things others had done.

A pizza delivery guy held the door for her as he exited her building. They shared a hello.

Sadie paused at the alcove of mailboxes. Might as well check, even though hers would probably be empty. Who knows? Maybe her hot new neighbor would be around.

Her heartbeat tapped in double-time as she glanced at the mailbox for apartment 714. *Joan Malone.*

Joan Malone sounded like a character from a classic detective movie. Though she looked like anything but. Sadie's style fit the bill more, with her love of vintage everything. Joan had a more modern flair with the undercut and tight pants.

Since Sadie worked odd days and hours, the likelihood of seeing one another again was either really good or really bad. Hopefully good, because Joan Malone was *hot*. That smile could let her get away with anything, and her *eyes*…

She hadn't been able to get those eyes out of her thoughts.

Footsteps echoed closer until someone rounded the corner. Her pulse catapulted at the sight of Joan Malone. Tonight she wore another short-sleeved shirt with a little diamond pattern and black skinny jeans.

"Sadie Eagan," Joan said, shifting her gym bag from one hand to the other.

"Joan Malone." Sadie tugged at the hem of her bright violet sleeveless top.

"Nice to see you again." Joan's voice was low and smooth, like the finest whiskey.

"Nice to see *you*." Sadie grinned. "I was just thinking about running into you."

"So you manifested me."

"I guess I did."

Joan looked at her with those amber eyes. There wasn't a word to describe them other than *remarkable*. Like they could reach inside you and take care of you.

Those eyes would get Sadie in more trouble than that smile.

Joan unlocked her mailbox. She stepped to the side and slid her hand in awkwardly sideways. Didn't most people shove their faces in to make sure they got everything? Or was Sadie the weird one?

"How was work tonight?" she asked, distractedly fumbling with her keys.

"Not bad. Got everything done I needed to."

"Are you a personal trainer? Sorry, I can't remember what you said you did."

Joan studied her junk mail. "A little bit of everything. Whatever they need help with."

Sadie nodded, pulling out the same advertisement for—funny enough—a window and glass company. "Which gym do you work at?"

"Do you have a local gym?"

"No," she laughed. "I prefer not to pay for bodily torture."

Joan laughed, too. "It's one across town. Kind of small. Caters to a specific clientele."

"Like CrossFit?"

"Not that kind of torture. It's, ah…specialized. Tailored to client needs. Pretty boring to talk about." She raised her arched eyebrows. "You're home kind of late. Were you busy at the coffee shop?"

How nice Joan remembered where she worked. "I work the late shift, so I'm usually home around this time," Sadie said, locking her mailbox.

Joan tore up and tossed her junk mail into the large recycle bin. Sadie was holding on to hers, just in case.

Her new neighbor stepped closer. Her citrus-ginger-pleasantly-sweaty scent floated through the air. "Did you get any good coupons in case you have a taco emergency?" Joan teased.

Sadie rolled the rectangular mailer between her palms. "Not tonight."

"Too bad."

If Joan kept looking at her with those eyes and that smile and the heat emanating off her body, Sadie was going to have a very personal taco emergency. The kind Joan could take care of.

"I get excited about a good deal," Sadie rambled on. "I used to clip coupons with my grandma and mom on Sundays when I was a kid. My sister and I had an unofficial competition to see who could find the best deal every week."

Amusement pulled at Joan's tempting lips as they walked out of the alcove. "Who usually won?"

"My sister. She's older and much more competitive."

"Where did you grow up?"

"The suburbs," Sadie said. "West Vector." *Where my mom wishes I still lived.* "You?"

"A tiny town nobody's heard of."

"Hmm. You strike me as a city person."

Joan considered that. "I guess I *have* lived here most of my life."

"Not cut out for small-town living?"

She pressed the "up" elevator button and stared straight ahead. "Not at all."

The elevator doors to their right opened. When they stepped in, Joan switched hands for her gym bag. Metallic clanking and clunking came from inside it.

"What do you have in there?" Sadie asked, glancing at the bulging nylon material.

"Hand weights. My workout clothes."

"You work out in a suit of armor?"

Joan chuckled, a delightful rumble in her equally delightful throat. "There's a metal water bottle in there."

The bag looked unusually heavy for something filled with clothes and gym equipment. How much did those hand weights weigh?

"I'm starting to think your gym uses medieval weaponry." Sadie took a step closer. "Do you have one of those spiked iron balls on a chain?"

Joan shifted the bag slightly behind her. "We used to, but too many people lost an eye."

"Seriously?"

"No." She laughed, but in a kind way. "It's just some hand weights."

She wasn't laughing at Sadie, nor did she seem to be lying. Joan's whole vibe was very trustworthy. Which wasn't something Sadie could say for most of the people she'd been attracted to in her adult life.

The doors opened on the seventh floor. Joan held out a hand to let Sadie off first. Sadie gave her a little smile. Everything about Joan Malone radiated kindness. Chivalry. Her sweet soft butch approachability.

Sadie slowed her steps as they neared her door. "How's your apartment? Have you unpacked?"

"For the most part," Joan said. "I like it so far."

"You're in a two-bedroom, right? All the ones on your side with the good view have two bedrooms."

"Yeah. It has a nice view of Friendship Park."

"Do you have vindictive pigeons on your side?"

"Vindictive what?" Joan laughed.

"There's this pigeon who constantly poops on my balcony. I can't sit out there or have plants or anything. It pooped so much on my tabletop cherry tomato plant last summer, I couldn't eat any of them."

"That's gross. Sorry. I haven't seen any, but I'll keep my eyes open now that I'm aware."

"You're probably okay because it's more open on your side," Sadie said. "I face the alley and high-rise next door."

"I'll consider myself lucky, then."

Sadie steered the convo away from pigeon droppings. "I love the layout of the kitchens on your side. I wish mine was a little bigger."

Interest flickered in Joan's eyes. How did interest cause eyes to flicker? "Do you like to cook?" she asked.

"I guess." Sadie blinked, then refocused on Joan's eyes. They looked normal again. Well, normal for her beautiful eyes. "I really love crafting coffee drinks. Experimenting with flavor combinations to try at the café."

Joan nodded in a non-eye-flickering display of interest.

"Are you a big cook?" Sadie guessed from her neighbor's enthusiasm.

"Yeah. I'm a bit of a foodie."

Excitement tingled through her stomach. "Do you like cooking new dishes, or going out to eat? Or both?"

"Both. I'm game for anything."

"Me, too." Sadie gave her a look that said she'd be game for anything with Joan.

They paused outside Sadie's apartment. Joan touched the crepe paper wreath. "This is cool."

"Thanks. I made it."

"You did?"

"With my own two hands." Sadie tucked the coupon under one arm to wiggle both sets of fingers.

"You make specialty coffees *and* craft projects?"

"I'm very handy and creative." *Two things my dates generally appreciate about me.*

"No kidding. Do you draw things? Like logos and stuff?"

"I can. I have. I wouldn't make a career out of it or anything, but I like doing it for fun."

Joan started to speak. Her gym bag bumped the cream-colored wall and its contents clanked. It made her flinch.

"That's cool," she said. "I should let you get some rest. Are you working tomorrow?"

"I am. Stop by if you're free. I'll take care of you."

"Thanks. I'll try to get there soon."

Sadie tapped her door key to Joan's upper arm. "I'll hold you to it."

Her eyes did that quick-flare thing again. They were extraordinary. "Goodnight, neighbor," Joan said.

"'Night, neighbor."

Joan walked to her own door. Sadie whisper-called, "My shift starts at one tomorrow."

"Okay," Joan laughed.

"Our Thursday specials are cinnamon dolce scones and the Avocado Madness sandwich on an everything bagel. We have three freshly brewed seasonal iced teas."

She laughed harder and went inside her apartment.

Sadie unlocked her door with a sigh. *Joan Malone.* There was so much to her. So many layers to unwrap.

Her eyes really were extraordinary. They weren't…well, they weren't mortal. Humans didn't have eyes like that unless…

No. That was wishful thinking. Wanting them to be the eyes of a Super. Joan couldn't be a Super. She lived in an apartment like an ordinary person. Had an ordinary person job.

Though there was something off about the whole "hand weights and a water bottle" story. Joan was in shape—oh boy, was she in shape—but something about her just didn't *feel* like she was a gym rat. She seemed more worldly. Like she spent her time out and about in the world.

A gasp escaped Sadie's mouth. She leaned against the wall. Joan wasn't helping people get in shape.

She was saving lives.

Was it possible? Could she be a Superhero?

Sadie dropped her keys and mailer to pull out her phone. SuperWatch glowed in her dark apartment. It was the go-to app for all things Super. Her default setting was (obviously) Vector City, so she went to the listing of local Heroes.

Joan definitely wasn't Lunk or Flight. Lunk was a huge white guy, and Flight was a middle-aged bald Black man. Maybe Race? Race was nonbinary, and Joan hadn't shared her pronouns— perhaps *their* pronouns. But something about a Super known for speed didn't match Joan's ease and comfort.

That left Catch.

Her heartbeat pounded as she gazed at Catch's full-length photo. A white woman in a navy-blue bodysuit. Skintight navy blue. Definitely in Superhero shape. Sadie had spent a lot of time admiring that body, and how Catch talked about justice and fairness, and just admiring her in general. She was a genuine hero.

What about reported activity? Sadie clicked on that option to see if there were any updates. Just some current Flight sightings, and one earlier of Lunk getting a giant ice cream sundae. Nothing about Catch, but that didn't mean she wasn't—or hadn't—been active.

This could explain Joan's eyes. All the things she'd absorbed.

Or taking in Sadie's blatant attraction. Or maybe her eyes did something to conceal their true color, and thus her true identity.

It was possible.

Uncertainty sliced through the elation in her chest. Improbable, though, that a Super had moved into her building and was queer and would be interested in a thirty-four-year-old slightly underemployed barista crafting art projects and squirreling away money for a café she was too afraid to open.

But still…

Sadie gazed at her door.

What if Joan was interested?

And what if Joan was Catch?

CHAPTER 4

The late afternoon sun caused sweat to trickle down Joan's back inside the rubbery material on her black-and-red Spark outfit. She wriggled as she sat on the roof across the street from Melvin's favorite weekday hangout. Tapping her heels against the brick ledge, she watched him pose to the delight of the eight women inside the brightly lit fitness center.

Well, manufactured delight. Brainwashed delight. Through Joan's eyes, Melvin was a dorky short guy in his strangely mauve-tinted Trick getup with fake muscles built into it. He could trick the norms, but the Villains knew he was not a big, buff dude.

A perky blonde squeezed one of his biceps and danced with glee. The other women cooed in admiration. Melvin grinned and said something that was clearly more mind control because everyone in the fitness center laughed heartily. Joan shook her head. Trick had the power to do some real damage but mostly went around making people think he was a stud. His ego was the most dangerous thing about him.

He could actually work out. Put in the reps to get the physique he desired. But no. Melvin only came to the gym to pretend. To lie. It was annoying to watch, but it was the best time to catch him without Irving and Ethel around. Mel gave them Mondays off from henching. Plus, he'd be too preoccupied to overreact to what she was about to do.

Joan scratched at where her facemask rubbed on the bridge of her nose, waiting for him to finish so they could talk. He hadn't stopped bugging Perry, and thus Perry hadn't stopped bugging Joan about telling Mel they wanted out of his schemes.

This place had an upscale clientele. Hot, rich women in designer workout wear. The sort of place Joan imagined when she told people she worked at a gym, though she saw herself more with the guys pumping iron in the back. Even if they grunted and postured way too much. Which was why she preferred to work out in the warehouse with Mark, sparring and using their powers on each other when they got frustrated.

Or mixing it up with Greta, not using her powers against her oldest friend (and honestly, her only true friend). Greta would absolutely take her down if Joan so much as even tried.

She leaned forward, bracing her gloved hands on the ledge. She needed to text Greta after this. It'd been a while since they'd hung out. She could pick her pal's brain about Sadie. Greta was one of the few norms Joan had allowed into her life, so she had that outside perspective. Although it was coated in a thick layer of criminality. Greta was hands down the best thief in Vector City and loved her chosen career. They never could see eye-to-eye on that versus Joan having no alternative.

Seriously, though, what to do about Sadie? She'd seemed interested in Joan's nerdy admission to being a foodie. (Only she hadn't let on just how nerdy she was about it.) And Sadie clearly wanted her to stop by Vector City Coffee for a sweet treat. She hadn't been subtle about *that* double meaning. Enough time had passed for it to be safe to stop by.

A smile tugged at her mouth. Sadie seemed so genuine, so sweet. Cute and creative and helpful. It'd be nice to talk over logo designs for a food truck. But neighborly flirting could only go on for so long before Joan had to either do something about it or put a stop to it.

It'd been pretty awkward having Sadie pick up on Joan's cut of the gold bars clanking in her bag. The hand weights story had been a good cover-up. Plus, she really did have a metal water bottle in there.

She wanted to get to know Sadie, but that brought the risk of Sadie wanting to get to know her. And she would think she'd be hanging out with a personal trainer who most certainly did not spend her time sitting on rooftops waiting to talk to Trick. Not exactly a great way to start things.

Ugh, enough already. This could go on all night. She pushed off the ledge and shot just enough fire from both palms to glide down to the sidewalk. She waved them out just before landing in a crouch. When she straightened, the flowing hair on her dark wig flopped over her face. She batted it back. Damn thing had a mind of its own.

She stepped into the street. An oncoming car braked sharply. The driver laid on the horn, then stopped when the woman in the passenger seat slapped the guy with both hands.

"That's Spark!" the woman screeched loud enough for Joan to hear through the open windows.

"Oh, shit." The guy raised his hands off the steering wheel.

Joan resisted rolling her eyes and continued to the fitness center. A deliveryman in a parked white truck jerked the brim of his ballcap low, like she wouldn't see him because he couldn't see her. Norms sure could be weird.

She pulled one of the glass doors open. The thumping beat of upbeat music filled the large space. Mel was still holding court by the treadmills. He did have one advantage over Spark: People weren't afraid of him when he used his powers.

He caught sight of Joan from his circle of admirers. Irritation flashed across his face. "What are you doing here?" he whined in his nasal voice.

"I need to talk to you," Joan said.

"Can't it wait? I'm busy."

"No."

The women stared blankly at her. People looked creepy under mind control.

Melvin changed his stance so he could show off his back. The women sighed and petted his Trick suit. Three weightlifter dudes nodded appreciatively from across the room.

Yuck. She had to get out of there. "I have an answer to your proposition."

Mel stopped posing and grinned. The women sighed again. "Why didn't you say so? Ladies, give us some privacy. Go back to what you were doing."

He waved a dismissive hand. The women moved away in a zombie-like daze.

"It's a short conversation," Joan said. "We're not interested. Leave us out of whatever you're planning."

Melvin crossed his arms. "Breeze must not have explained things the right way."

"No, he explained it. You want to lord over the city and then take the show on the road."

"Exactly."

"That's not our style. We're not interested."

"Now, Spark…"

She took a step back, signaling this was over. "We've never had grand plans of domination. We don't want that kind of attention. We like being in the shadows."

"We shouldn't have to be in the shadows," Melvin said. "Look what we can do. What we can get if we work together."

He gestured around the gym. It was like a scene out of a horror movie with all the people exercising at a steady, monotonous rhythm.

Wrinkling her nose, Joan said, "Yeah, no. This is disturbing. Taking away free will isn't cool."

She turned to go. Mel hastened to get in front of her. "Stealing isn't cool, but you do it all the time. Breeze has taken chunks out of half the buildings in the city. That's not cool. We work with the skills we have."

Joan kept walking. "I don't have to justify our decision. Just wanted it to be clear."

"But you haven't heard about my magnificent plan!" Melvin cried, falling in step beside her.

"Not interested."

His nostrils flared, which meant a tantrum was coming. "This is all your fault. All your idea."

Joan sighed and told him, "It's all three of us. Get Hide and Volt to do your dirty work."

"You'll reconsider when you hear about my plan."

She paused her stride long enough to guess, "First you take over Vector City, then you mind control your way into taking over the other big cities. Even though you'll have to get through all their Supers *and* their Villains, which is honestly ridiculous."

"That's where Spark and Ice and Breeze come in." Melvin gave his dorky grin.

"We're gonna be wherever we want because we won't be the most wanted Supervillains in the world. It's ludicrous and unsafe, and we want no part of it."

"You're just having the jitters."

"I don't get the jitters." God, talking to him was like reasoning with a six-year-old.

"Urgh, damn it, Spark!" Melvin growled.

Three of the women shook their heads. Mel was too distracted to direct his power. They comprehended that Supervillains were standing right by them and screamed in fright. The rest of the women came to, shrieking and running in all directions to get away.

Melvin waved his hands and said, "Look what you did!"

"This is because of you, numb-nuts." Joan ducked as the blonde flailed her arms.

"Don't hurt us!" she begged. "Please! I have a child!"

She was screeching so loudly, Joan covered one ear. "I'm not gonna hurt you. Stop screaming."

The weightlifters moved toward them, cautious but intent. Joan moved into a fighting stance, ready to throw a couple of punches if need be.

Melvin narrowed his eyes at the men, and they stopped. Then he held out a hand, moving it across where the women scampered about. "Let's have no more of that," he told them. "Settle down."

They quieted, going slack.

"Everyone was having a good time until you showed up," Melvin said.

"Can't you get your jollies doing something else?" Joan said, relaxing her stance. "They're not your playthings, Mel—"

She halted before saying his name. There were some things that just weren't done. No exposing true identities, (mostly) not using powers against each other. Honor among thieves.

Melvin sneered at her. "I would've liked to get in on that shipment of gold bars you hauled in last week."

Figures that he'd found out about that. "We don't share everything," Joan said.

"*Gold bars,*" he emphasized. "That's something you share."

"Maybe if you showed up to one of Breeze's weekly meetings once in a while..."

"They're boring."

"That's fair," she had to agree.

"I'll come if we can discuss my plan. You three are an integral part. It only works with all of us."

"Then think of a new plan."

"I'll bring donuts," he said, like that would make everything right.

The women inched closer, drawn to him, and gently pawed at his shoulders and arms. A camera flashed through one of the windows. Shit, there were non-mind-controlled people gathering outside.

"Can we get out of here?" Joan said. "We're drawing a crowd."

Narrowing his eyes at the front windows, Melvin said, "Way to ruin my fun."

He started to raise a hand to direct his thoughts, only the door flew open to Catch demanding, "Stop your wrongdoing this instant, Trick and Spark."

Great. Darlene was the literal worst.

She stalked toward them. Joan fisted her hands while Melvin pushed the women in front of him and ran for the back exit.

"Really?" Joan yelled at him. Then she said to Catch, "Go after him. He's the one—"

Catch weaved between the women, intent on Joan.

"I'm not doing anything. Trick's the one messing with people."

"What do you want from these honest citizens?" Catch said.

"To get away from them," Joan said. The women were coming out of their stupor and would start screaming again. She took a step back to prepare for Darlene's onslaught and—

Shit! Her foot caught on the base of a tall exercise machine and she tumbled into it, slamming her shoulder on the way down. Pain shot through her, making her swear.

She tried to straighten and barked at Catch, "Go get Trick. He ran out the back."

"Your diversion doesn't fool me." Catch held her palms out 'cause she'd take any flames thrown at her and give them right back. Totally unfair.

"What diversion? Look at these people. They've obviously had their minds messed with."

Sure enough, the women got all screechy about Spark and yay that Catch was there. So much for keeping a low profile.

Her shoulder throbbed with a sharp ache. Joan pushed away from the machine and leapt over the cushioned bench. The women shrieked.

Darlene chased after her. Just the thing Joan wanted to do today—have it out with a Super because Melvin sucked. Perry could damn well talk to him from now on.

They burst into the alley. Catch did some fancy jump and

tackled Joan to the ground. Her shoulder smacked the blacktop so hard, she saw stars.

Anger flared fast. Her hands burned to release the fire bubbling under her skin. She pressed them on Catch's chest. It wouldn't hurt her but was hot enough to make her loosen her hold.

Joan twisted and scampered away. "Chill out. I was trying to get him to stop."

"Like I'd believe any of your lies," Darlene said as she stood.

"It's true. Now you've lost him. Nice work."

"Two Villains gathered together means you're up to no good."

"Sometimes it just means brunch." Joan scanned the alley. A dumpster with one side open, a pile of garbage bags down a ways, three closed second-floor windows to the right, four to the left.

Darlene did her palms out thing again. "Hit me with your best shot. You know you have no effect on me."

"Yeah, and you know shooting fire back has no effect on me."

"I'm not letting you escape justice."

"I'm really not in the mood," Joan sighed. "Rain check? How's Thursday? Around noon?"

"Accept the consequences of your actions, Villain."

God, she was so overdramatic and annoying. Everything was black or white, right or wrong. "How do the other Supers put up with you?" Joan said. "Nobody talks like that."

Darlene charged ahead. Joan vaulted up to the covered side of the dumpster. "You're picking a pointless fight," she said.

"You're a Supervillain scaring people and putting them in harm's way."

"I'm about to put *you* in harm's way."

She jumped off the dumpster and tried to make a run for it. Darlene caught her and spun her around, holding tight to steal some fire. Joan shoved her hard. Hot flames formed between her hands. The same happened between Darlene's palms.

"Why don't you ever listen?" Joan snapped. "I'm not working with Trick anymore."

"You're bad apples who belong together."

Her flames crackled in irritation. The staunch Superhero would never listen to a Villain. Not when she thought they were all the same. Might as well give Catch what she wanted from Spark.

"Well, I'm in the mood for a fight now," Joan said.

CHAPTER 5

Sadie set another folded towel on the pile beside her on the couch. The nightly news played on TV, a drab contrast to her cheerfully decorated apartment. They replayed the shaky amateur video of what they were calling a "Super catfight" between Catch and Spark yesterday.

The two were in a back alley beating the crap out of each other. Catch kept absorbing Spark's blasts of fire like it was nothing. It was wild to watch. Where did Catch store all that excess energy? Their catfight was more like a firefight with them shooting flames at one another.

It was hot in more ways than one. Two agile women in form-fitting, neoprene-like outfits. Catch in blue covering everything but her eyes and mouth. Spark in a similar black number slashed with red, only with long dark hair waving about.

They finally resorted to a good old-fashioned fistfight. You couldn't make out what they were saying, but Spark was clearly angry. Well, what did she expect, getting caught by the city's greatest Super? She shoved Catch against a brick wall, then blasted into the air with two streams of fire.

A warm blush spread across Sadie's cheeks. What if that awesome Super was living across the hall?

She hadn't seen Joan in almost a week. As in, Joan hadn't stopped by Vector City Coffee. As in, Joan could've just been busy at work.

The uptick in Villain activity could also maybe, possibly be the reason. The Supers had been in the news for days—more so than usual. SuperWatch was full of sightings. Catch had mostly been in the thick of things.

Her phone jingled on the other side of the deep plum couch. She didn't have to look to know it was Mom. Who else called regularly at ten o'clock on a weeknight?

She swiped on the screen and set the call to speakerphone. "Hi, Mom," she said, steeling herself for what was coming.

"Are you watching the news?" Mom's soft voice was colored with concern.

"Why?"

"There was another incident. *Another* battle with those Superheroes. There was fire. A lot of fire. On a busy Monday afternoon."

"I saw that."

Before Sadie could assure her mother the Super catfight had been nowhere near her, Mom said, "What if that happened by where you work? What if instead of a man falling through your window, a ball of fire shot through the café and hurt you?"

"This looks like it was by some warehouses down by the river," Sadie fibbed, bringing the corners of a pink washcloth together.

"Those people bring destruction to every part of the city."

"It's not that bad."

"You need to be careful. It's so dangerous there."

"Our overall crime rate is less than any other major city," she recited by habit.

"I don't care about other cities. I care about the one my daughter lives in."

"I'm fine, Mom. I'm folding laundry in my apartment. My building is very secure."

"Stay away from the windows."

"Ha ha."

"I'm serious," Mom said. "Did you move your bed yet? It's too close to a window."

"My building is safe. There's no reason for any Hero or Villain to be near it." Unless to live in it, of course. In, say, apartment 714.

"If you feel unsafe, you can come home." Mom was the one feeling unsafe after the Lunk-through-the-window affair.

"I don't feel unsafe," Sadie said. "You know I love it here. Can you trust me a little?"

"I do," Mom said, her tone filled with *No, I don't.*

Not like Sadie could entirely blame her. She hadn't exactly made a lot of smart moves. But still... "Where I work is fine. I like it and what I do."

"Where you work is dangerous!"

"It's been a little unusual at VCC, but the damage is always repaired."

Mom grumbled something that sounded like "They shouldn't have to keep repairing things."

"The Supers paid to get our window replaced. Ten thousand dollars just appeared in the café's bank account. They gave us the money for it, and I think for the other times, too."

"That's the least they could do," Mom said.

"They didn't have to. It was very kind of them."

After a deep sigh, Mom said, "All I'm saying is we don't have these problems in West Vector."

Because it's too boring in West Vector. Changing the topic, Sadie said, "How's Dad's garden doing? Any tomatoes yet?"

"We have a few cherry tomatoes just about ready to pick. The peppers and cucumbers are growing steadily. Are you growing anything on your balcony?"

Ugh, she'd told Mom countless times about the vindictive pigeon. Why did she never remember? It was one more terrible thing about living in the big, bad city. "Not this year. I don't get a good amount of direct sunlight. What I've planted in the past hasn't done very well."

Mom went on about plants that did well in indirect sun. Sadie finished folding her hand towels. Joan could probably grow whatever she wanted on her sunny balcony. If she had time in between fighting crime to do a little container gardening.

Okay, this was silly, and all kinds of presumptive. She should just leave Joan a note saying hi. Pass along her phone number. If Joan was interested, she'd text. If not, they'd be friendly neighbors.

"Oh, you know what," Sadie said, doing her best *I just thought of something* voice. "I promised to loan something to one of my neighbors. I should bring it to her before it gets too late."

"What are you loaning?" Mom's tone went to *Oh no, not again.*

"Sugar. For baking something."

"Just some sugar? Not a hundred dollars or your dead grandmother's pearl earrings?"

Sadie stifled a groan and forced out, "A cup of sugar. That's all."

Mom made a sound that was part disbelief, part relief.

"I got Grandma's earrings back. Not everyone I date is a jerk."

This time, Mom's snort was ripe with skepticism.

"I'll call you this weekend, okay?" Sadie said. "Tell Dad to text me pictures of the garden."

"I will. Take care. Look both ways when you walk to work. Are you still walking home in the dark by yourself?"

"We'll talk this weekend. I really have to go."

They said love yous and goodbyes, and then Sadie hopped off the couch. Mom meant well. She didn't like how often Sadie's kindness had been exploited by the wrong people. But the overprotective thing didn't help. It was probably what made those types of people attractive in the first place. Like she could prove her parents wrong about all her life choices by rebelling against societal norms. By not settling down in the suburbs with a nine-to-five office job and sensible partner.

Hanging out with a Superhero would be one heck of a subversive move. Mom was scared of anyone with abilities beyond what most of the population possessed. The rest of the family thought they were a public nuisance more than anything. They hadn't seen firsthand all the good the Supers did.

In her slightly cluttered kitchen, she pulled a pink-polka-dotted page off the notepad on the side of the fridge.

Hi neighbor!
Let's swap coffee recipes when you're free. Stop by my apartment or Vector City Coffee.
Sadie

She added her phone number, then folded it in half. She wrote Joan's name on one side, stopping herself from drawing a heart on it like a dork. Then she scuttled out of her apartment before she lost her nerve. Her day-off-work sailor shorts and green-and-white striped shirt were cute should Joan be home.

Sadie knocked, then listened for movement inside.

Nothing.

Oh, well. Crime fighting—or personal training—could happen anytime, day or night.

Joan didn't have a wreath or mat or anything to personalize her doorway. Where could the note go so it wouldn't get lost?

Sadie tried sliding it between the door and doorjamb. Several beeps sounded from inside, like an alarm. Uh-oh.

She left the note sticking out and backed up. She was halfway to her place when the door cracked open. Several seconds later, Joan peeked through the opening.

"Hi. I didn't think you were home," Sadie said.

"Sadie," Joan said, visibly relieved for some reason. "I hoped it was you."

Hooray! "I was just leaving you a note." Sadie gestured at the folded paper on the carpeting.

Joan scooped it up and read it. A grin stretched across her face. "Sorry I haven't gotten around to stopping by the café. Work's been…"

"That's okay. I figured you were busy."

"Yeah. There's been some coworker drama."

Sadie nodded. "That's always fun."

She approached Joan in her open doorway. Her new neighbor wore gray sweatpants and a red T-shirt beneath a short-sleeved plaid shirt. Her brunette, chin-length hair hung loose and wavy.

Joan swung the door closed. "Still unpacking," she said. "Kind of a mess in there."

"If you need to use a fully functioning kitchen, mine's available."

"Thanks. I've been hoping we'd run into each other."

Sadie leaned in and jokingly bumped Joan's shoulder with her own. Joan winced and hunched forward.

"Oh my gosh, I'm sorry!" Sadie covered her mouth in embarrassment.

"It's okay. I hurt my shoulder at work."

Wait a second. Joan had a jumbo adhesive bandage across her knuckles. "What happened?" Sadie asked.

"Just…y'know… Sometimes equipment is in the wrong place."

And actually, now that she was really looking, there was a bruise forming under Joan's left eye. "Holy moly, you're a mess," Sadie said. "Can I get you something? Do you need anything?"

"I'm good."

"Want me to beat up whoever was so negligent at your gym?"

A smirk tugged at Joan's lips. "Sure."

"Was it a coworker?" Sadie punched a fist into her palm. "Let me at 'em."

"It was indirectly caused by a coworker. I appreciate the offer, but it might make things worse."

"I have something that's really good for bruises. Come over for a minute."

Joan hesitated, looking back at her door.

"Unless you were in the middle of something," Sadie said.

"No, I was watching the Vultures lose another game. Let me grab my keys really quick."

She dashed back inside. Why did she have to lock her door to run across the hall? Unless she was planning on staying, in which case, that was *okay*. Or maybe she'd been robbed before. Maybe she had expensive workout equipment. It wasn't fair to assume anything.

Maybe she's a Superhero who doesn't want me to see her secret lair.

Joan came back out and smiled. "What coffee concoctions have you been working on?"

"I'm experimenting with Madagascar vanilla. Seeing what pairs best with it."

She moved slowly across the hall. Seriously, how did she get *that* injured working at a gym? Sadie lightly touched Joan's short shirtsleeve and said, "I hope you filed a workers' comp claim. You really got banged up."

"It's all part of the job," Joan said. "How's work going for you? Did you get your broken window replaced?"

"Yeah, it got fixed the other day. Oh, guess what? Someone anonymously gave us a huge amount of money."

"Really? Do you think it was to cover the repairs?"

"It had to be," Sadie said. "Why else would the Supers do that?"

Joan paused outside Sadie's door. "The Supers?"

"We assume it's from Lunk, since he's the one who broke the window. Isn't that thoughtful? I mean, you wouldn't expect any less from the Supers."

"So you assume it's from Lunk."

Sadie set a hand on her chest. "Personally, I do. Amit—my boss—thinks it was from the Supers in general. He said it's guilt money, so he doesn't care who it came from."

"Amit might have a point," Joan mumbled.

Hmm. An odd thing to say. Maybe she had some inside information...

They entered Sadie's cozy inner sanctum. She followed Joan's gaze straight to—whoops, the bras and panties hanging on the drying rack. "Laundry day," Sadie said.

She gently guided her guest into the kitchen, even though the rack was still visible beside the couch. The plain C-cups were more functional for work than the pretty ones she reserved for dates.

Joan focused on the gadgets lining the counters. The espresso machine and makeshift coffee station. She zoned in on the small food processor. "Is that the newest model?"

"No, the old one. The new one's a little bigger. I like this one because it saves space but still has a large enough capacity for what I need."

"I have the old one too but am looking to upgrade."

Sadie pulled her bin of bandages and various ointments from a cabinet. She found the much-used tube of arnica gel. "I'm always getting bruises from banging into stuff at the café," she said. "This really helps reduce swelling and discoloration. You can rub it into your shoulder to help with aches and pains. Use it twice a day."

"That's nice of you to share," Joan said. "I'll buy you another one."

"Okay." Sadie unscrewed the cap and squirted a bit of gel onto her fingers. "Let me put some on now."

Joan started to speak, but stopped when Sadie dabbed beneath her eye. Her fingers felt extra chilly against Joan's warm skin. "Sorry my hand's so cold," she murmured.

"That's okay," Joan said. "It feels good."

Sadie took a step closer to softly pat the gel. Joan was a little bit taller, so she tiptoed up to get level with the bruise. That gingery bite mixed with citrus wafted off Joan. Her mesmerizing eyes looked into Sadie's, heating her deep inside.

"That should do it." Sadie lowered her heels but kept her gaze locked on Joan's.

"Thank you for fussing over me," Joan said. "I don't get fussed over very often."

"Well, that's a tragedy. Come over anytime you want to be fussed over."

Sadie gave her a smile that said she meant it. Joan's grin grew sheepish. She scratched her eyebrow with the bandaged hand.

Sadie touched her wrist. "All this from a coworker error. Do you want to talk about it?"

"It's just..." Joan wrinkled her nose in an unexpectedly cute move. "I stood up for something, and the guy reacted like a whiny man-baby. A client mistook the situation. I tried to smooth things over, but tripped and fell into some equipment. That's why I'm all banged up."

"Was it the man-baby who left the equipment in the wrong place?"

"More or less," she said. "That was part of what I'd been trying to tell him. Safety, and what's best for everyone."

"That should be important to everyone you work with."

Joan pursed her lips. "My coworkers can be pretty self-absorbed. But he's the worst."

"He sounds like a jerk."

"Definitely a jerk. Anyway, it all sounds way more interesting than it actually was. My job's pretty boring."

Sadie stepped over to the arnica gel on the counter. How awesome would it be to rub it into Joan's shoulder? Okay, to get her hand inside Joan's shirt? Welcoming heat exuded off her neighbor like the steam radiators in her last apartment, and she wanted to soak it in.

"Can I treat any other spots?" Sadie asked.

"Oh, no, I'm good."

She nodded at the adhesive bandage. "What about your hand?"

"It's just a scrape."

"Scrapes need love, too." Sadie handed the tube over. "Put it on before you go to bed."

The bandage spanned Joan's knuckles. They looked a little

bruised, too. Like from punching something hard, such as a person's face.

Her heartbeat stuttered.

Like the bruise on Joan's face.

"It works well on minor burns, too," Sadie said. "In case you have any from…anything."

Joan's eyes warmed to liquid amber. "I'll keep that in mind."

This wild theory about her being Catch was looking less and less wild. There were too many coincidences. Too many—

"This is really nice of you," Joan said.

"Just being neighborly," Sadie said with a cheeky grin.

"Then I'm glad to have you as a neighbor."

"I'm glad, too."

"I owe you for taking care of me like this."

Sadie tilted her head. "What do you have in mind?"

"Dinner?"

Yes, yes, YES! "Dinner would be lovely."

"There's a food truck festival in Friendship Park this weekend. I've been looking forward to going. I'd love to have you join me."

"Sure. That sounds fun."

"As a date, by the way," Joan said. "It'd be a date."

"I appreciate the clarification," Sadie giggled.

A half-smile pulled Joan's lips upward. "Hey, it can be hard to know if a woman's interested in you."

"I'm interested in you, Joan Malone."

Her grin widened. "I'm rather intrigued by you, Sadie Eagan. And your taste." She gestured around the kitchen. "I feel like I'm in one of those vintage shops on the east side of the city."

"That's what I was going for."

Joan's gaze rested on the bras and panties. No, wait, the TV. The weathercaster pointed at plentiful sunshine across the area.

"We should have perfect weather on Saturday," Sadie said. "I'm off on Saturdays. Does that work for you?"

"Saturday would be great. I should let you get back to watching the news."

Waving at the TV, she said, "That's unimportant. I'd be more than happy to talk to you about food processors."

"Then we'll have nothing to talk about on Saturday," Joan said with a wink.

Anticipation swizzled up Sadie's chest. "There's also coffee grinders," she teased.

Joan glanced at the TV again before turning toward the door. Maybe she didn't want to see herself on the news.

Some gentle probing was in order. Sadie followed her and tried to be casual. "Oh, hey, sorry. I haven't asked for your pronouns. Mine are she/her."

"Me, too. She/her."

Okay, Joan wasn't Race.

She held up the tube in the hallway. "Thanks again for this. I feel better already."

Sadie gave a little curtsy and said, "Glad me and my top-notch dabbing skills could help."

"I'm definitely feeling your healing energy."

Her hands stilled on her shorts. *Feeling. My. Energy.*

"Absorbing it, like the arnica gel?" Sadie asked carefully.

Joan smiled. "Something like that."

Holy crap!

"Have a good rest of your night, neighbor," she said. "I'll text you when I get to my place so you have my number."

"Goodnight, neighbor." Sadie's voice came out all breathy. "I can't wait 'til Saturday."

"Me, too."

They shared a wave. She watched until Joan made it safely inside her apartment. Her legs jellified and she had to hold on to the door as she closed it. It really did feel like some sort of energy transfer had happened between them.

Joan felt my energy. She absorbed my energy.

Wait, wait, hang on. Joan had reacted funny to the idea that Lunk had given the café money. It had to have been Catch, because she knew about the window. Because *Joan* knew about the window.

Sadie squealed and danced in a circle. "You're going on a date with a Superhero! A nice girl for once. The *nicest* nice girl!"

She had a date with Catch. Well, Joan, but they were one and the same wonderful woman.

She squealed and spun again. Finally, a date with someone sweet and good and honest. A true protector. Someone who'd look out for her rather than ask to borrow five hundred dollars, or lie about not being married, or simply ghost her.

Superheroes did not ghost.

CHAPTER 6

As predicted, the weather was perfect for a Saturday afternoon stroll through Friendship Park. Joan studied the elaborate paint job on an Asian fusion food truck done in shades of red, orange and yellow. Two rows of trucks and other mobile vendors lined the large, open greenspace. The air was filled with conversations, mouthwatering competing scents, and happy pop music playing nearby.

Sadie took a bite of her shredded chicken empanada. She'd been very patient with Joan nerding out and asking the vendors a bunch of questions. "Thanks for humoring my curiosity," Joan said, and gave her a smile. "In retrospect, this maybe wasn't the best idea for a first date."

"When you said you were interested in food trucks, I didn't know you meant, like, *interested*," Sadie said, eyes widening in an exaggerated expression of fascination.

"I tried to warn you in my texts."

"You did."

"I'm learning a lot, so I appreciate it."

"I don't mind." Sadie grinned at her. "It's cute how excited you are."

"Thanks."

She looked cuter than cute with her old-school, curled red hair and 1940s-style green dress with little yellow polka dots and espadrille sandals. Her fire-engine red nails coordinated with her bright lipstick. The deep V on her dress highlighted the twin swells of her delectably more-than-a-handful breasts.

Joan took care not to drop any ground beef from her empanada on her buttoned-up, short-sleeved patterned shirt and black pants. In crowded situations, it was best to play it safe and blend in. Nobody needed to notice her. If anything, someone might stare at her bright white new kicks with red stripes.

She adjusted her black Wayfarer sunglasses—a necessity in public due to her eyes occasionally flaming up when something triggered her.

They walked past the big rock with a plaque commemorating the creation of the park. Its metal had tarnished with age, but one could still read the inscription about how a Supervillain attack had damaged the area's buildings beyond repair. It lauded the Heroes for thwarting the worst assault in Vector City's history.

Sadie chose a wrought iron bench beneath a large, shady tree. She set her cup of horchata between them. Joan did the same, then pulled her stash of business cards and menus from her back pocket. Mark had already scoped out the festival and texted her the names of a few specific trucks to check out. Their plan was to come back tomorrow and take extensive notes.

"So many," Sadie teased. "The vegan truck is my favorite so far. That was the best chicken and waffles I've ever eaten, and it wasn't even real chicken."

"I've had their food before," said Joan. "Everything they make is perfection."

"My empanada's really good," Sadie said, poised to take another bite. "How's yours?"

"It's interesting. I'm trying to work out the blend of spices." Joan munched on hers. Cumin, chili powder, a hint of oregano.

She flexed her sore hand. That arnica gel did help, but it took time to recover from smacking her gloved fist repeatedly into Catch's facemask. That thing was made out of a lightweight but strong-as-hell material. She almost wanted to ask Darlene what it was.

Melvin. What a dick. Running away and letting someone else fight his battles for him. Unnecessary conflict was so…unnecessary. And Darlene thought all conflicts were very necessary. On the bright side, it'd caused Sadie to fuss over her. It might not be so bad to get clobbered if Sadie was there to take care of her.

Sadie smiled over her empanada. "You're really trying to figure out those spices," she said, laughing.

Joan blinked and refocused on her food. "Oh. Yeah. It's rich and complex."

"Do you want to try mine?"

"Sure."

Sadie held hers out for Joan to take a bite. The chicken was missing one more layer of flavor. "Good, but I like mine better," Joan said.

She offered hers for Sadie to sample. Sadie wrapped her fingers around Joan's hand and took a small nibble. She chewed, nodded, then said, "Yours is better. I'd get one, but I have to save room for those fancy strawberry shortcakes."

"Those look so good."

They grinned at one another. The whole afternoon had been fun and relaxed. Sadie was really easy to talk to and joke with. Her warm brown eyes were constantly filled with good humor. Her whole vibe was so comfortable and comforting, you never wanted to leave its orbit. She was beautiful and charming and made you feel like you'd known each other your whole lives.

The way she'd fussed over Joan the other night… Plus, she'd texted every day to see how Joan was feeling. No one outside of Mark had ever done that.

And she was into learning more about Joan. Which wasn't as

bad as she'd thought it would be, since Sadie seemed to like nerdy foodies. Joan could give her nerdy foodie for days.

Ah, damn it. It wasn't fair to pretend she worked at a fitness center. Another "gym injury" would for sure raise suspicion.

"So." Sadie took a sip of her drink. "How come you're so interested in food trucks?"

"It's a dream of mine to have one someday," Joan said. At least she could be honest about that.

"Really?"

"Yeah. My broth—" No, better play it safe and not call Mark her brother. "—cousin and I have been brainstorming ideas for what we'd do if we had our own food truck."

Sadie's thin eyebrows drew together. "You'd rather run a food truck than…work at a gym?"

"It'd be something different. And I'd get to make delicious food for lots of people." *More honesty.*

"What kind of food would you serve?"

"I love hot gourmet sandwiches, so we'd do those. Easy things to eat on the go, like these." Joan wiggled her empanada. "Mark—my cousin—is a genius with sauces and toppings. He'd handle those. He also makes really good ice cream. Simple meals crafted from quality ingredients."

"That's a great idea," Sadie said. "Put your unique twist on familiar favorites."

"That's what we're going for. Cool how you picked up on that."

"I *am* in the food service industry."

"I should be turning to you for advice," Joan said.

"Anytime." Sadie nudged her leg with one foot. "Do you have a name picked out? An overall concept?"

"We were thinking about calling it Hot and Cold."

She considered that. "Hot sandwiches, cool prices? No, wait. Hot servers, ice cream to cool you down."

Joan chuckled and couldn't help saying, "You're so cute."

Sadie just grinned.

"We'd like a turquoise, pink and white theme. That's why I asked you about designing logos. Maybe someday we'll need one."

"Sure. Just say the word."

"I will." Having a logo would make Hot and Cold feel more real. More attainable.

They finished their empanadas in silence. Sadie dabbed at her mouth with a napkin. "It's too funny that's your dream. I've been saving money for years to open my own little café."

"Really?" Joan said, pleasantly surprised.

"Yeah." A dreamy smile played about Sadie's lips. "It would have the same cozy atmosphere as my apartment. Comfy pillows and cushions, lots of color. It'd be drinks and pastries. I don't want to deal with food prep. Oh, but maybe I could partner with you to sell your sandwiches pre-made."

"Or you could open an adjoining food truck."

"Or we could have one mega truck. Food out of one side, coffee out the other."

"A food semi," Joan joked.

"Or you could park your food truck in front of my café." Sadie tilted her head. "I wouldn't mind."

They shared another smile, which seemed to be the thing they enjoyed most—grinning at each other like big dorks. "What's the name of your proposed café?" Joan asked.

"I don't really have one. Maybe something kitschy and catchy. Or something simple like Sadie's Café."

A loud *pop* banged nearby. Joan jumped up and fisted her hands. Smoldering fire burbled under her skin. She peered over her sunglasses to survey the area.

A little boy held the string of a broken balloon up to his parents. *Whew.* Just a freakin' balloon.

She released a deep breath to let the fire subside. *Just a kid. Just a balloon.*

Sadie watched her with wide eyes. Joan pushed her sunglasses back and sat. "Loud noises," she said, like that might explain.

"Yeah, that scared the bejesus out of me."

Sadie snuck a glance at her. Whether she was respecting Joan's privacy or trying to figure out how to ask *What's up with you and loud noises?*, it'd be best to pretend like that hadn't just happened.

Joan took a big gulp of horchata. The cinnamon-y rice drink heated as it traveled to her stomach. "So what's the holdup on opening Sadie's Café?" she asked.

"The cost." Sadie made a face. "The initial expenses to get it going, but also the insurance. Banks don't like to loan money to new businesses because they know you have to spend a fortune on property and liability insurance. Those rates are ridiculous."

"Insurance is really that expensive?"

"It's ludicrous," Sadie stated. "Witness what happened at Vector City Coffee. Three property damage claims in one year. Our rates are always going up."

"I didn't know that." Joan never had to worry about stuff like insurance. She couldn't even go to a regular doctor due to the whole shooting fire as a preexisting condition thing.

"It's part of living in any big city." Sadie tapped her on the knee. "Definitely shop around for the best quote if you do get a food truck."

Joan quirked her eyebrows. "Any tips on the best companies?"

Sadie gave her the inside scoop on insurance companies, and which grocery stores were best for buying in bulk, and how to get equipment and supplies at a discount. They inched closer, voices growing quieter. It felt good to sit there sharing secret dreams. Reassuring. Sadie had thought about this café as much as Joan and Mark had about their food truck.

Sadie rested her fingers on Joan's forearm. "Can I admit something to you?"

Please don't let my skin be burning hot. "Sure."

"I'm scared I might not be able to run my own business. Like, do all the paperwork and hire people and worry about profit and loss statements. It's a lot of work. I don't know if I could hack it. I'm a creative type, not an analytical type."

Joan hummed in sympathy. "Have you thought about a business partner? Someone who's good at that stuff?"

"I have. I asked Amit about it once. He's been the manager of Vector City Coffee since it opened. But he doesn't want to start from scratch. He's married and settled in a good routine. He likes where he's at."

Sadie stared down at her dress. It was the first time she hadn't been upbeat and confident about something. This was a deep confession she was trusting Joan with.

Her heart twinged.

"I'm sorry, and I hear what you're saying." Joan rubbed her date's cool hand. "For what it's worth, you strike me as the sort of woman who goes after what she wants."

"I usually am," Sadie said. "I think I just want this so bad. Like, more than anything."

"It's scary to go for something you want that much. But I think you can do it."

"You do?"

"I do," Joan said.

Sadie dragged her fingers along Joan's arm. "Can I tell you something else?"

"What else?"

"You have very sexy forearms."

Desire bloomed from her core, flowing through her veins like warm tropical waves. She brushed Sadie's thick hair back. "Now that's a prime example of a woman who goes after what she wants."

Sadie pinned her with a sizzling gaze. "I really want to kiss you. If that's okay with you."

Okay? More like hell-to-the-yes. Joan leaned in and murmured, "See? It's already working."

Their lips met softly but surely. No hesitation from Sadie. Joan returned the same energy, reveling in the feel of Sadie's mouth, the slight taste of sweet drink and savory food.

They parted with smiles. Sadie dropped another quick kiss on Joan's appreciative lips. Joan ran her thumb down her date's chin.

Sadie sat back and exhaled deeply. "I have to admit something else."

"Oh yeah?" Joan stared at those luscious red lips. "What's that?"

"I know your secret."

Time crashed to a complete stop.

Joan blinked and managed, "What secret is that?"

"You know." Sadie glanced over both shoulders. "That you're Catch."

What? "I'm what?"

"You're Catch." She held up a hand. "I know you have to keep it a secret, and I don't expect you to talk about it. I just wanted you to know that I know so you don't have to hide it. I promise not to say a word to anyone."

This was…just…*what?* "What makes you think I'm Catch?"

"Your suspect gym injuries. You act weird around doorways. How you said you absorbed my energy the other night. The way you've been watching the crowd." She touched Joan's cheek. "But it's your eyes that gave you away. They're like nothing I've ever seen."

Damn it, her eyes *would* give her away. Joan pulled back slightly.

"Also, the mysterious payment after I told you about the window. I don't know if it was you personally, or the Supers—"

"It was me," Joan stated. Those assholes were not getting the credit for her kind gesture.

Sadie's smile brightened. "It *was* you!" She looked around, then leaned closer. "Thank you. That was so thoughtful."

Sadie thought she was freaking *Catch?*

Sadie thought she was a Superhero?

Sadie wanted to be with a Superhero.

Joan's heart sank. "So you only wanted to go out with me because you think I'm…"

"No," Sadie said, shaking her head. "I wanted to jump your bones the first time I saw you. You are one hot woman, Joan Malone."

More than you know. "But it's a contributing factor."

"Well, I'm not gonna lie and say it's not. But not why you might think." She gazed down at her lap. "I totally admit I'm eager to please and help people out. I'm an open book, and that's been taken advantage of. And yes, I've been attracted to bad boys and girls and other folx in the past. But you're…" She waved a hand at Joan. "You're better than a good guy. You're *the* good guy. I feel safe with you. I hope that's not weird to say. But it's true. I feel like…"

She shook her head again, then covered her mouth. Then uncovered it to add, "I've admired you for a very long time, that's all."

Admired Catch.

Well, shit. Sadie wanted to date someone who wouldn't take advantage of her. In theory, Joan fit the bill. She was overall not a terrible jerk and never took advantage of kindness. She hadn't seen much of it in her life, and it was sacred.

But she was a Supervillain. And had broken *a lot* of laws. And she was lying to Sadie. Even if she denied being Catch, she'd still be lying about the gym. Lying about the true nature of her injuries. No way would Sadie have wanted to fuss over a Villain.

Sadie looked at her with those big brown eyes. She was the good girl here. And Joan really liked her and appreciated her.

A glimmer of something akin to hope flickered in her chest. She didn't have to confirm or deny. And there could be a nugget of truth. Several nuggets. A pack of nuggets. They could get to know the truest parts of one another and see if anything more developed.

A lie of omission was still a lie, but it was the only way she could finish this date and possibly snag another one and, yes, get to feel Sadie's soft lips again.

Nobody had ever accused Joan Malone of being noble.

"There are things I can't tell you," she said. "That's true. It's for your own protection. The less you know, the safer you'll be."

Sadie nodded in understanding.

"But I'll be as honest as I can with you, okay?"

"I know you will."

They were silent for a few moments. Sadie slipped her hand in Joan's and laced their fingers. "Do you really want to open a food truck?"

"I really do," Joan said, squeezing her hand.

"You'd give up fighting crime for that?"

"Like I said, it's something different. I haven't really been able to live a normal life. I wouldn't mind the change."

"But the city needs you," Sadie said.

"The city will be fine without me doing what I do. Or, I don't know, maybe I could do both. I don't know if I can just walk away." She really had no idea if Melvin would let her, or let Mark or Perry, either. He was so hell-bent on villainous victories.

A group of chattering teenagers settled on a blanket near them to take advantage of the shade. Having this conversation in a busy public place was not a good idea. Even kissing Sadie—lovely though it was—could attract too much attention.

Sadie followed her gaze toward the food trucks and crowd. "I'm sure you don't want to talk about this here."

"It's safer if we don't," Joan said. "I am serious about that. It's not in your best interests for anyone to find out you... I don't want you to get dragged into that world."

"Plus, we're on a date. We're supposed to be getting to know each other." Sadie held out her other hand. "Let's gorge on strawberry shortcake and ask each other embarrassing questions."

Joan took her hand gratefully. She dropped a kiss on Sadie's cheek, taking in the scent of her smoky rose perfume. The less they talked about secret identities, the better. And it sounded like she really did want to get to know boring old Joanie.

It was much safer for everyone if Sadie got to know Joan and not Spark, and definitely not the fact that she wasn't Catch.

If there was a recipe for the perfect date, this was it. Sadie laughed with Joan as they approached her apartment. Delicious food, fun conversation for hours, sharing secret dreams, sharing secret identities, maybe sharing some other things very soon…

"So that ended my brief childhood aspiration of becoming a roller-skating veterinarian," Sadie said.

"Too bad," Joan said. "That's an underserved market."

"What did you want to be when you grew up?"

"Hmm. I don't really remember. Nothing as cool as a veterinarian on wheels. I did want to help people, though."

Sadie opened her mouth to ask if being a Superhero had been on the list. No, she didn't want to focus on that. Didn't want Joan thinking she was some fangirl interested in Catch. Which she sort of was, but she was mostly interested in this funny, confident, mind-numbingly attractive woman beside her.

She'd barely paused in front of her door before touching her fingertips to the row of buttons on Joan's shirt. Their kiss had been *hours* ago. Every molecule in her body wanted to do it again. She was practically vibrating in anticipation.

"I think I still have my roller skates at my parents' house," Sadie said, fingering the button just below Joan's throat. "We could go for a roll along the riverwalk so I can show off my mad skills."

"I'd like to see those mad skills." Joan tilted her head and lightly settled her hands on Sadie's waist.

"So that's a yes for another date?"

"A big-time yes."

They leaned in. Sadie's breath hitched in her throat. Joan's lips were so warm. They captured Sadie's, the pressure increasing from gentle, then more sure, then firm. Sadie glided her hands across Joan's shoulders. Joan released a small sigh. Her fingers moved lower to Sadie's hips.

She opened her mouth at Joan's gentle prodding, moaning when their tongues touched. She explored the feel, the taste, the pulse of Joan Malone. Everything about her drew Sadie in, inching her closer until her chest mashed into Joan's and her hands slid around to feel the band of Joan's athletic bra through her shirt.

Joan kept the pace leisurely, swiping her tongue languidly across Sadie's. A jolt of desire rocketed down her body, making her knees go weak. *Whoa.* Joan was such a good kisser, it was actually weak-in-the-knees good. Sadie sucked her tongue deeper and released a throaty groan.

Joan's heat seeped into her like afternoon sunshine. *So. Flippin'. Good.* Her fingers bunched the skirt of Sadie's dress, a clear sign she wanted to hitch it up and get underneath.

Despite the protesting in her head, Sadie drew back. Joan's grip loosened. Sadie turned just enough to fish her keys out of her pocket and unlock the door. She grasped one of Joan's hands and started leading her into the darkened apartment.

Joan hesitated, her captivating eyes bright amber. Sadie quirked her throbbing lips and murmured, "Come inside."

"Oh, I, uh…"

No way was she misreading the situation. At least she didn't think so from the way Joan appeared to be mentally undressing her. "Let's continue this in private."

"Believe me, I'd like to," Joan said, almost painfully. "You're, ah…" She reached up and skimmed her hand through Sadie's hair. "You're so gorgeous."

Sadie pressed a lingering kiss on the back of Joan's hand connected to hers. "I can't stop looking at you. Can I see more of you?"

Joan closed her eyes for a moment. Then she gently extracted her hand. "Let's take this a little bit slower. Get to know each other better."

Oh. Okay. "Sure," Sadie said. "If that's what you want, of course. I didn't mean we *had* to do anything. You can just come in for a nightcap."

A rueful smile tugged at Joan's lips. Probably from the way Sadie had unintentionally said *nightcap* all wink-wink, nudge-nudge.

"You're great," Joan said, sliding her hands in her pants pockets. "And you're really sweet. I can't wait for our next date."

"Ditto," Sadie assured her.

"I want to respect you. You deserve to be respected. So I'm gonna say goodnight now."

Uhhh, thank you? "I respect your wishes, so..." She took a step closer. Joan met her halfway for a soft kiss. "Goodnight."

"Sweet dreams," Joan murmured.

"Oh, they'll be more spicy than sweet."

Joan laughed and kissed her again before moving away.

"Text me when you get home so I know you got in safe," Sadie joked.

"I will."

Joan slowly strolled to her place. Sadie's gaze dropped to the tight ass inside those black skinny-leg trousers. The energy surrounding Joan seemed to fill the hallway, pulling at Sadie, taunting her.

Ugh, she had to go inside and deadbolt her door before she succumbed to it.

She sighed and melted onto her beige carpet, splaying her arms and legs. She was a little disappointed and would *definitely* need to take care of the throbbing in her pink panties. But Joan liked her—respected her—enough to not rush things. She'd listened to and acknowledged Sadie saying she'd been too open too soon in the past.

Joan didn't want to be like the others, but she was already

nothing like them. A heroic person in real life as well as her, well, professional life.

Sadie's phone vibrated in her pocket. A giddy grin stretched across her face as she wrestled with her skirt to retrieve it.

Made it home safe and sound.

Then another text appeared.

Today was perfect. Thanks for everything.

"Today *was* perfect, Joan Malone," Sadie said. She squee-ed and rolled onto her stomach to type her reply. The night didn't have to end just yet.

CHAPTER 7

Darkness surrounded Joan as she peeked inside the air duct opening on the roof. Well, the enlarged opening she'd created via some light torching.

Breaking into the auto museum on the far north end of the city wasn't exactly what she'd envisioned for hanging out with Greta. Though hanging out with Greta often meant literally hanging from something. She had to talk to someone about her date with Sadie, and Mark had been all about Day Two of gorging on food truck offerings.

Greta checked her harness and its line, her sleek black ponytail swinging. "So you've been texting with her?"

"Off and on since last night." Since the end of their date when it had nearly killed Joan to walk away. "She's at work right now but is on a break."

"They've been texting *all day*," Mark whined. He was lying on the roof, holding his stomach and moaning because his Ice getup fit too close for comfort after finishing an ill-advised second Cubano sandwich.

Joan unzipped the chest pocket on her Spark bodysuit to make sure she hadn't missed a text. Their outfits were similar in their black and striped designs, though Mark's was streaked with a deep blue. He'd also opted to get a dark wig attached to his facemask.

"She has some ideas for the Hot and Cold logo based on what we saw this weekend," she told her brother.

Greta readied to slide into the ductwork. "You two and food trucks," she drawled.

She slipped through the hole, sitting back and testing the line. Greta's petite frame made thievery easy. It also provided a good cover for her to move about unnoticed. Unless someone called her an "exotic beauty." Joan had borne witness to Grets throat punching more than one ignorant dude for saying that because of her half Japanese, half Filipino background.

Damn, no new response below Joan's last text. Sadie had been teasing her with little hints about her hidden tattoos. How many were there? And where were they located?

Her heart skipped a beat seeing the magical three dots appear. Then Sadie's text.

> Two. Let's just say you can't see them when I'm fully clothed

> What about partially clothed???

> Maaaaaaybeeeee 😊

Damn it, she could've seen them last night. But she had to sort out the whole *You're Catch* situation before that could happen.

Mark groaned as he crawled over. "This seems like the least straightforward way to get in."

"There are motion detectors all over and pressure sensors on the floor," Joan told him.

"Why not turn them off?" He mimed typing on a keyboard and went, "Bleep blop blerp."

"Why are you here again?" Greta said, her voice echoing.

"I was already with him," Joan said. "He wanted to tag along."

"I wanted to see you pull this off." Mark leaned into the duct. "Which car are you eyeballing?"

"None of them," said Greta.

"Then why are you doing this?"

"Someone bet her ten grand she couldn't break into this place without setting off an alarm," Joan said.

"Easiest money I've made all year." Greta slowly lowered a few feet.

Mark squinted in confusion. "So you're not taking anything?"

"What would I do with a fancy old car that needs to be unloaded fast? I want cash to renovate my apartment in France."

"I love your apartment in France," Joan said. It was in a gorgeous wine region. The local food was some of the best she'd ever eaten in her life.

The light from Greta's headlamp glinted off the metal ductwork as she glanced up with a sly grin. "We had some good times there."

"We had some great times." They'd spent a few weeks there the last (and final) time they thought they could make things work between them.

"So, wait." Mark still wasn't getting it. "You're just doing this for shits and giggles?"

"She does everything for shits and giggles," Joan said, and Greta laughed in agreement.

"I enjoy my money," she said. "Unlike you two. 'I pay my rent. I bought my car with cash.'"

"Joanie steals cars." Mark loved to point that out.

"One car, one time, when I was young and dumb," Joan said.

Greta's headlamp beam bobbed side to side as she shook her head. "You felt so bad, you returned it."

"I couldn't justify why I'd done it."

"For fun? Because you could?"

Speaking of why it never worked between us...

The car episode should've been exhilarating, but had left her feeling sad. Mark had been enrolled in culinary school, and she'd felt lost without him accompanying her on Spark escapades. It'd prompted her to try going legit. The call center job she got fired from for the suspicious fire in her cubicle.

Customer service was not her strong suit.

"I didn't need a sports car," Joan said. Then she grinned. "But I did need that Migano statuette I picked up a few weeks later. I liberated it from a rich guy's office."

"Is that the bronze horse on your shelf?" Mark said.

"Yeah. I love it. I look at it every day."

True, she loved the bold lines and deep carvings on the little sculpture. It also acted as a reminder of what she was good at. The world she belonged in. A middle finger to the norms who'd never tried to understand her.

"Wait," Greta said. "Didn't you take it from your old boss's office or something?"

"The owner of the call center," Joan said.

"That's right."

"I was still working through some anger management issues in my twenties."

Mark snorted. Greta's smile was barely visible. "Perry was so proud of you," she said. "*I* was proud of you. A Migano belonging to the man who fired you. That was a sweet score."

"It was."

It had been at the time. Gaining Perry's approval used to be so important. He'd been glad when Joan took a liking to art, so he'd taught her all about what was worth money and what was to be appreciated. And that revenge was a dish best served on really nice china.

Then Mark flunked out of culinary school for always making dishes that were too cold. Their little family had been reunited. For a while, she was happy just being Spark.

A new Sadie text appeared.

Have to get back to work but I'll think about
colors for the hot and cold logo and will text you
later 😊

Looking forward to it.

At least one norm understood her desire for something different. Joan put her phone away, then called down to Greta, "Sadie's so nice. She's a genuinely nice person."

"And here you are helping with some light B and E," Greta said. "What are you going to do about the fact that you're not a personal trainer or whatever story you told her?"

"She…" Joan glanced at Mark. He would laugh his ass off if he knew who Sadie thought she was. "I really don't know. She thinks I'm looking for a career change with the food truck and everything."

"Yeah, but she'll eventually find out when you get too worked up and fire flies out of you."

"No hiding that. You of all people know sex can be a complicated affair for me."

Mark made a pretend grossed-out face.

Nodding, Greta said, "Like you might melt a metal headboard if you're handcuffed to it."

"I told you the handcuffs were a bad idea," Joan said.

"At least I got a new bed out of it."

"You're welcome."

"*Stop*," Mark groaned. "But also, that was hilarious."

"It was." Greta laughed at the memory. "We were running around my house, naked, trying to put out the—"

"We don't have to rehash the particulars of that story," Joan said.

She could never jump into bed with a woman. There were things she had to do first to ensure her body temperature stayed down. Shoot off a few fireballs in the shower beforehand. Plus, other women knew she was Spark. They expected a certain level of heat. Sadie would expect her to absorb energy, not emit it in a fiery blaze.

"Mark has it so much easier," she said.

"Why?" her brother said.

"You get worked up to room temperature when excited in a personal way."

"So? Room temperature feels good to me."

"Is that why you're such a little slut?" Greta teased.

"You laugh, but that's a part of it," Mark said. "And I have a healthy and active social life, thank you so much, common thief."

He leaned farther into the duct opening. The empty wrapper and napkins from his Cubano fell out from where he'd tucked them in his glove and skittered down the vent.

"Oh, shit," Joan muttered.

They froze for several long seconds, waiting, listening.

"Damn it, Mark," Greta snarled.

"My bad," he whispered loudly.

No alarms were audibly or visibly triggered. Greta continued her descent cautiously. There could still be a silent alarm.

Mark pulled his phone out. "I'll send in a hot tip that Spark and Ice were seen breaking into Allegria Tower. The Supers love high-profile action more than some car museum alarm going off."

"True," Joan said. At most, the cops might show up. Though Greta would lose her bet, which was the far scarier possibility.

Greta landed at the horizontal split in the duct. She unclipped from the line, saying, "Let me drop into one of the cars and do a video call proving I got in. Then we can talk about what to do with this nice girl."

As she crawled off, Mark peered over the side of the roof. "Aw, crap. We did something."

"*You* did something," Joan pointed out.

"No, I mean..." He gestured with his chin. "Race just showed up."

"Shit. Greta's gonna kill you."

"She won't get caught." Mark waved and called, "Hey! Up here! Long time, no see. What have you been up to?"

"The usual." Race's calm voice carried up from street level. "What are you up to?"

"Oh, y'know, just hanging out. Joanie's here. Come say hi, Joanie."

She sent Mark a wary look, but complied to take the heat off Greta. "What's up, Zee?"

When no one was around, they usually reverted to real names with Zee. The Heroes also knew all the Villains' actual first names. Irving was especially bad about inadvertently using them in public. His invisibility made him forget he could still be heard.

Zee stood with hands on hips, off-white Race gear bright in the harsh floodlight. "We got a report of some suspicious activity," they said.

Mark gasped. "How terrible. We'll keep our eyes open for anything untoward."

"Uh-huh. You, uh..." Zee cocked their head. "You wouldn't mind coming down here, would you?"

"Aww, what's the problem? You can't zigzag up the side of a building?"

"Not yet."

Resting his arms on the roof's edge, Mark said, "Where's your flyboy? Why don't you send Flight up here?"

A long pause, and then: "He's on vacation."

"What?" Mark turned to make a face at Joan. "You get vacation days?"

"Deservedly so, yes," Zee said.

"Are they paid?"

"Of course."

"My tax dollars pay for you to take vacations?"

"Do you pay tax dollars?" Zee said at the same time Joan said, "You don't pay taxes."

Mark hunched over the ledge. "Do you get medical and dental insurance?"

"That's all taken care of," Zee said. "Vision, too."

"Come on. Nobody gets vision coverage. That's an urban legend."

"We do."

Mark grumbled to himself. Joan shared a look with Zee. She never really minded dealing with them. Race had always been the least greedy of the Supers. The least *Justice no matter what.* They were actually kind of chill considering super speed was their forte. She'd never admit to it, but Zee cracked her up with their dry wit. In another life, they would've been friends.

A black SUV careened around the corner and screeched to a stop. The rear door flew open, and Lunk charged out.

"Yippee!" Mark cheered. "It's a party now."

A young white guy scuttled out from the driver's side. He looked uncomfortable in the dark suit hugging his thick frame.

"New sidekick?" Joan guessed.

"Hi, New Sidekick," Mark said. "I'd learn your name, but the Supers go through you so fast."

The floodlight glinted off New Sidekick's glasses. "The main entrance is to the right," he said, looking at his phone. "There's a rear entrance to the left, and a big garage door beyond that."

Zee pointed up. "They're on the roof."

Joan and Mark waved. "Greta had better hurry up," she muttered through her teeth.

"Give me a boost," Zee told Lunk.

Lunk cupped his huge hands under one of Zee's feet. Mark shot down a blast of ice, covering the blacktop. Lunk wobbled like a newborn colt but managed to fling Zee into the air. He then slipped and fell on his ass.

Zee tumbled awkwardly onto the roof. "You wanna take this one?" Mark asked, gesturing to them.

"It's all you, Mr. Second Cubano with the Errant Wrapper," Joan said.

Mark cracked his knuckles. "I've gotta work off that second Cubano, anyway."

Zee raced over. Mark sprayed ice around both of them so Zee couldn't get a solid footing. Joan left them to their sliding and fighting and moved to the duct hole. The faint beam of Greta's headlamp bounced around the metal.

"I'll have to piggyback you out of here," Joan said. "Race and Lunk showed up."

A string of angry curses echoed upward.

"I don't think it was an alarm. Probably just us being up here, or that little fire I created."

"It better not be an alarm. I called my guy from a sweet cherry-red convertible. Even took a few selfies."

"I'll vouch for you making good on the terms of your bet."

"Damn right you will," Greta stated.

"Joanie?" Mark called. "A little help?"

"In a second," Joan said. Zee and Mark were across the roof inside a flurry of ice shavings.

She blocked Greta creeping out of the hole as best as she could. Greta unhooked from the line and said, "Let's go."

"Hang back for a sec. I don't want anyone to see you."

Lunk stood with New Sidekick at the rear entrance. "They have to be misdirecting you," New Sidekick said. "There's something going on inside."

"Stand back. I'll put a stop to it." Lunk dug his fingers into each side of the steel door and wrenched it free. The top of the door recoiled and clonked him on the head. He went down like a felled tree.

"Daaaamn," Greta cackled. Joan simply shook her head.

A shrill alarm began to wail, instantly sobering Greta. "Son of a bitch," she ground out.

"Mr. Lunk?" New Sidekick bent down, gently slapping the prone Super's cheeks. "Mr. Lunk? Can you hear me?"

He'd be fine. Hard to tell if Lunk was concussed since he lived in a perpetual state of confusion.

New Sidekick prodded Lunk some more.

"He's better than the robotic sidekicks were in Destine," Joan noted.

Greta winced. "Ooh, yeah. That was a whole mess."

"*Joanie!*" Mark shrieked.

Whoops. Zee had swirled Mark into an ice shell with their super speediness.

"Light it up," she yelled, running over to him.

Mark managed to get one hand free. He blasted ice at the same time Joan shot a steady stream of fire. The elements connected to form a burst of steam. It rose and thickened, clouding across the rooftop.

Joan set her other hand on the frozen shell and melted it enough for Mark to get free. They used the haze to sprint across the roof and lose Race.

As soon as she spied Greta, Joan called, "Get on."

Greta hopped up and pressed herself flush against Joan's back. Joan took several running steps and blazed fire from both hands, careful to keep it out to the sides. They floated over Lunk stirring into consciousness.

"What happened there?" Mark said as he flew alongside them.

"Knocked himself out," Joan said.

"Again?"

A few blocks later, they coasted down to the dark alley where Greta's van full of equipment was parked. She pushed off Joan, shaking her arms and legs. "You get hot when you fly," she said.

"You say that every time," Joan said.

"Not a complaint. I would love to be able to do what you do. Without all the side effects."

"Yeah, well, those are part of the deal."

They got into the back of the van, Joan and Mark quickly pulling off their masks. Joan unzipped her suit to air out. Her white tank top stuck to her sweaty skin.

Her phone vibrated. She pulled it out, smiling at Sadie's name on the screen.

What about a few rainbows and pride flags on
your food truck? Represent LOL

Her smile faded. Here Sadie was, thinking about Hot and Cold
at her regular person job while Joan was making a getaway from
the Supers with her Supervillain brother and thief best friend.
She'd told Sadie she was having a quiet night with them. This
didn't exactly qualify as a quiet night.

Mark chuckled at his phone. "I love SuperWatch. Catch went
to Allegria Tower to get us. She's so predictable."

Catch. Ugh. Shit. Would Sadie know Catch was out and about?
Would she think Joan was texting her while patrolling the streets?

"Sadie again?" Greta said. She set her harness on the narrow
work counter.

"Yeah."

"Then why the long face?"

"She thinks I'm someone else," Joan said. "A way better
person than I am."

"And that's a problem?"

"Of course it's a problem."

"You can't tell her who you are." Greta stated this as fact.

"I just wish I could steer her away from assuming I'm a good
guy."

"You're the most decent person I know."

Mark beat Joan in quipping, "That's not saying much."

Greta gave them both a withering glare. "I'd tread lightly here.
If this goes on for any length of time, the truth will literally come
out. She'll freak the fuck out if you have one of your melty sex-
plosions. And you're too horny not to sleep with her. I'm
surprised you haven't already."

"Because I'm lying to her," Joan said. "I don't like lying to
her."

"But you *can't tell her,*" Greta emphasized.

"*I know.* That's why this sucks."

"Well, I don't know what to tell you. Be a skeeze like your brother and hit it and quit it."

Mark shot her a stink eye and said, "Nobody says skeeze anymore, you sad, pitiful norm who dreams of having superpowers."

"I'd do a hell of a lot more with them than you."

The two of them playfully ribbed each other while Joan stripped out of her Spark suit. She was completely stuck in this situation with Sadie. The actual truth couldn't be an option. She'd be putting more than herself at risk.

Telling her she wasn't Catch was the obvious solution, but that sucked, too. Sadie would be all, *"Why did you lead me to believe you were a Superhero?"* And Joan would have to be all, *"Because I like you and didn't want to correct you and also so you'd think I was good and honorable and not know I'm who Catch fights against."*

It would only open the door to more questions she couldn't answer. Or more lies that would repel Sadie. Telling her she wasn't a Super meant she was a liar. Another jerk in Sadie's long line of jerks. No coming back from that.

Shit.

CHAPTER 8

Mondays weren't usually Sadie's favorite, but this Monday was going to be all right. Joan had promised to stop by Vector City Coffee for a custom drink and chat.

She checked her reflection in the back of the glass display case, fluffing her bangs. Amit caught her and laughed. "What's their name?" he said.

"Joan." She didn't bother feigning surprise at his assumption.

"And how did you meet Joan?"

"She lives across the hall." Sadie smoothed out her apron. Straightened her happy yellow shirt with the fluttery butterfly sleeves.

Amit reclined against the counter and crossed his arms. "You've seen where she lives. That's already a step above who you're normally interested in."

"Yep. She's gainfully employed, too." *Defending our city from harm.*

"Wow," her boss teased. "Better put a ring on this one quick."

Sadie laughed and pushed him toward the check-out tablets. "I found a nice one for a change. We had a date on Saturday, which was great. When I invited her in at the end, she said, 'I want to respect you, so I'll say goodnight now.' Can you believe that? Someone who actually respects me enough to wait?"

"I bet you made out." Amit waggled his thick, dark eyebrows.

"Obviously." The way that woman did things with her tongue defied description.

Sadie fanned at the flush creeping across her face. Just thinking about kissing Joan made her hot and bothered. And her *forearms*. Good lord.

She cleared her throat and told Amit, "She's really nice and open and easy to talk to. Her texts are so funny. We have a date planned for tomorrow night. She's going to cook for me. She's stopping by this afternoon before a work thing."

That was what Joan had called it. What did a *work thing* entail as a Super? So many questions rattled around her head, but they weren't things Sadie could ask about in a text message.

Amit gave a chin nod to a regular customer as he entered and headed for the restrooms. "I have to be your grouchy voice of reason and remind you to keep your eyes open."

"I will," Sadie droned.

"They always seem great at first. Then you get roped into pet-sitting three ferrets for a month. Or bailing the person out of jail."

"She broke up a bar fight. That's why she was arrested."

"Keep telling yourself that," Amit said.

It'd be great to tell him *Joan is Catch, Amit,* but that was a secret she had to keep very quiet. Joan was counting on her to do so. She had a point—the bad guys would love to know how to get to her so they could catch her unaware. Well, not on Sadie's watch.

Nyah returned from lunch, tying on her gray apron. "Did I miss meeting your hot neighbor?"

"No," Sadie said. "She hasn't been in yet."

"Did you hear about this one?" Nyah raised her pierced eyebrows at Amit. "She has a job, no pets, *and* a permanent residence."

"There has to be a catch," Amit said.

Sadie stifled a giggle. *There's a Catch, all right.*

"She's in a band. Or has some bizarre hobby."

"She does have some ideas about opening a food truck. Good ideas. I'm brainstorming a logo with—"

"There it is," Nyah laughed.

Sadie narrowed her eyes. "What?"

"She's gonna hit you up to invest in this food truck."

"No, she's not."

"She'll at least get you to do a bunch of unpaid labor," Amit said.

"It's just for fun," Sadie told them. "I don't know how serious Joan is about it. She's gathering information and resources right now."

She was also appreciative of Sadie's input, and oh yeah, was a *Superhero*.

Nyah shared a look with Amit and hummed an "Mm-hmm."

"It may or may not happen. Her job keeps her pretty busy."

"Mm-hmm."

"You can ask her about it as long as you don't act this weird."

"Mm-hmm." Nyah stepped from behind the counter to collect the dirty mugs off a nearby table.

"I assure you, this one is different," Sadie promised them. It was so annoying to have to justify everything to her coworkers, to her friends and family. Nobody trusted her to make good decisions.

The door opened to a familiar figure. Her pulse triple-timed. Joan wore a black baseball cap and sunglasses and a collared white shirt with tiny black dots and salmon pink, straight-legged pants. Pants Sadie very much wanted to slip a hand inside and explore.

"Hey there, Joan Malone," she all but sang. Her grin stretched as wide as the counter.

"Hi, Sadie Eagan." Joan smiled in her sexy, self-assured way. She pulled her sunglasses off so Sadie could revel in the amber-gold of those exquisite eyes. "How's your workday been going?"

"Good. A little busy earlier, but good."

Joan turned to stare at the wall of windows along the front of the coffee shop. "Looks nice. You'd never know there have been so many disasters."

Sadie glanced up through her lashes. "We had a thoughtful and generous donor."

Amit sidled up to her, giving Joan a deep glower.

"Joan, this is Amit." Sadie gestured between them. "Amit, this is Joan."

Joan gave him a warm greeting.

"So Joan." Amit studied her suspiciously. "What do you do for work?"

Joan's eyes darted to Sadie. "I work at a gym."

"And you get a steady paycheck from this?"

"More or less." Her lips twitched.

"Don't give her the third degree," Sadie said.

"Somebody has to," Amit said. "Have you been convicted of a crime, major or minor?"

Joan grinned. "I haven't."

"Clean driving record?"

"Yes."

"And you're single? Not in any sort of complicated relationship with an ex?"

Sadie rolled her eyes. "She lives across the hall."

"I don't have a secret wife hiding in my apartment," Joan said. She seemed to be enjoying this, fortunately, because Sadie was not.

Amit gave Joan an up-and-down appraisal. He wound up to ask another inappropriate question, so Sadie gestured to their regular customer. "A valued patron is waiting, Mr. Manager."

His frown suggested he wasn't done yet, but he turned to take the guy's order.

"Sorry," Sadie told Joan. "He's trying to protect me."

"It's all good. I like that you have someone looking out for you."

Nyah walked over with the tub of dirty dishes. Sadie introduced the two. Her coworker said, "I heard you like to cook."

"I do," Joan said.

"What's this about you opening a food truck?"

Joan shot Sadie another quick glance, then said, "It's something I've had an interest in. I'm learning more about everything involved with them. If I do it, I want to do it right."

"They're a lot of work."

"I thrive in high-stress situations."

Nyah considered her for a moment, then gave a decisive nod. "Okay. As long as you respect my girl here, we're cool."

"Thanks," Joan said. "I'll do my best."

Ny continued on her way, pausing behind Joan to raise her eyebrows and mouth, *"Wow."*

Sadie gave her a look in return like *Right? I told you this one was different.* Joan kindly pretended not to notice.

"So what can I get you?" Sadie pointed at the black-and-white menu board on the wall.

Joan surveyed the options. "Why don't you surprise me?"

"Okay." Not like she hadn't been thinking about what Joan would want. "I have just the thing. Hot coffee's okay, right?"

"Hot drinks are my jam."

Sadie whipped up an espresso with cayenne pepper and honey. She poured a steamed whole milk heart on top. Offering Joan the paper cup, she said, "One Kick Me Up to go."

"Thank you. Aww." Joan smiled at the heart. "Cute. I've never tried to make latte art. Will you teach me how to do it?"

"Of course." *In the morning, in my kitchen, after…*

Joan took a hearty sip. A really hearty sip for a piping hot drink. Her eyes widened. "Wow. That's good."

"I thought you'd like something with a little kick."

"Yeah. Whoa. It *is* kicky. In a good way."

"Would you like something to eat?" Sadie asked. Amit brushed past to get to the cold brew.

"I just ate. Maybe next time." Joan reached into her front pocket. "How much do I owe you?"

Sadie waved a hand. "On the house."

"No, no. I pay my way."

Joan pulled out a twenty. Hmm. She'd paid in cash on Saturday, too. Did she even have credit cards? Could she get one, or was this an easier way for her to keep a low profile? How did she make money, anyway?

Sadie moved to the nearest tablet to ring her up. She made a slight show of it so Amit would notice. Joan was so clearly not using her for anything.

"Keep the change," Joan said.

"Are you sure?"

"I'm sure."

"Why, thank you." Sadie sent her an appreciative glance. "Gorgeous *and* a good tipper. My, my, my." *And a Superhero. The complete package.*

Joan grinned, then looked around. "I like your design ideas for Sadie's Café better than this. Something more colorful."

"You're into color?" Sadie said…to the woman wearing salmon-colored pants.

"I like a bit of chaos in my life."

They stepped to the edge of the counter. Sadie slid a cute (and practical) rainbow-striped tennis shoe toward Joan's bright blue sneakers. "You do like a pop of color."

"I do." Joan lounged sideways against the counter. "Are we still on for tomorrow night?"

"I still have tomorrow off, right, boss?" Sadie said to Amit.

He pursed his lips. "We'll see."

"That means yes." She gave him a dirty look.

Joan leaned in. "I can't wait to make you dinner," she murmured.

"I can't wait for you to cook for me." Sadie peered over her shoulder at Amit. "Did you get that? She's cooking for me *inside her apartment.*"

He grumbled and waited on the next customer.

Joan's citrusy fragrance mingled with hot coffee and milk. "Hopefully I won't have any kind of work emergency."

Nodding vigorously, Sadie said, "Of course. I understand if you have work emergencies."

"They do crop up."

"I totally understand. You don't have control over…"

"Client activity," Joan supplied.

"Exactly. That's why I told you I…" Sadie raised her eyebrows. "*Know.* I get it."

Joan lightly nudged her with an elbow. "It'd have to be something very important to keep me from you."

How sweet and considerate. Sadie nudged her back. "As long as you text me or whatever, it's fine."

Joan's phone buzzed in her front pocket. "Speaking of." She checked the screen, pulled an irritated face, then said, "I should get going."

"Enjoy your work thing," Sadie said.

"It's just a meeting."

"You have meetings?"

Joan laughed to herself. "Weekly meetings with agendas. I did tell you my job can be pretty boring."

Was that true? Being a Superhero meant meetings and agendas? With who? "What's usually on your agenda?"

"Last week's incident at the gym will be on it. Perry's not thrilled with how it went down."

"Perry?"

Joan's lips parted in a way that conveyed she'd said something she shouldn't have. "He runs the meetings," she said.

"Is he the guy in charge?"

"No, he's the one who likes meetings. Nobody's really in charge."

Hmm. Could Perry be Flight? He was the most senior of the current Supers, and it seemed like he was the number-one guy. Or maybe they had a coordinator. A sidekick who functioned as their manager.

Nyah was not so subtly lurking nearby wiping down tables, so it wasn't the right place or time to get into it.

Joan slid her sunglasses back on. Amit loomed over Sadie, saying, "What's with the hat and glasses? Are you an undercover FBI agent?"

"Yes," Joan deadpanned. "Don't blow my cover."

Nyah chuckled loudly.

"Seriously, Amit, knock it off." Sadie stepped away from him.

"I'm just making sure," he said.

"Shocking fashion news: People wear ballcaps and sunglasses when it's bright and sunny."

"Or when they're trying to disguise themselves."

Sadie ignored him, even though he was right. Joan took a long drink from her cup. Damn, her lightly tanned arms were sculpted works of art.

"Let me walk you out," Sadie said. "Ny, I'll do the garbages."

Her coworker thanked her, then saluted Joan with the cleaning rag. "Nice to meet you."

"Nice meeting you," Joan said. She pointed at the octopus covered in armor tattooed on Nyah's forearm. "Is that OchoStrike?"

"Oh no," Sadie muttered.

Ny's face lit up. "Yeah. You know *Sea Voyage Five*?"

"I've played it a little. I have friends who are really into it."

"Cool. I'm part of the Five Hive." Nyah called over to Amit, "We got another Hiver here."

"I like gaming," Joan said, which seemed to marginally interest Amit.

Sadie couldn't help the cringe pulling at her mouth. Not that she disliked video games, per se. It was the being subjected to countless hours of the people around her obsessing over them.

Ny started down the rabbit hole of asking Joan what her favorite weapons were to use against the giant mutant starfish. "I have to run," Joan said, "but next time I'm here, we can talk about it."

"Yeah, okay. Wave on."

"Wave on." Joan leaned toward Sadie as they headed to the entrance. "I've only played it a few times. I'm not super into gaming. Don't worry."

"Whew." Sadie wiped her brow in exaggerated relief.

"I only play them when someone else wants to."

"So we're not going to have a ten-hour marathon tomorrow night?"

"Not gaming, no." Two bright spots flickered behind Joan's sunglasses.

Giddy delight zipped through Sadie. Their bare arms brushed, sending jolts of awareness through every nerve ending. The flickers glowed more intensely.

They paused at the door. "Thanks again for the coffee," Joan said.

"Thanks for finally stopping in." Sadie touched her fingertips to Joan's arm because she was dying to touch those arms. "Have fun at your boring meeting."

Joan gave a small laugh. "I'll text you later."

"You'd better. Wave on, OchoStrike."

She laughed again, giving Sadie that mesmerizing smile, and squeezed her hand. Sadie's knees liquefied. An unconscious absorption of energy, but worth it.

Joan exited the coffee shop, still smiling but definitely aware of her surroundings. She looked carefully both ways before heading toward a dark luxury sedan. It was going to be interesting hanging out with a Super. Sadie would have to do a bit of truth-stretching about Joan's job as well. But it was for good, and for Joan's protection.

She sighed happily. Getting to spend time with Joan was worth all of it.

CHAPTER 9

Joan lounged in her apartment doorway. It was easier to wait for Sadie than turn off the alarm system. She still had no idea what to do about this situation, but was one hundred percent certain she couldn't wait for this date.

Sadie's door opened. A moment later, she appeared in a long, flowing, indigo-blue halter dress. Her hair had been swept into an updo with little tendrils framing her face. She was barefoot and smiling and carrying a bottle of red wine. And did not appear to be wearing a bra.

Excited anticipation thrummed through Joan's bloodstream. "Good evening, neighbor," she said.

"Joan Malone," Sadie purred. She gave Joan a brief kiss filled with promise. "You look nice."

"You look..." Joan raised her eyebrows, taking in the vision that was Sadie Eagan. "Breathtaking."

Sadie's grin widened, and she breezed inside. Compared to her goddess-like appearance, a burgundy button-down shirt and dark-wash skinny jeans was pedestrian.

Joan hastened to lock the door. The only person she wanted was already there, glancing about the apartment, absently swinging the wine bottle. Sadie met Joan's gaze, and then her eyes slid down to Joan's mouth.

They joined to share a deep kiss. Joan cradled Sadie's face in both hands, gently tugging her closer. Her taste was like a fruit-filled pastry, tart and delicious with every bite. Sadie moaned her approval and wrapped her arms around Joan.

Ooookay, they had to slow down. Joan pulled back and got a throaty groan in response. "Dinner before dessert," she murmured.

"Rude." Sadie gave her a quick kiss and slid her arms back. "But it does smell great. What are you making?"

"Per your request for no seafood and nothing that requires too much prep or too many dishes…" Joan took her hand and led her to where the cast-iron skillet and prepped ingredients sat on the kitchen island. "Steak and spring vegetable mix with a spicy mustard sauce. The herbed garlic butter rolls are ready to go in the oven."

"Yumola." Sadie held out the bottle. "I brought wine-flavored wine. I don't know anything about wine, but the woman at the store recommended this."

Joan accepted it and read the label for the young cabernet. "This will pair nicely. I've got some of Mark's strawberry ice cream for dessert. It's fantastic, so save room."

"I will definitely save room for dessert." Sadie's direct stare left no doubt which dessert she was craving more. "Can I have the grand tour?"

"Um, sure." Joan set the wine down. Inviting anyone into her home was a rare occurrence, let alone showing them around. Opening up her private sanctuary.

Sadie's eyes widened at the shelves of books and art pieces, the original abstract paintings on the walls. "Wow. This is a lot fancier than I was expecting."

"I have fancy taste," Joan joked. *And sticky fingers.*

The bronze Migano horse statuette glowed in the late-day sunlight as if to back that up.

They moved past the mid-century modern gray couch. Sadie looked out the sliding glass doors. In the near distance, the cityscape surrounded Friendship Park. Sunshine dappled through the trees onto the green grass.

She pointed at the park and said, "Do you stand here imagining your food truck down there?"

"I haven't, but now I will." Joan considered the view. She gestured to one of the buildings with retail space available at street level. "Sadie's Café could go there. I could park Hot and Cold across from it at the edge of the park."

"Now you're talking."

She couldn't resist running her fingers down Sadie's back. Yep, definitely no bra under the wavy material.

Sadie turned and wound her arms around Joan's neck. "I love how you keep talking about my café. You even call it Sadie's Café. It feels validating. Like my dream is valid."

"Because it is." Now Joan couldn't resist skimming her palms across Sadie's slim hips.

They kissed, deep and open-mouthed. Joan licked inside Sadie's sweet mouth. Her heartbeat pounded and her blood began to boil. Literally. This attraction burned way too strong.

She slid one hand across Sadie's lower back and pulled the other off her body. Then she flicked a few tiny sparks off her fingers to get rid of some of the building fire.

Sadie ran her hands down Joan's sides, pressing her chest into Joan.

Joan shook off more sparks behind Sadie's back.

"Mmm." Sadie nibbled on Joan's lower lip. "The appetizer is scrumptious."

"We're never gonna get to dinner at this rate," Joan teased.

"I can't help it. You draw me to you like...*whoa*. I'm powerless, like a Villain fighting against you."

That was one way to douse her fire. Joan eased back. "I don't want you to feel powerless."

"I don't mean it in a bad way," Sadie said. "It's just...y'know... how you are."

A bright flare of irritation replaced the fire bubbling inside. "Anyone who considers themselves heroic wouldn't use their powers on someone not expecting or deserving it. I would never do that to you."

Sadie blinked, then gave a small smile. "Of course not. I think my mind's making more out of my jelly knees when it's just normal I'm-hot-for-you jelly knees."

"I get it. I'm feeling it, too."

"Let's continue the tour." Sadie claimed her hand and tugged. One capture a Villain wouldn't try to evade.

She stopped outside the bedroom and peeked in. Joan had done a thorough inspection to make sure there weren't any piles of cash or extra Spark apparel in any of the dresser drawers or the closet. Sadie struck her as the sort of woman who'd spend the night and grab a piece of her lover's clothing to wear the next morning.

They passed the bathroom, then Joan halted near the second bedroom. "That's my office," she said. "It's locked and off-limits. Sorry."

"Ooh, what do you have in your office?" Sadie made quote fingers with her free hand. "Free weights? Gym equipment?"

A very illegal computer system. My old Spark outfit with a big hole in the armpit. A safe full of gold and money. "That's one of those things I can't tell you. For your own good."

Sadie stared at the keypad on the handle. "I respect that. You need to keep things safe."

"I need to keep *you* safe. You shouldn't know about this stuff."

She rubbed Joan's back. "Well then, make me dinner."

They went to the kitchen. Sadie sat on one of the cushioned barstools. Joan grabbed two wineglasses from a glass-front cabinet. Now she was horny *and* slightly annoyed. She shouldn't be leading Sadie on, but Sadie had gone all in on assuming Joan was

Catch. And assuming a lot of things about Catch. If she knew the real Darlene, she'd be singing a whole different tune.

Ugh. This had to get released before it built up. Joan set the glasses in front of Sadie, then slid the wine bottle over. "Can you open this while I wash my hands?"

"Sure."

After giving her a corkscrew, Joan turned on the faucet. She quickly formed a small fireball between her hands. As soon as it flickered and rotated, she shoved it under the running water. It fizzled out in a whisper of smoke. She checked over her shoulder to make sure Sadie was preoccupied with the wine.

Much better. Joan released a cleansing breath. She could've cooked the entire dinner in her bare hands with all that simmering heat.

As she rubbed the seasoned strip steak with olive oil, Joan asked, "So what's your story, Sadie Eagan? What was it like growing up in West Vector?"

"Like the most average childhood ever. A very ordinary house in a very ordinary suburb. It wasn't bad or anything. Just…"

"…ordinary," Joan finished.

Sadie popped the cork out of the wine bottle. "I was always a little too funky for West Vector. I came to the city for college and never looked back."

"Which school?"

"The City School of Design. I wanted to go into fashion, and then textiles, and furniture design for a hot second."

Joan nodded. She could see Sadie being into all of that.

"I worked part-time at a café for living expenses and stuff. By the time I graduated, I realized the thing I enjoyed doing the most had nothing to do with what I'd studied in school. So I kept working at the café." Sadie rolled her eyes. "Much to my parents' extreme disappointment."

"They spent all that money on your education, and then…"

"And then I kept working the same job." She poured wine into one of the glasses. "Well, I did end up getting promoted to assistant manager, but I didn't like it. Too much paperwork and not enough making drinks and interacting with customers. That's my favorite thing to do."

"Did you quit?"

Nodding, Sadie said, "Eventually. As if my parents weren't disappointed enough, then I worked for a few years at one of those cabanas along the riverfront. The ones that sell margaritas and fish and chips."

"A change of scenery?" Joan guessed.

"Yeah." Sadie slid the second full wineglass toward Joan. "I was going through some stuff. An annoying breakup where I had to move out unexpectedly."

"Sorry to hear that."

"It's okay. I got really good tips at that job, so I don't regret it at all."

Sadie took a sip of her wine. She'd alluded to past partners taking advantage of her. Since Joan was trying not to be an asshole despite the obvious lying and all, she asked, "How come you had to move out? Why wasn't it the other way around?"

After a bigger gulp of wine, Sadie said, "It was her place. I had moved in. Rather impulsively after a week."

An uncontrollable chuckle rumbled in Joan's throat.

"I know, I know. Classic queer woman move."

"At least it wasn't after the first date."

"That's what I told my family," Sadie laughed.

"Are you close with your family?"

"I'm not *not* close with them, if that makes sense. I just don't have much in common with them. Everyone's very 'marriage, house, kids, corporate office job.' I don't visit a lot, but I talk to my parents every week on the phone."

Sadie rolled her eyes and started to say something else. When she hesitated, Joan prompted, "What?"

"Nothing. Just that talking to them is usually my mom worrying about how dangerous it is in the city. And my dad and sister like to point out all the things a smart girl like me could be doing with her life."

Joan groaned at that.

Sadie tucked one of her tendrils of hair behind an ear. "It's like nobody trusts me to make my own decisions, so I keep making bad decisions despite not wanting to. It's a cycle I can't seem to get out of." She scrunched her nose. "Sorry, that was kind of deep."

"No, I get it."

"It's like, maybe if I had a little support, I'd be more confident. It's hard to stand by what I want when there's a part of me that knows no one will approve."

Joan nodded. "That makes total sense."

"Does it feel like that with your food truck dream?" Sadie asked, swirling the wine in her glass.

"More than you know."

She wanted to share just how much she understood, but right now it was more important to show Sadie she supported her.

"Does your family know about your plans for Sadie's Café?" Joan wondered.

"I've told them I'd like to open my own coffeehouse. They think that means I want to be a barista for the rest of my life. They don't really get it. They keep waiting for me to get a *real* job and make *real* money."

"Live an ordinary life," Joan said.

"Exactly."

"You enjoy what you do. That means more than a paycheck."

Sadie gestured with her wineglass. "See? That's what I try to explain to them. Who cares if I want to be a barista? I like my life. I like what I do."

"And you're good at it."

"Thank you."

Joan set the steak in the hot cast-iron skillet. It sizzled on contact.

Living an ordinary life meant very different things when one was about a corporate office job and the other was not having people flee in terror because you shoot fire. Funny how Sadie thrived on being extraordinary. Joan had a lot of days where she wished for a slice of ordinary.

Sadie cleared her throat. "I know it's none of my business, and you totally don't have to answer, but..." She adjusted on the stool. "How do Supers make a living? Do you get paid by the city or something? I've always wondered how you can afford to, like, buy food, and pay for rent and utilities."

The honest answer was: "Supers are given everything for free. Whatever they want. The city and its people are very generous to their heroes."

"Oh. I was thinking there's a line item in the annual budget for Superhero salaries."

"There should be one for Superhero damages," Joan muttered.

"Hmm?"

"I have to preheat the oven for these dinner rolls."

She washed the raw meat and oil off her hands to end that line of conversation. She couldn't pretend like it was okay that the Supers cruised into any place in the city and walked out with bags of freebies. Or were all too happy to ask for an unlimited allowance from the mayor. *Take, take, take.*

They did the same things the supposed Villains did, only were welcomed with open arms.

Joan grabbed a pair of metal tongs and checked the steak. Then she preheated the oven. She could tell Sadie was thinking about more questions. Why couldn't they just talk about food and movies and normal things? Did she ever get to be ordinary on a date?

"Would you mind if I asked you a few questions about your abilities?" Sadie held both hands up. "Mostly because I'm curious, but also so I know what I might be in for. Like, in case you suck out my energy accidentally, or—"

"I definitely won't do that," Joan said. "You don't have anything to worry about. I can control myself."

"Supers are born with their powers, right? Have you always been able to do what you do?"

"Yeah. I started noticing it in childhood. And then noticing nobody else could do these things."

"You weren't like the other girls, huh?" Sadie laughed.

"I wasn't like the other kids, no."

"That must've been hard. Especially in a small town."

"Yeah, it was. I…" *I had Mark to go through it all with me.*

It'd been really confusing to have a brother who also didn't know any better, only to discover the other kids in school weren't like them. Lots of whispered conversations in Mark's bedroom about how they should keep it between them because something was really wrong with them.

"Mark was great. He's always been there for me. He's gay, too, so we bonded a lot over stuff. We were the oddballs in our tiny town."

Sadie smiled and commented on how nice that was. It sucked having to lie to her about being a twin, but there had long been speculation that Spark and Ice were siblings, and twins at that.

"In a lot of ways, you could say Mark's been the only person who really gets me," Joan said.

"What about your parents? I get the sense they're not in your life that much."

"That was their decision." The lack of emotion in her tone matched the dull feelings in her chest.

Sadie tilted her head. "Do they not know who you are? I can't imagine parents being ashamed of having a Superhero as a daughter." She released a small gasp. "Oh, unless it has to do with your sexuality."

"No, it's not that." Joan turned the steak. "We never—I mean, I never came out to them. But they had to have known. It was pretty obvious."

"Do you think they know about the other thing?"

"I sometimes wonder about that," she answered honestly. "It's not like they…"

Painful memories tightened her throat. Fuck, she hated talking about anything that'd happened in her old life. How many nights she laid awake, mulling over whether Mom and Dad suspected the Supervillains shooting fire and ice in Vector City were their screw-up children.

"It's not like Mark and I didn't cause problems," she finished.

"What do you mean?" Sadie looked at her, an eager earnestness in her expression. Curiosity but kindness in her eyes. The way she tended to look at Joan, like getting to know her was the single most important thing in the world.

The only reason Joan could open up to her. Or even wanted to.

"When I was young, I didn't have a good grasp on my unique talents," she said. "I caused a lot of damage. Not on purpose. I wasn't sure how to turn it on and off, and it wasn't like there were any guidelines for how to control it. You just have to figure it out as you go."

Sadie nodded in understanding.

"It got to be too much. Mark and I... Mark was around for a lot of it." *He caused some of it, too.* "Our parents decided it would be best for everyone if we packed up and got out of town. That's why we came to Vector City."

"How old were you?"

"Sixteen."

Sadie's eyebrows shot up. "Both of you?"

"Yep."

"You were *sixteen* and your parents kicked you out?"

"We were."

"What did you do that made them...?"

How to tell the story as truthfully as possible? "High school was tough for Mark. He was shy and quiet and skinny in a town that prided itself on its football team, y'know?"

"Oh, I know all about that," Sadie said.

"He got bullied a lot. I had no problem sticking up for him. I, uh... I got really mad this one time. The douchenozzles on the football team were harassing him. So during lunch, when no one was around…" Joan held up a hand. "We really didn't intend to do anything, I swear. But back then when I got mad, it was next to impossible to control myself. I sort of blew up their equipment shed. The place where they stored all their stuff for practices and games."

"Joan!" Sadie gasped, eyes wide. "You didn't!"

"Oh no, I did. And then Mark flooded it. With a hose. To put out an, um, an electrical fire."

In retrospect, it'd probably looked a little funny having an angry girl who always wore a dark flannel and jeans fuming outside the equipment shed while her preppy brother begged her to chill the hell out before she did something she'd regret.

The fire came anyway. A big blast that blew the metal roof clear off. Mark did his best to extinguish it, but his icy bursts ended up making the shed a smoky, smoldering, useless pile of debris. One more mess those troublesome Malone twins had created.

Sadie leaned on her forearms. "How did you blow it up? Where did you get the energy to do that?"

"Oh, I, uh…" Shit, how to explain that? "I had a lot of emotion, and Mark had a lot of emotion. I fed off both of us, and it just kind of happened. Like I said, things were pretty out of whack until I learned how to control my abilities."

"Wow. So did you get caught?"

"Someone saw us running away from it. We had a reputation for being troublemakers, so it wasn't hard to put two and two together. We got expelled."

"Joan." This time, Sadie's voice was soft.

"That's when our parents—mine and Mark's—decided they'd had enough of our shenanigans. They didn't know how to deal with us anymore. Figured we'd do better in the city. They gave us a little money to start over. So we did."

"You were just kids." She shook her head in short, jerky movements. "Did you tell them Mark was being bullied? That what happened was an accident?"

"We tried to, but..." Joan shrugged. They'd already been labeled bad seeds. Something that continued in Vector City.

She didn't want to get into the guilt she still carried over getting them kicked out. That *she* was the reason, not Mark. That Mark had had his life upended because of her. She knew on one level he didn't begrudge her, but deep down, that didn't make it any easier. She'd been his protector but had let him down. It had never happened again, and never would.

"Have you talked to your parents since then?" Sadie asked.

"I used to, once in a while. Mark stayed more in touch with the people back home. We called when we got our GEDs, stuff like that." Joan paused. "But it's been a while."

"You should be so proud of what you've accomplished."

"A girl's gotta do what a girl's gotta do to survive," Joan said.

"I can't believe this. It makes me so mad." Sadie leaned back. "I hope they do know you're Catch. So they understand you were trying to get a grasp on your abilities while defending someone you care about."

A pinch squeezed her heart hearing that name. "I'm sure they suspect there's more to the story. But they for sure don't think I'm Catch."

"Well, it is so totally their loss."

Okay, enough was enough. She had to tell Sadie she wasn't Catch. It wasn't fair to lead her on, especially if they were gonna sleep together. Even if it meant saying goodbye. Even if it meant revealing her true identity. She'd made it clear by now she was not a norm.

"There's something I need to tell you," Joan said.

A noise sounded at her door. Keys jingling. *Shit.*

It swung open to Mark's familiar, "Why aren't you answering your phone? And why is your alarm off?"

He stopped short when he spotted Sadie at the island.

Joan leapt to keep him from saying anything. Why had she given him a key? "What are you doing here? I told you I was unavailable tonight."

"Something came up." Mark peered around her. "Is this Cute Neighbor Sadie?"

"Yeah, this is Sadie." She pointed the tongs at her brother. "This is Mark. The *cousin* I told you about." She gave him a meaningful look. "Right, cuz?"

He squinted at her, then said, "Yes. Your cousin."

Sadie wiggled her fingers in a little wave. "Nice to meet you. Joan was just telling me about you."

"Oh, she was?"

"She was. Wow, you have the bluest eyes I've ever seen."

"What's up, cuz?" Joan said, a tad too anxious. "You don't usually stop by unannounced." Another lie. He did it all the time.

"There's a family emergency. With Uncle Mel."

Shit. "Uncle Mel's acting up again?"

"Oh yeah, he's..." Mark trailed off, darting a glance at Sadie. "Needs help moving. Tonight. Like, now."

Ugh. That meant Trick wanted their help in stealing a big haul. "Did you tell him we don't want to help him move anymore?"

"Remember the last time you tried to tell him that? He won't take no for an answer."

Ugh. Mark wouldn't be here unless Melvin was being particularly douchey and uncooperative. Joan was the one who wouldn't cave in and could make Mark and Perry stand firm.

Damn it. She still had to protect her brother and her...well, her Perry.

Sadie slid off her barstool. "It sounds like you have a work emergency," she said. "Or a...family emergency?"

Joan looked to her, to the cut-up vegetables, to the steak that needed a turn, to the doughy dinner rolls nestled on a baking sheet. Then to Mark waiting expectantly. Well, this sucked.

"I'm sorry," she told Sadie. *For our date ending. For leading you on.*

"Joanie will make it up to you," Mark said.

"I hope so." Sadie picked up the baking sheet. "Can we refrigerate everything for a rain check?"

"Everything but the steak," Joan said. "It's half cooked."

"I can take it back to my place and finish cooking it. So it doesn't go to waste."

"It can finish cooking. It's almost done."

Mark snagged the cutting board filled with green veggies. "Joanie can put together steak sandwiches for you tomorrow. Has she told you how good her sandwiches are?"

"She's alluded to that," Sadie said.

Joan helped them put everything in the fridge. Then she turned off the stovetop and oven. This *sucked*.

As Mark headed around the island, Sadie leaned close and whispered, "Mark knows about…you…?"

"Oh, yeah. He knows."

"I didn't realize you had more family in the city."

"It's found family. Mel's not our real uncle. And we have a guy who's like our big brother who took us in when we were young."

"Perry," Mark offered, because of course he was eavesdropping. "He's a loveable curmudgeon. He'd dig your fashion sense."

"Ohhh." Sadie nodded slowly, comprehension spreading across her face. "Perry, with the weekly meetings. Your *uncle* and *big* brother."

Crap, she was thinking Flight and Lunk. "It's not who you think it is," Joan told her.

"I get it. Found family, with people who understand you."

Mark watched them curiously. She was gonna have some explaining to do.

"It's really not," Joan said. She didn't have time to get into it and wasn't about to do so in front of Mark. "I'll tell you more another time."

Sadie squeezed her hand, letting her fingers linger. "Stop by if you get home early."

"I will," Joan said. *I want to. I wish I didn't have to leave.*

Damn Melvin.

CHAPTER 10

Mark waited until they hit the sidewalk before giving Joan the third degree. "What was all that cousin stuff about? Does she know about your alter ego?"

"Something like that," Joan said.

"I thought you didn't want her to know you're a Villain."

"She doesn't think that." Joan avoided his gaze. "She...thinks I'm Catch," she mumbled.

"She *what*?"

"She thinks I'm Catch."

Mark burst into loud laughter.

"Shut up. It was a misunderstanding, and now I don't know how to get out of it."

"She thinks you're Darlene?" Mark snickered. "That's hilarious."

"It's not. I need to tell her the truth, but..."

"But you don't want her to run screaming down the street because you might set her on fire."

"Exactly. She keeps saying how she feels safe with me, and trusts me." Joan scrubbed at the back of her neck. "I don't know how to come back from that. I've been pretty honest with her."

"Not that honest," Mark chortled.

"I was about to tell her when you barged in."

He shook his head and went around to the driver's side of his tricked-out electric-blue sports car. "Dude. How did this happen?"

"She figured out I have powers and assumed I had to be a Superhero. Which means Catch."

"She didn't think you could be a different Super? What about, I dunno, Amazing Woman?"

Joan made a face at him as she opened the passenger side door. "Amazing Woman retired years ago. She's probably dead by now."

"She's practically immortal. She could still be around and be in good shape."

Amazing Woman was from the old days when Supers had super-gendered names. Her impenetrable body was essentially indestructible inside and out. By the time she'd stepped away from her duties, she was something like seventy years old but barely looked a day over fifty. You couldn't blame her for being burned out. She'd retired before Spark and Ice's time, so they'd never interacted with her. All Perry ever said about her was, "She was the most hard-headed person I ever met."

"I hope I look slightly better than a hundred-year-old woman," Joan said as she sat on the shiny leather seat. "The point is Sadie does think I'm Catch, and it sucks."

"It does suck. She's a cutie pie."

"Isn't she?" Warmth pulsed through Joan's chest.

Mark started the engine and said, "She's just your type, Catch."

He released an evil cackle that got louder when she backhanded his arm.

Joan ignored his ribbing and calling her Catch on the short drive to their hideout. She'd half expected Sadie to freak out from that story about the equipment shed. Maybe a small part of Joan had told her as a test. A gauge of how much Sadie could tolerate, or would want to tolerate. But Sadie had clung to the idea of Joan heroically defending Mark, because Joan was a Superhero even before becoming a Superhero.

She didn't usually feel so bad about lying. This gnawed at her head, at her heart, at her bones. The deep-down facts of what she'd told Sadie were true, but that wasn't enough. It wasn't right. Sadie didn't deserve it. And the longer this went on, the harder it would be to come clean.

They parked inside the warehouse and quickly changed into their gear. Mark pulled at the tight crotch on his bodysuit. "I'm not wearing the right underwear," he grumbled.

"What's the deal with tonight, anyway? What does Mel want us to do?"

"Perry said it's cut and dry. A special art exhibit's being delivered to the museum. Eighteenth-century paintings."

"Art." Joan snarled in annoyance. "He picked the thing Perry and I can't resist."

"He knows you love pretty things." Mark snorted and added, "And that I'll go along with whatever you do."

"I made it clear we don't want to be a part of his schemes anymore."

"That's why he's trying to sweeten the score."

They could decline the job and get Melvin off their backs, and she could hurry home to have dessert with Sadie, and then *have dessert* with Sadie. If the rest of her tasted as good as her lips…

Only that would require having a conversation Joan was so not looking forward to having.

Perry came in through the back entrance, Irving and Ethel with him. All three were dressed for the task at hand: Perry in gray for Breeze; Ethel in black and yellow for Volt; and Irving in deep green for Hide.

"We're really getting the band back together," Mark muttered.

"We don't have to do this," Joan reminded him.

The twins stared at the hench-people. They didn't like each other, but had found it necessary to tolerate one another for the greater good. Er, well, the greater bad, as it were.

Irving acknowledged them with a brisk nod. His straight brown hair poked out of his facemask. Ugh, his terrible halitosis wafted through the air. It was a hilariously cruel joke that he had the ability to be invisible yet could be detected by his foul breath. It got worse when he was nervous before a job.

Ethel scratched at the warm beige skin of her nose. Still the blandest individual on God's green earth. She didn't even shoot off electricity in a particularly interesting manner.

Joan turned toward Perry and said, "Don't be tempted by shiny things. We're turning this and all other jobs down."

"Fine," Perry grumbled. Then he murmured, "Could we start after I take a look at what's in the shipment?"

"No." Joan crossed her arms. The rubbery material of her gloves squeaked against her suit.

"You should commit to Trick now," Irving said. "Before his big plan is set in motion."

"You're either with him or against him," Ethel droned in her monotone.

"Against." Mark waved his hands around. "How much clearer can we be?"

Ethel slid a glance in Perry's direction. He was their weak link. Trick knew how to push his buttons because Perry loved nothing more than art. The older, the better.

Stepping in front of him, Joan said, "We don't need more paintings, and they're too hard to sell quietly. This is where we draw the line."

Footsteps clomped from the hidden side entrance. "Are you sure about that?" Melvin said.

Jesus. His lavender Trick ensemble had gotten an upgrade to add more faux muscles. And a flowing cape. And did he somehow look taller? Lifts in his boots, maybe?

Everything was a lie with him.

His henches scurried over like obedient puppies. "Looking good, Trick," Irving said. He grabbed both sides of the cape and fluffed it out.

"We're ready for tonight's plan, Trick," Ethel said.

"Excellent." Mel turned to the others, elbowing his cape so it flapped slightly. "What's this about not wanting to check out a sweet score of eighteenth-century Flemish masters?"

Perry whimpered softly.

"We don't steal from museums," Joan said.

Melvin scoffed. "When did you grow a moral code?"

"A rich private collector is one thing. I'm not taking anything from a museum. That art's for everyone."

"You know most of it is on loan from some private collection. I've had enough of your holier-than-thou attitude."

"Then stop trying to rope us into doing your dirty work." Joan looked to her brother to back her up. "We said no more, and we meant it."

Mark crossed his arms to mirror her. "We're out, *Melvin*," he said.

"It's *Trick*, damn it," Mel whined.

"It should be *Asshat*," Joan said. "Just because you didn't want to hear what I had to say doesn't mean the conversation didn't happen."

"Joanie…"

"Don't *Joanie* me. I shouldn't even be here. This pulled me away from something very important for something I don't want to do."

Melvin held his hands up like he was trying to calm the situation. One of them got tangled in his new cape and he had to wrestle it free. "Let's go over the plan before you make any rash decisions."

Joan rolled her eyes at Mark and sighed deeply. He did the same.

"How about we sit?" Mel said.

"How about I give you a new hole to pee out of?" Joan swirled her hand and brought a roaring flame to shoot upward.

Ethel clapped a bolt of lightning at her. Perry blew them both out with a rush of air. "Knock it off," he half-heartedly warned.

Melvin cleared his throat loudly. "Hide will go in and scout the area. Once we have eyes on the score, I'll key in to the movers and tell them we're authorized to take everything. Breeze and Volt will help me load the truck. Spark and Ice, you run defense outside in case there's trouble. Can't have you damaging the paintings, and plus—"

"Ethel could damage the paintings," Mark pointed out.

"I focus my energy," Ethel monotoned. "You two spray yours everywhere."

Mark wound up with a dirty retort, so Joan interrupted with, "Hard no. I'm done with this conversation."

Perry shuffled his boots, obviously torn about what to do. The Flemish masters were among his favorites—he already had three oil landscapes in his condo. Getting his hands on them was an evergreen itch he had to scratch.

"*Perry*," Joan gritted between her teeth.

"There has to be a VanderHooven in the shipment," he said. "*A VanderHooven*. The Holy Grail of—"

"Come on, dude."

"I've never taken a VanderHooven."

"Do it some other time."

"I didn't mention the best part," Melvin said. "Spark and Ice aren't directly involved. You can have a clear conscience about the job."

Joan snorted and drawled, "That's how you're trying to justify this? We're not technically involved, so we're not technically working with you?"

"There's a little thing called aiding and abetting," Mark said. "We neither want to aid nor abet."

Mel was characteristically unconcerned. "You're just bystanders. Tell yourself whatever you have to so you feel better about the job."

His words poked at something in Joan's gut. Wasn't she doing the same thing with Sadie? Letting her think whatever she wanted so Joan could benefit?

Oh, shit. She was no better than freakin' Melvin.

"It's a no," Joan said. "Period. End of story."

Her body flooded with adrenaline. She didn't want to be as villainous as freakin' Melvin.

She pushed past him and headed for the back entrance. "I don't care what you do. Leave me out of it. For good."

She shoved the steel door open and took a few running steps. Strong, concentrated flames blasted from her palms, and she shot into the air.

In the dim early evening sky, she flew past rooftops, office building windows, satellite dishes. The wind whipped her long wig.

She'd never liked stealing from places like art museums and hated destroying parts of them. Doing it because freakin' Melvin wanted to made it infinitely less appealing.

Sadie's beautiful face filled her thoughts. Her bright smile, her zest for life, the way she kissed Joan with fervor and stared into Joan's eyes like she *knew* her.

She didn't want to be as bad as Melvin. But could she be as good as Sadie imagined her to be?

I want to be the woman Sadie thinks I am.

Her flames lost momentum. She glided down to a dark, deserted alley, landing in a low crouch. Her entire adult life had been spent in dark places. Sadie was a chance to move into the light.

Only she couldn't be. Joan hadn't been honest, and once she came clean, Sadie wouldn't want anything to do with her. She wanted Catch. A Superhero.

What if I went legit? What if Mark and I open our food truck? What if—

Movement rushed up and stopped a few feet away. It was Race.

Great. Her brief burst of flying had attracted enough attention to alert a Super.

Joan flared stuttering flames with her hands, poised to strike. "Go away. I'm not up to anything."

"Just a fire-fueled evening stroll through the air?" Zee said.

"I wasn't causing any trouble."

Zee shielded their eyes with one off-white glove. "Point those somewhere else. I come in peace."

"What do you want?"

"To talk."

"Right," Joan snorted. "Supers always just want to talk."

"This time, I do."

She merged her weak flames into a ball. "About what?"

"Is it true you're done with Trick?" Zee asked.

"Yes. I'm sick of his shit."

They nodded once. "I believe you."

"That's a surprise," Joan said, and meant it. "Do your cohorts share your belief?"

Zee paused before answering. "They're less keen on taking your word for it."

"They think it's a trap."

"I want to give you the benefit of the doubt. You and Mark are the only ones in that bunch with any common sense." Zee stood watchful, but not poised to strike. Really, any time they stood still was good. If they wanted to, they could wrap Joan up in something secure in seconds.

Joan waved her hands to extinguish the smoldering fireball. It didn't have much juice thanks to her using so much energy as a flying propellant.

"Listen." Zee walked toward her. "Can't you convince Trick to give up his whole *First Vector City, then the world* plan? You told Darlene you tried talking to him. She doesn't believe you, but I do."

Freakin' Darlene. "He won't listen to me. He doesn't listen to anyone. His lackeys do whatever he says. Mark and I stand up to him, but we can't stop him."

Zee crossed their arms. "Once he starts in on civilian mind manipulation, we quickly lose control of a situation."

"I get that it's hard to stop him, and harder to keep him contained." Joan took a step back, not that such a small distance would matter should Zee want to capture her. "But you guys need to do something. He's grown drunk on his self-made power. He even got a cape."

"He what?"

"He got a new cape attached to his suit. It looks ridiculous."

"Channeling big Flight energy?" Zee half-laughed.

"I guess."

They hesitated for a long moment. "I shouldn't be telling you this, but he's our priority right now. We're doing all we can. Any help you could provide would be—"

"I know he's planning on—"

Joan clamped her mouth shut. She'd rat Mel out if she could force herself to look beyond their Villain Code. They didn't snitch, didn't turn each other in. The bad guys were still her people, for better or worse.

Plus, if Mark or Perry decided to take part in the museum heist, she'd be putting them at risk. That was something she'd never do, not for anything or anyone.

Zee stared at her intently, dark eyes shining against the golden skin peeking through the eyeholes on their mask. "He's planning on what?"

"Taking over the city," Joan offered weakly.

"Do you know how? Has he filled you in on his plan?"

She focused on a nearby pile of trash bags.

"Come on, Joan. Help us. You and Mark can help bring him down."

"What will you give us in return?" she asked. "Immunity? A free pass?"

"Well, no, but possibly a moratorium on—"

"Possibly? So, what, your jerk friends can double-cross us?

Not a chance." Sparks flickered from her eyes. Zee had picked the wrong night for this.

Zee planted their hands on their hips. "You're a criminal. I can't wave a magic wand and erase everything you've done."

"But you could let me and Mark go. And Perry, if he goes legit. Mark and I want out of this life. We're making plans. We want Perry to come with us."

"Perry will never stop. I tried telling you that years ago."

"You just wanted me and Mark to join you."

"I didn't want you thinking you didn't have a choice."

"We didn't," Joan stated. "We were homeless street kids. The Supers did nothing to help us. *Nothing.* You all treated us like shit. Didn't even offer to buy us food. Oh, wait. You never pay for anything. You couldn't even give us a free meal."

Zee didn't respond to that. They couldn't. They knew the Supers had failed two angry kids with superpowers. Bad seeds once again.

"Perry took us in. He helped us control our abilities so we—"

"So you could use them for his benefit."

"So we wouldn't destroy the city. You should be thanking him."

The heaviness of an old, unresolvable argument hung between them. A small part of her had always wondered what made Perry so vehemently anti-Super, and vice versa. It went deeper than just the Hero/Villain conflict. It sometimes felt like his life of crime was to spite them. The more he villained, the more he was determined to villain. That had to be why he didn't like the idea of going legit.

"I can talk to the others," Zee said. "See what we can do for you."

"That's not a good enough guarantee."

"What good is a guarantee to a Supervillain? You could very well double-cross *us.*"

"I would if you didn't uphold your end of the deal."

"Then why should I trust you?"

"Why should I trust *you*?" Joan countered.

"If I was here to capture you, I would've done it by now."

"Yeah, and I'd have burned through whatever you'd try to contain me with."

Zee cocked their head. "Let me put it another way. If you don't want to be lumped in with all the Villains, don't lump me in with all the Supers."

Hmm. Good point. "Maybe," Joan answered slowly.

"We don't always see eye to eye."

"They're total jerks."

Zee looked like they wanted to agree, but changed their mind. "You and I have more in common than you want to admit."

"What, that we're both stubborn? Sarcastic? Think Darlene's a pain in the ass?"

"She's very dedicated to our cause."

Joan rolled her eyes.

"Do I have to point out the obvious?" Zee gestured at their off-white outfit, then at Joan's black-and-red getup. "We're part of a larger community."

They gestured back and forth again. "We're both queer," Joan realized.

"And Mark. Did you ever stop to think that's why I've been lenient on you two all these years?"

"Lenient?" Joan fisted her hands.

Zee's mouth pulled into a little smirk. "Like I said. You'd already be on your way to jail if I wanted it."

Ugh, Zee was still a smarmy Super at heart. But they wanted to do the right thing—the *right* thing, not the stringent, by-the-rules thing.

Joan sighed, the weight of the evening sitting on her like Lunk. "Look, I'll think about it, and I'll talk to Mark. But you're probably on your own."

Zee nodded, then shifted their feet. "As a gesture of good faith…"

They zoomed away, barely leaving a puff of dust.

Joan slumped against a nearby brick wall. Could she ever really trust a Super? Could the Supers trust her? Would Mark laugh his ass off at the idea of a shaky alliance? They'd tried to go legit before, and it never stuck. Villainy was the life they knew. The one they were good at.

This time could be different. They had a plan. They had the food truck dream and a way to utilize their powers to benefit their business. And maybe they could even get off Vector City's Most Wanted list, even though that would require turning on three people who were sort of like family. Or at any rate, who were no better than Big Liar Joan.

Then she could come clean to Sadie. Tell her yes, Spark had been a thieving liar, but that life was behind her. Joan would be one hundred percent honest with Sadie from then on. Sadie could be an important part of New Law-Abiding Citizen Joanie.

She needed time to think this through. And to talk to Mark. And Perry, if she could convince him to start a new life. Only Zee had a point—Perry loved the thrill of the heist. The making (and taking) gobs of money.

She slunk out of the alley to walk back to the warehouse. A young white woman carrying a grocery bag took one look at her and screamed and dashed across the street. Up ahead on the side-walk, two Latino men elbowed each other.

"Damn, it's Spark," one said.

They stared at her, either frozen in fear or waiting to see what she'd do. One of them pulled out his cellphone. Possibly to take a photo, possibly to report a Villain sighting.

Ugh. Joan wanted to tell them to chill out. Spark wasn't on the prowl tonight. She turned and ran in the opposite direction. Away from anyone thinking she would do them harm.

CHAPTER 11

Sadie banged on her sliding glass door. The vindictive pigeon stared back from where it was sitting on her balcony railing.

"Go away!" she yelled, banging harder.

The pigeon studied her for an unhurried moment, then hopped around until it faced out. Then flapped its wings and took flight, dropping two big glops of poop on the back of her patio chair.

"*Noooo!* You suck so hard!"

Another day, another victory for that jerk.

Her phone chirped from the kitchen with the text tone she'd selected for Joan. A tone she'd heard a lot that morning as they made plans to walk to work. She cast a forlorn glance at her poop-covered chair, grumbling, "Stupid rat with wings. I hope you eat rotten garbage, and I'm an animal lover."

On my way out now.

"You can't ruin my day, you gross pigeon. I get to see Joan to make up for our interrupted date."

She gathered the two metal travel mugs and her keys off the kitchen counter. It would've been much nicer leaving Joan's place after a wonderful night together. Per the text she'd sent at one a.m., it had been a rough night.

Sadie exited her apartment, carefully balancing the mugs. A door opened across the hall, followed by Joan saying, "Let me help you with that."

"Good, because one of these is for you."

Joan trotted over and snagged the red tumbler. "I was kidding about the coffee in my text."

"Coffee is never a joke with me," Sadie said.

"It wasn't at all necessary, but thank you."

She made sure her door was locked, then turned to Joan. They both leaned in to share a brief but lovely kiss. "Hi," Sadie murmured.

"Hi." Joan pulled her into her arms and squeezed tight.

"Aww." Sadie nestled against Joan's warm chest, taking in her citrusy scent, the feel of her hard body. "This is nice and unexpected."

"I'm just glad to see you."

"I'm glad to see you, too."

They drew back slowly. Sadie dragged her fingers along one long sleeve of Joan's thin black button-down shirt. Her vivid red pants and white sneakers were much more Joan Malone, and complementary to Sadie's hot-pink shell top, lilac-colored capris and rainbow sneakers.

Joan kissed her on the cheek and grinned. She seemed awfully chipper for someone who'd gotten home late. Though it *was* a little after noon.

"What kind of coffee are we having today?" Joan asked, glancing at her mug.

"I made you a little something with ground ginger steamed into the milk."

"Ginger?" She took a sip, then *Mmm*-ed in delight. "Sadie. You are spoiling me rotten."

The way Joan said her name caused a thrill to zigzag up

Sadie's spine. "I believe I told you I'm more than happy to fuss over you."

Joan took another sip. Her *Mmm* was lower, throatier. Speaking to what else Sadie could do to fuss over her.

Sadie twined their fingers as they moved toward the elevators. A sweet kiss, a big hug, holding hands as they drank coffee... A girl could definitely get used to this every day.

She opened her mouth to ask how things went last night, but Joan spoke first. "So you enjoyed the steak?"

"It was really good." Sadie glanced up with a little smile. "I got hungry and ate the whole thing. Sorry."

Joan laughed and squeezed her hand. "That's okay."

"I didn't want it to go to waste."

"Hey, I deserve that for leaving. When can we have our rain check dinner?"

"Not 'til Saturday," Sadie sighed. "I have to work every night until then."

"We could make it breakfast or brunch. I can scare that pooping pigeon off your balcony."

"You literally just missed it."

"Darn. I'll get it next time."

Joan was smiling, and had her hair pulled back in a tiny bun, and she just looked so damn adorable and snuggly, and she genuinely wanted to make up for...

Why *was* she so chipper? Was it simply a good mood from fighting crime or whatever she'd done last night? There had been no news about major Super activity, but that didn't mean she hadn't been doing something important. It'd been significant enough for her to step away from a very promising date.

"I make a really good frittata," Joan said.

Sadie blinked and stirred out of her reverie. "I'm sure you do," she said. "Did everything go all right last night? It sounded pretty important."

Joan drank some coffee. "Nothing ended up happening. At

least not with me and Mark. We have to have a serious discussion with Perry about something today."

"So this was a found family thing? Not a work thing?"

"My found family is usually a bit of a work thing."

"I'm only asking because you're not as tired as I figured you'd be, and if it was related to your job..." Sadie trailed off, biting her bottom lip.

Joan tapped the elevator button with her elbow. Cradled her coffee against her chest. Rubbed the back of Sadie's hand with her thumb. "I want to be as honest as I can with you," she murmured.

"I appreciate that, and I know you can't give me the specifics. I just thought you'd be exhausted after last night's activities."

"It ended up being some frustrating meetings."

"And you're having another family meeting today?"

Joan took a sip of coffee. "Another meeting."

Huh. That was somehow more confusing. "You're really just having meetings? That's not code for something?"

"It's really just meetings. This one's less formal. Just Mark and Perry."

"I can't believe you ditched me for a meeting," Sadie half-joked.

"It sounds weak, I know, but I had to be there." Joan looked at her with those arresting amber eyes. "I had a good talk with Race. At a different meeting. Some new things came up."

Hmm. A talk with Race, but not the others. "So Mark and Perry," Sadie said. "And Uncle Mel. Are they...?"

The elevator doors to their left opened. A twentysomething Black man glanced up from his phone as they stepped in. Sadie raised her eyebrows at Joan, telegraphing she had to answer when they were alone.

She felt bad poking into Superhero affairs, but she had a long history of people not being fully forthcoming with her. Joan had said her "uncle" and "big brother" weren't who Sadie thought they were, but who else could Uncle Mel and Perry be but Flight and Lunk?

And where did Mark fit into the equation? He had unusually bright blue eyes. Joan always referred to her cousin with *he* and *him* pronouns, so he wasn't Race. Was he a sidekick? An ally who assisted in the fight against crime? Maybe he was an unknown Super. Or he could really just be Joan's cousin, sworn to secrecy.

How did all the puzzle pieces fit together?

The elevator reached the lobby. Sadie firmly held Joan's hand and all but dragged her away from the other residents milling about.

"So." She leaned close and murmured, "Mark and Perry. How are they both work and family?"

Joan's chest rose and fell with a deep sigh. "It's really not what you think," she said. "Like, it's *really* not what you think."

"Can you tell me who they are to you?"

"I can tell you they're not…" Her voice had dropped to a near whisper. "Heroes."

Sadie matched her volume. "They're not Flight and Lunk?"

"Not at all."

"And Uncle Mel?"

Joan snorted. "Definitely not."

They exited their building into the brilliant sunshine. Joan released another deep breath. "We've had a miscommunication. I need to tell you… That is, I should've told you…"

She glanced across the street. Her eyes widened.

"Princess! No!" a woman screamed.

Joan took off running straight into traffic. Sadie's blood froze as she helplessly watched Joan scoop up a fluffy little white dog. A large SUV squealed to a stop right in front of her.

Joan leapt on top of the hood, then took two big steps and pushed off the windshield with one foot. She landed in a crouch, cradling the dog. Then she jogged to the sidewalk and held the dog out to a middle-aged white woman.

"Here you go," Joan said.

"Oh, Princess!" The woman hugged her dog tight. The little pup wiggled and licked her face all over.

Joan patted its body. "I had a dog like this when I was a kid."

"How did you do that?" the woman asked, clearly in awe.

"I used to be a gymnast," Joan said smoothly. Still holding her coffee like she'd just taken a stroll to the break room.

There was a pause in traffic, so Sadie made her way across the street. Her pulse pounded with a rush of relief. That had been terrifying and incredible to watch. Obviously, Joan was in shape to do the things she had to do. But seeing her in action, being so athletic, was...

Why *had* she jumped out of harm's way? Not that anyone should voluntarily let a car hit them. But Catch could absorb a blow like that. Sadie had witnessed her stop a train. Wouldn't it have been easier for Joan to just stand there?

"Are you okay?" Sadie asked, grasping Joan's upper arm.

"I'm fine. So is Princess." Joan smiled at the dog.

"Thank you," Princess's mom said. "Thank you so much. She's my baby."

"Happy to help. You behave yourself, Princess."

The woman moved one of the dog's legs up and down to wave goodbye.

Sadie slid her hand down Joan's arm. "I can't believe you ran in front of all those cars."

"I grew up with a dog who looked just like that," Joan said. She took several steps back on the sidewalk.

"It was pretty awesome."

"Sometimes I do nice things."

"Of course you'd save a dog. But why did you do the fancy gymnastics instead of absorbing the impact?"

"Well, I *am* in disguise." Joan gestured to her clothes. "The thing with a secret identity is keeping it a secret."

Oh. That made sense. Everyday people did not stop cars with their bare hands. A hero was a hero, no matter what they wore. "It's all about the goodness on the inside," Sadie said.

Joan took another step back, surveying the area. "Yeah, and speaking of secret identities..."

"Yes." Sadie grinned. "Mark calls you Joanie. Which I love. Can I call you that? Bear in mind no matter what you answer, I'm going to call you that."

A brief smile flitted across Joan's gorgeous face. "That's cute. But I need to—"

"Or what about Joanie Maloney?" Sadie mused, then giggled hard. "A play on both your names. That is too adorable. There's no going back now. You are henceforth Joanie Maloney forever in my mind."

"Okay, sweetheart, but—"

Sadie surged forward to wrap her arms around Joan's neck and plant a big wet one on her mouth. Good god, Joan could call her *sweetheart* in that low, silky voice 'til the end of time.

"Sorry," Sadie breathed. "You were saying?"

Joan looped her arms across Sadie's lower back. "I completely forgot."

"I'm proud of you for rescuing Princess, Joanie Maloney."

Her eyebrows drew together in concern. "I want you to be proud of me."

"How could I *not* be?" Sadie gave her a peck on the cheek before untangling her arms and travel mug. "That's probably the smallest good thing you've done this week."

Joan dropped her arms. Pulled her sunglasses from her shirt pocket and put them on. She glanced around, then said, "Can we go over there for some privacy?"

She jutted her chin at the small greenspace in front of the tall office building next door. Sadie followed her to the narrow stone path outlining the grass. "I didn't mean to talk about Supers and everything in public," she said, keeping her voice down even though they were alone.

Joan gulped her coffee.

"I'm just trying to figure out how your family fits in with your work stuff if they aren't involved." A new idea sprang to mind. "Are they with the police? Some special task force that works with the Supers? Or the mayor's office?"

"Nothing like that," Joan said.

"I guess I don't understand how you can have one found family, and then another family with the Supers—"

"The Supers are *not* my family," she stated firmly. "They're work acquaintances."

Her vehemence was rather unexpected. "Oh," Sadie managed. "I figured they would understand you, because—"

"Mark and Perry are my family." Joan kicked at a small rock. "That's the truth. Perry has been like a father figure. He let Mark and I live with him for years. He taught us how to survive. How to harness my abilities so I wasn't so destructive. I don't know what would've happened if he hadn't done that. I was with them last night while also having to deal with Super activity. The meeting with Race."

"Okay."

She looked over at Sadie. "Remember the man-baby I told you about? The one who doesn't care about the safety of others?"

Sadie nodded.

"That's Uncle Mel. Or really, just Melvin. I don't want to think of him as any kind of family."

"So when you got beat up by Spark last week, Melvin was there?"

"He was the reason that fight happened. He's an asshole and is up to no good." Joan clutched her coffee tightly. "He needs to be stopped. Mark and Perry are trying to help me stop him."

"Oh. I just thought Spark was being a jerk."

Joan flinched. "Spark's not... She's not the worst of..."

"Um, she shoots fire. That's pretty scary." Sadie swirled her coffee. "You're lucky you can absorb it and give it back to her. A taste of her own medicine."

Joan stared at her tumbler for a long moment. "Spark's not really that bad," she said quietly.

"*Shoots fire,*" Sadie said.

"And that automatically makes her bad?"

"She's a Villain. Literally the definition of a bad guy."

"Not all Supervillains are inherently bad. Some do bad things because they had no other option." Joan looked up, meeting Sadie's eyes. "It's hard to go through life scaring everybody off because you shoot fire, or ice, or lightning bolts."

"Yeah, but you can suck the energy out of people. And Race can literally run circles around us. You use your gifts for good. It's a choice."

"Is it?" Joan stopped and fully faced her. "There's no real hope of living a normal life with these *gifts*. You can't just get any job. It's hard to work in customer service when a client pisses you off so badly that you melt your phone. And computer and desk. There are some powers that make it impossible to exist in normal society."

"I guess, but…"

"Even if you try to hide, the truth comes out in the end. Breeze went to college. He got an MBA. But he ultimately couldn't pursue his passion for curating art."

"Not legally," Sadie drawled.

"Sometimes they try to go legit. Spark and Ice have tried. We're not…" Joan's mouth twisted. "We're not meant to live like the norms."

"The norms?"

"Regular people, like you."

"Ah."

Sadie's heart lurched from the hurt expression wrinkling Joan's face. Clearly, this was a sore spot. "I'm sorry," she said, rubbing Joan's shoulder. "It has to be hard for you. I didn't consider the drawbacks of being so extraordinary."

Joan dug her thumb into her travel mug. "I'm just saying not all bad guys are bad. And not all heroes are heroic. I could tell you things about the Supers that would…" She shook her head.

Like what? "Some people—I'm definitely not one of them—but some people say the Supers create as much damage as the bad guys they're trying to stop. Is it things like that?"

"Yep. They never offer to rebuild. Just expect people to be

grateful and show their gratitude with a bunch of free shit. Not that they ever share that free shit, even with folks who really need it."

"You pay for things," Sadie pointed out. "You paid for the window at VCC, and you've paid for food and coffee with me."

"I'm not like them," Joan said.

Another thing she'd never considered: Joan didn't have a good relationship with the other Supers. They always appeared to work well together. Maybe that was just for show. A united front in the face of crime.

"Did something happen?" Sadie asked gently. "A rift between you and the other Supers?"

"You could say that."

"Can I ask what it was about?"

"We have different ideas about some things," Joan said.

"That's why you've been spending so much time with Mark and Perry," Sadie guessed.

"For sure."

They began to walk again. "But you all ultimately want the same thing. Justice, safety, fighting the good fight."

"That's what all Superheroes want." Joan's eyebrows quirked. "Sometimes, that's the only thing they can see. They don't always notice when a Villain tries to do some good."

"Wow." Adoration flowed through Sadie's bloodstream. "You can see the good inside a Supervillain. That's so noble. And honorable. You're kind even to your archenemies."

A strange sort of sadness played across Joan's face. "Remember that about me, okay?"

"How could I forget?" Sadie said, tucking her arm through Joan's.

Her gaze swept over the travel mug in—

"Joan." She stared at the deep ridges that hadn't been in the red metal a few minutes ago. "What happened to my tumbler?"

Joan lifted her thumb out of the rut it had created. Her other fingers rested inside more grooves. "Shit," she muttered. "Sorry. That happens sometimes. I'll buy you a new one."

"Was it because we were talking about superpowers?"

"No, it's... Sometimes when my emotions run high, stuff melts."

"Yikes."

"Oh, yeah."

Trying to keep things upbeat, Sadie joked, "Absorbing the caffeinated energy from the coffee?"

Joan pushed her sunglasses back.

"I'm sorry." Sadie squeezed her arm. "Your powers aren't a joke. I shouldn't be so flippant and nosy."

"It's okay to be nosy. I'd be curious if I were you. And I don't want you to feel like you can't ask me things."

"So you still cause a little damage when you're upset?"

"When I'm strongly emotional, yeah. A little." With a smirk, Joan added, "I don't incinerate equipment sheds anymore, so progress."

"Very good progress." Though the metal tumbler might not agree. It was *melted*.

She nestled her arm more snugly through Joan's. "I appreciate you telling me all you have. And I'm sorry you're having problems at work. With your coworkers."

"Thanks," Joan said.

"It's nice you have Mark and Perry to turn to."

"It is."

"And..." Sadie glanced up through her lashes. "You have me. I like you for exactly who you are. If the other Supers can't see how great you are, well, that's their problem."

Joan stopped walking again. Her lips parted like she was about to say something.

She drew Sadie into a tight hug instead.

Sadie rubbed her back, feeling the tension knotted in Joan's muscles. Her work problems were really weighing on her. That could explain why she wanted to open a food truck. And why it'd be an unobtainable dream. It was hard to be ordinary when every-thing about you was extraordinary.

"I really like you," Joan murmured against her ear. "For exactly who you are."

Her heart swelled. "Maybe I can help you be more average while you help me climb out of mediocrity."

A balmy breeze of laughter rushed out of Joan's mouth and traveled down Sadie's neck. "That would be great."

"But you still have to save dogs," she teased.

"I will always save a dog."

Joan kissed across her cheek, landing a soft one on Sadie's lips. She claimed Sadie's hand and said, "Let's get you to work. Making you late won't win me any favors with Amit."

They stepped off the stone path onto the sidewalk. Joan's palm was abnormally warm. Not in a painful way. Just a...

Sometimes when my emotions run high, stuff melts.

Had that story about melting office equipment been about her? Another unfortunate error by young Joan? She'd said she'd caused a lot of damage. Things had been bad enough for her parents to send her away.

Sadie wanted to ask. Should ask. Like, *really* should ask. It wasn't too nosy. But all she did was ask Joan questions about being a Superhero. And about the other Superheroes. There was more to her than that, and she was probably tired of talking about all that. It wasn't the only part of her, and Sadie didn't want her thinking that was the only thing she found interesting.

Joan kissed the back of her hand. "So the thing about liquids is their instability. They're hard to control in terms of temperature..."

Sadie half listened as a tiny sliver of doubt threaded through her. Why would Joan have these problems? Too much excess energy stored in her body from being Catch? And how did she know so many details about what the Villains did?

She shook that away. *Come on, Sadie.*

Past hurt was making her suspicious of a literal hero. Joan

wouldn't lie to her. She wouldn't have risked injury—or revealing her true identity—to save a dog's life. And it was her duty to know the goings-on of the Supervillains. She was a kind, sympathetic person who saw them as more than just the enemy.

Joan was amazing, and she really liked Sadie, and she needed to be supported. Fussed over.

Joan Malone deserved only the best, and Sadie was going to give that to her.

CHAPTER 12

Joan Malone was a coward. A lying, villainous asshole of a coward. Because she couldn't tell Sadie the truth.

Even though they were enjoying a lovely impromptu Thursday morning brunch, reality screamed at her from all sides. The apartment paid for with ill-gotten funds, the keypad on her office door in her periphery, the picture of her and Mark and Perry on their annual blowout Christmas trip to the Caribbean stuck to the side of the fridge.

And Sadie sitting with her socked feet on the bottom rung of Joan's barstool, nibbling on eggy frittata, happiness personified as they chatted about Sadie's Café. Thinking she was hanging out with the most noble Superhero around.

Joan had tried to tell her yesterday. She really had. But then Sadie saw her rescue that little dog, and kissed her soundly, and made Joan forget for a few moments that she wasn't heroic. She didn't want the admiration shining in Sadie's brown eyes to dim.

Sadie thought of Spark the way all norms did. Not like Joan could say *I'm actually the scary menace you're afraid of.* The new plan was to show her all Villains weren't bad. That Spark was no saint, but not a fire-breathing monster.

Joan tipped her tall coffee mug back to catch the last drops of the cappuccino Sadie had infused with cinnamon and nutmeg. "You definitely need to put this on the menu."

"It's similar to a seasonal offering at VCC," Sadie said. "I use a lot of pumpkin spice syrup in the fall and winter."

"You could do this one for the holidays. Add a little gingerbread man cookie to the mug."

"Oh, wait until you see what I whip up around the holidays." She waggled her eyebrows.

"Looking forward to it," Joan said, squeezing Sadie's thigh through her green pants.

Sadie rested her hand on Joan's. "My latte art gets very yuletide-y."

Lacing their fingers, Joan said, "Will you show me how to do latte art tomorrow? Brunch date at your place?"

"Sure."

They shared a smile, then turned back to their plates, still holding hands. "I can picture how Sadie's Café would look in the fall and winter," Joan said.

"So cozy. I'd switch out the pillows and some décor for rich earthy tones and leaves. And lots of twinkle lights in the winter. Not that we have cold winters, but I want to make it feel like you're stepping out of the snow into a warm, woodsy cottage."

"I love that. We should be taking notes for all this stuff."

Sadie made a vague shrug, focusing on her piece of sourdough toast. Her phone chimed on the island countertop with a new text. She glanced at it, groan-grumbling.

"More crime?" Joan guessed.

"Mom wants to make sure I got the links to the articles. All three of them." Sadie rolled her eyes.

Her mom had been texting about recent crimes in Vector City. A news item about the art museum robbery the other night, one about a sculpture stolen from the front yard of a historic home, another about an art gallery that got hit last night. Joan hadn't been aware of the last two.

"Let me text her really quick so she knows I'm okay." Sadie

slipped her fingers free. "I try not to complain because I know my parents mean well."

It seemed more like they were smothering her, but what did Joan know about a good parent/child relationship? From the way Sadie acted with each message, it was clear she was being sensitive to Joan's strained parental situation, which was thoughtful.

As Sadie typed, Joan checked her phone. Nothing new under Mark's last text.

> P never came home last night. Still not home unless he's taking one of his epic dead to the world naps.

Perry had done his usual disappearing act. That wasn't unusual when he didn't want to face someone or something. He knew Joan was mad at him for doing the museum heist despite not wanting to be seen around town with Melvin and Company. If he was out there doing jobs with—or worse, *for* Melvin…

It was going to be damn near impossible to get him to cut back or lay low. And no way would he do anything to help the Supers. Perry didn't have a different dream to pursue. Stealing a Vander-Hooven *was* his dream. She and Mark couldn't foist their dream upon him if he didn't want it.

Sadie pushed her phone across the island. "I told her I'm having brunch with a friend so she'll hopefully get the hint."

Speaking of dreams… "Did you tell her we're talking about Sadie's Café?"

"There's no point. She doesn't think it's real."

"You know what you're doing, and you're really excited about it. I'd say that's as real as anything."

"Yeah, but…" Sadie wrinkled her nose. "I haven't done anything about it in thirty-four years. I can't blame my family for thinking I never will."

"There's no timetable for these things. I'm thirty-five and considering a career change."

"I know," she sighed.

"Listen. This was delicious." Joan touched her empty mug, then nodded at the fridge. "And you made that cold brew chilling in there that smells like vanilla paradise. You're teaching me about tasty beverages. I can tell it's your passion."

"It's nothing, really," Sadie said, staring at her lap. "I'd rather talk about your food truck."

"We've talked plenty about that. Today's about you and your dreams."

"That's just it. A far-fetched dream."

"What you want is important," Joan told her. "Don't discount it because you think it's not possible. I can help you figure out the business part of things. The loans and money stuff. We can learn about it together. But honestly, you already know way more than you're giving yourself credit for."

Sadie wrapped loose arms around Joan's torso. "Thank you."

"You're welcome."

"No really, thank you." She dropped a quick kiss on her lips. "You make me feel like it could be possible."

"Good. That's our deal." Joan tucked Sadie's hair behind her shoulders. Her insides twisted at the fact that she was also making today about Sadie to take the focus off herself. It'd been just boring old Joanie with no discussion of the Supers. The normalcy she'd been craving for so long. How could she give that up?

A shy smile spread across Sadie's beautiful face. "I don't talk about my café with anyone. Not even my friends. But I like talking about it with you."

"I'm here whenever you want to toss ideas around." Joan ran a thumb down Sadie's cheek. "And for taste-testing."

Her grin intensified, warming Joan's heart. "It's so nice to trust each other with our secrets."

Joan wrenched her lips up and forced out, "Yeah."

Sadie kissed her cheek before sliding off her barstool with a sad sigh.

"Do you need to get going?" Joan said.

"Soon. Thursdays are pretty busy. It's Amit's day off, and I'm de facto in charge when he's not there. But I'll help you clean up."

She stood, too. "Don't worry about it. I toss everything in the dishwasher."

"Then I'll help you toss everything in the dishwasher so you can walk me to work."

Sadie tilted her head up, signaling she didn't have to leave just yet. Joan took her time meeting her for a soft kiss. God, she could kiss Sadie for a decade straight and not get tired of it. Their kisses weren't the usual feverish rush toward getting naked. They were for fun, for exploration.

For Joan, not Spark.

She kissed Sadie deeper, their tongues meeting with equal need. The heat that rushed through her body wasn't fire. It was sweeter, lighter. Something like delight. Joy. Excitement at a true connection. She had no doubt Sadie sex would be amazing sex, but it was okay to wait and enjoy the anticipation.

Sadie hummed, pressing her fantastic breasts into Joan's. Ooookay, now the heat was turning molten with desire.

"Dishes," Sadie moaned miserably. "Day job."

"Boo."

They slowly separated, letting their fingers linger as long as possible. As they gathered the dirty dishes, Sadie's phone chimed. She read the screen, shaking her head. "I swear, next she'll tell me our near record number of days without rain is a result of Super activity."

"We don't control the weather," Joan said. "At least not the Vector City Supers. Oceanview has Ether, that one Villain who can manipulate clouds and moisture in the atmosphere."

His name was Derek and he was kind of a tool, but he threw kickass parties on the beach.

"My family's part of that group of people I told you about," Sadie said. "The ones who think Supers are overrated and destructive and are why it's so dangerous in the city. My mom especially doesn't trust them. Well, you."

Joan carried her plate and mug toward the dishwasher. "I don't blame them."

"She's gotten more paranoid since Lunk crashed into VCC. Apparently, I work at the most dangerous coffee shop in the world."

"I mean..." She couldn't help snorting. "You kind of do."

"Don't you start," Sadie laughed.

Because she was genuinely curious, and also as a temperature check, Joan asked, "What would your parents think about you hanging out with one of *those people*?"

Sadie set her dishes on the countertop. "They'd probably jump in the car and try to drag me back to West Vector. But I wouldn't go. I'm safe with you."

Shiiiiiit. But hey, even if she was Catch, Sadie's parents wouldn't like her. So that was something.

"I look out for the people I care about," Joan said. That much was true.

She went back for their water glasses. Her phone lit up with a text from Mark. One to both her and Perry.

Perry where the fuck are you?????

She shook her head hard enough for Sadie to notice. "Oh no. Is my mom texting you now?" she teased.

"It's from Mark."

"Better a text than having him interrupt another date."

"I should warn you that'll happen again. Mark stops by all the time."

"If he wants to hang out with us, that'd be fine. I'd like to get to know him better. He's so important to you."

"Yeah, he's..."

He's your brother. She doesn't even know he's your damn brother.

Maybe the truth could come out in bits and pieces. Chip away at the lies. She could get one out, then lead to more important ones.

Joan set the glasses next to the dirty plates. "I have to tell you something."

"Okay." Concern filled Sadie's eyes.

Drawing in a deep, steadying breath, Joan said, "Mark isn't my cousin. He's actually my brother. My twin brother."

"Oh."

"We keep it a secret for both our safety. No one needs to know we're twins, or even that we're siblings. I didn't want to lie to you, but we don't tell anyone other than people who know us really well."

"Oh," Sadie said again. She gradually nodded. "Okay. That makes sense. His eyes are like yours. Is he—"

"He's not a Superhero." Joan was quick to quell that notion.

"Okay. You keep it under wraps. I get it. Now I see how Mark's connected. Thanks for telling m—" Sadie's eyes widened. "Wait. Then it was just your parents who kicked you out?"

"Yeah."

"Both of you?"

A twinge squeezed Joan's heart. "Yep."

"Wow. Two kids." Sadie took a step closer and set her cool fingers on Joan's forearm. "Do you have any other siblings?"

"No, it's just us."

"Your parents sent their only two kids away?" She shook her head in disbelief. "Wow. I mean… *Wow*. No wonder you don't talk to them."

"The only slightly good thing was that Mark and I had each other. When I say we've been through everything together, I mean *everything*. I…" Old, familiar pain coursed through Joan's veins. "I still feel guilty for what happened."

"Why?"

"The equipment shed thing was my fault. Getting expelled. I took away his future without giving him a choice."

Sadie sucked in a small gasp. "Joan. That wasn't your fault. You were kids. You didn't know how to control your abilities."

"Consciously, I know the adults around me failed us. But that doesn't take away the sting. It's why I'm protective of him."

"You were protecting him even then."

"Yeah," Joan said. "He was the one who first thought about a food truck. I think part of why I want to do it is because he really wants to. I do, too, but I want to do it for him as much as for me."

Rubbing her arm, Sadie said, "He's lucky to have such a caring sister."

"I'm lucky to have him."

Joan welcomed the hug Sadie enveloped her in. She rested her chin against Sadie's temple, soothed by her embrace, her compassion. It felt good to talk to someone about this.

"I'm so glad you have each other," Sadie said, and squeezed tighter.

"Me, too."

She pulled back enough to give Joan a small smile. "I bet you're the older twin."

"I am. By eight minutes."

"Thank god. I'm a much better match for oldest kids. I'm the youngest and used to being spoiled and getting exactly what I want."

Humor brimmed in Sadie's coffee-colored eyes, and she was visibly trying not to laugh. But the levity was nice, and the idea of giving her everything she wanted was pretty damn appealing. It helped tamp down the nerves over trusting her with some serious inside information.

Maybe it was a mistake to tell her about Mark, but she wanted Sadie to know. Wanted her to know everything.

"I hope I can spoil you as much as you've been spoiling me," Joan said, massaging Sadie's lower back.

"I hope…" Sadie tiptoed up to nuzzle Joan's nose. "We can spoil one another." She glanced behind Joan. "Shoot. I need to get going."

"I can drive you if you're worried you'll be late."

Sliding back, Sadie said, "As long as we leave, like, now, we're good."

Well, crap. Not like Joan could toss out *By the way, funny story about my secret identity. Have fun at work!*

They headed for the island to grab their phones and keys. She'd finally gotten a text from Perry.

> Went out of town. Will explain later. Job tomorrow night. Não se preocupe.

He only told them not to worry when he meant it.

A job tomorrow night. Probably selling some of that art he stole. Not that she wanted any part of it, but for Perry, it could be her last job. Mark's last job.

Spark and Ice's last job.

"I'm officially a fan of your frittata," Sadie said, strolling toward the door.

"I'm officially a fan of Sadie Eagan."

"Well, aren't you cute, Joan Malone?" She grinned as Joan joined her. Damn, she was adorable.

Hmm. *Spark and Ice's last job.*

They exited the apartment. Easing into more truth-telling, Joan said, "So what do you really think about my wanting to change careers?"

Sadie cocked her head, taking her time before answering. "Can you walk away from what you're doing? Like, can you stop doing it?"

"I don't know," Joan answered honestly. "Could I stop cold turkey? I'd like to think so, but…"

"Sorry, I meant are you allowed to retire? I know"—Sadie mouthed the word *Supers*—"retire when they get old. Are you allowed to step away while you're still in your prime?"

"Yeah. I mean, nobody's beholden to anything. The nice thing about having an alter ego is you can just stop being them and be your true self."

"Maybe you can cut back your hours? Go part-time?" She giggled. "Part-time crime fighter sounds like someone who dons a cape and tights and patrols their neighborhood in their spare time."

There was one thing Joan was fairly certain about. "If I stop, I have to stop completely. Make a clean break. It'd be too easy to slip back into that life."

A neighbor approached with two bags of groceries. They exchanged hellos with the tall person rocking an all-denim ensemble.

Once they were out of earshot, Sadie said, "I imagine it'd be hard to walk away in times of need. Maybe you could be around for, like, the really big stuff. When the you-know-whos are really wreaking havoc."

"Hopefully, what I'm working on will put a stop to most of the havoc."

"That would be great."

Going for a joke, Joan said, "Then I can just save the occasional dog, or a cat up a tree."

Sadie gave her a close-mouthed smile. "You do so much more than that. You literally save people's lives."

"That's a bit extreme."

"Don't be so modest." She leaned into Joan's side. "I saw you save a busload of children from an oncoming train. You're a hero."

Shit. That'd been the biggest win of Catch's career. Even Joan had to admit she'd been impressed by Darlene's heroics. "I didn't do that," she whispered.

"Well, okay, if you want to get technical, Race pushed the school bus off the tracks. But you stopped the train."

Her stomach bottomed out. *Fuck.* "I didn't do that."

Sadie held her palms out. "I don't want you to think I'm a superfan or anything. I'm kind of embarrassed to admit this, but I've had a huge crush on you for years. Ever since I saw you do that. I was there."

Shit fucking shit. That was why she was so excited about Joan being Catch.

Joan paused a few feet from the elevators. Dread swam around her head, making her a little dizzy. "Sadie…"

"I know, I know." Sadie bit her lower lip. "You're used to people gushing about how much they adore you. You've probably gotten marriage proposals."

"No, it's—"

"I really do like you. Please don't think I'm only interested in that other thing. You trusted me enough to tell me about Mark. I hope you know I'm totally here for you. You can trust me."

"I do."

The *but* sat on Joan's lips, a breath away from letting the truth out.

But you shouldn't trust me.

Something passed over Sadie's face. Like she sensed the *but.* One of her eyebrows scrunched lower as she studied Joan.

This was it. The door was open. She had to push through and accept the consequences for once in her goddamn life.

Sadie's expression softened. "It makes you uncomfortable to talk about this, doesn't it? That's a whole other world, and I get the feeling you don't like your worlds to intertwine."

The words lodged in Joan's throat. *I'm not Catch. I'm a big-ass liar.*

"It's okay. Really. We can stick to talking about the world I'm in. I'll stop embarrassing you."

"You're not. It's just… I'm not who you think I am."

"You think I've built you up in my head all these years," Sadie said.

"No, you see the Supers how most people see them."

"Your concern's not unwarranted. I tend to leap headfirst into relationships. One of us should be cautious."

"Don't put this on you," Joan said.

"Let's do this right. Or at least try to do it right. Foodie Joan and barista Sadie, hanging out and eating a lot of really good food."

She brushed her fingertips down Sadie's cheek. "That's exactly what I want," Joan murmured.

Sadie had given her the perfect out. Not talking about Supers? Done. Focusing on what was brewing between them? Done and done.

Now would be a great time for an interruption. Another neighbor, or an elevator arriving. Or a text. Anything so Joan wouldn't feel so damn guilty.

The seconds ticked by.

Sadie laced their fingers together. "I also hope to do other things," she said.

"Adult things?" Joan said.

"Mm-hmm."

"Yes, please."

A beautiful, wide smile graced Sadie's face, and goddamn, Joan couldn't do it. She was a shit. She was a giant pile of shit.

The only way out of this was to get out of villainy. She could come clean after the fact.

Sadie squeezed her hand, then tugged her toward the elevators. Joan blew out a shaky breath. To be fair, she *had* tried to tell her. Had actually said the words *I'm not who you think I am.* Sadie could have asked for an explanation.

At this point, she wasn't even sure Sadie would believe her. She was so hung up on all things Catch, she'd probably view it as Joan just being modest. Or protecting the Supers the way she protected Mark. It was kind of impressive how Sadie had such a one-track mind.

Sadie's phone trilled with a different text tone than before. She pulled it out of her back pocket. "It's work. Jeez, sorry for all the interruptions today."

"It's okay."

"Tomorrow, can we silence our phones and not look at them?" She glanced up with intent. "I want to focus on you and me."

"You and me," Joan echoed.
She could absolutely focus on just the two of them.

CHAPTER 13

Warmth from Joan's body and the hot frothy milk seeped into Sadie's core. Her kitchen had felt small before, but never this intimate. She slid her palm across Joan's lower back and watched her try to pour another milky heart on top of the espresso.

Joan laughed and gave a little cry of frustration as she dragged a crooked line down the center of the foam. "Ahh, I'm so bad at this."

"You're doing well," Sadie said, rubbing her back. "It takes practice."

"I'm too distracted. I'll have to practice at home." Her gaze swept over Sadie in that mentally undressing way she'd been doing all morning. They'd gone from wolfing down tasty yogurt parfaits to making out to Sadie teaching Joan how to pour latte art to making out to this one last attempt.

"Your instructor's a tad distracted, too," Sadie said, skimming her hand down to Joan's hip.

"I mean, your lips are right there." Joan lifted the small metal pitcher and dropped a kiss on Sadie's mouth. "And your cheeks." She kissed both. "And your nose." She brushed her lips across it. "And this neck of yours, Sadie Eagan." She nipped at the tender skin just below Sadie's earlobe.

Sadie grabbed the pitcher and set it on the counter so she could pull Joan against her and kiss her properly. She dug her fingers into Joan's waves of hair while Joan cupped her butt.

"You taste so good," Joan rumbled before licking inside Sadie's mouth.

She grunted somewhat unsexily in response, backing against the counter, parting her legs to let Joan know it'd be one million percent fine if she wanted to haul her up to the top.

Joan pressed against her. Her thigh crept between Sadie's, fingers teasing the skin above the waistband of her blue cigarette pants.

Ungh, she didn't really want their first time to be an under-the-clothes kitchen quickie, but she'd take literally anything at this point. Joan was so freaking hot and got her so freaking hot, it was a wonder Sadie could form a single coherent thought around her.

Joan touched several spots near Sadie's hips. Then her lumbar region. Uh, if she was searching for erogenous zones, she was way off.

"What are you doing?" Sadie giggled against her lips.

"Guessing where your secret tattoos are," Joan said.

"Ah."

Her fingers wandered under Sadie's striped shirt to her lower spine. The touch sent electric prickles through her skin. "Can I see them from the back?"

"Maybe," Sadie said.

"Here?" Now her hands were on Sadie's hips.

"Maaaybee."

Joan took her sweet time tortuously grazing her fingertips across the skin around Sadie's waist, pausing above her bellybutton. "Can I see them from the front?"

Yes, yes, sweet Sappho, YES. "Maaaayyybeee."

Her eyebrows quirked above those liquid amber eyes. "Not even a hint?"

"I don't like spoiling the surprise. Plus I love what your eyes are doing right now."

Joan leaned back slightly. "What are they doing?"

"They change colors. Like they go from light to dark, kind of in a swirl." Sadie nestled her hands on Joan's strong shoulders. "It's really cool."

She blinked a few times, then dragged in a deep breath.

"Feel free to do some in-depth ink investigation," Sadie said. She pushed her chest up, knowing damn well the scoop-neck on her shirt gave Joan a generous view of the girls. Joan was always sneaking glances at the girls.

The swirling eye colors intensified as Joan stared at the twin swells. She probably didn't even notice the stretch marks. Her energy seemed to heighten. It was a little intense.

In the near distance, Joan's phone buzzed. It'd been vibrating off and on, but they'd been ignoring the outside world.

Her fingertips curled into Sadie's waistband, close to one of her secret tattoos. "I want nothing else in the entire universe than to discover your secret tattoos. But I have to— I mean, I need more time. I mean, *we* need more time. To do this. To do it right, like you said yesterday."

She was adorably flustered. Confident Joan didn't seem like she'd be nervous about sleeping together, yet she kept hesitating. Maybe it was an energy absorption thing. Maybe sex felt kind of weird for her. Or incredibly wonderful if there was an energy exchange. Regardless of her reasons, they were valid and worthy of respect.

"Whenever you're ready," Sadie said, cradling Joan's face in her hands.

"I'm so damn ready, sweetheart. You have no idea."

"Oh, I have a pretty good idea," she laughed as her heart soared. *Sweetheart.*

"You have to leave soon for work, and I've got a work thing. I'm not rushing this all-important ink exploration."

"I don't want to rush it, either."

Joan wrinkled her nose in that unexpectedly cute way. "I wish we could stay in this little cocoon we've created between our apartments. Leave the outside world…outside."

Sadie drew her close for a kiss. "Friday nights are usually dead at VCC. I'm home by ten-thirty."

"That's not late at all," Joan said, toying with the button on Sadie's pants.

"And tomorrow is Saturday, which just so happens to be my day off."

"You can sleep in."

"I can be up late tonight." She kissed Joan again. "Very late."

"Then let's pick this up at ten-thirty."

"I'm gonna be thinking about it all day." *Yessss! Finally!*

The intensity of Joan's kiss left no doubt how much she was looking forward to it, too. "I already think about you all day," she said.

"Smooth. Very smooth."

"Just speaking the truth."

Like Joan would ever tell her anything but the truth.

A piercing alert wailed out of her phone. Joan instantly shifted into Super Mode and pulled away. She grabbed her phone, then started for the door. Then paused, face wrinkling in irritation.

"Is everything okay?" Sadie asked, rushing over.

"Yeah," Joan breathed. "My friend set my home alarm off."

A few text messages sat above the alarm notice.

> Cute security system. Im in your living room.
> Where r u?

> My locator says you're here. I have to talk to u

> Dammit do I have to set this shit alarm off to get
> your attention

The contact was just the letter G. Whoever G was, they had utterly ruined the moment.

Joan raised her phone. "Greta, uh, has a key but not the alarm code."

It looked like Greta had set it off on purpose. "Is she one of those friends who expects you to drop everything whenever they need you?"

"No, she's really not." Joan sent a reply text. "I need to reset the alarm. Want to come with? Say hi?"

"Sure." Ooh, maybe Greta was a Super from another city.

A petite East Asian woman with long black hair lounged in Joan's apartment doorway, arms crossed over a leather jacket. "What's the deal?" she said to Joan. "Mark answered my text before you."

"Mark answers texts in the middle of sex," Joan said.

"You guys have to—" Greta's focus swiveled to Sadie.

"Sadie and I were having breakfast."

Pleasure replaced wariness as Greta gradually smiled. "Sadie. I've heard a lot about you."

"Hi," Sadie said. Delight danced through her. Joan had talked about her!

"Greta's one of my oldest friends." Joan raised her eyebrows at her pal.

Hmm. Greta was very pretty, and looked to be in really good shape, and had perfectly round nails tipped with black polish, and a couple of unique rings.

And a penetrating gaze she fixated on Sadie. "You're wondering if Joan and I have slept together," Greta said. "We were on and off for a while but make better friends. I have no interest in her. She likes you a lot."

Joan ducked her head in embarrassment, but Sadie grinned. "That's refreshingly candid," she said. "Thanks. I appreciate honest people."

A look passed between the friends. Was Greta part of the found family, like Perry?

"How did you two meet?" Sadie asked. "Through work?"

Greta burst out laughing.

Joan thought for a moment, then said, "We met at a gym where we were both working out." She chuckled. "Oh man, I just remembered *that's* why I started saying I work at a gym. That was the origin of my fake job."

Sobering, Greta said, "Wait, you know about…"

"That I don't work at a gym," Joan said.

"*What?* You told—" Greta darted a glance at Sadie. "You know?"

Sadie nodded and started to say the secret was safe with her, but Joan interjected, "This isn't the place to talk about this." She waved her hands at the hallway. "And Sadie has to get to work."

"My real job," Sadie joked.

Joan touched her arm. "If you want to grab your stuff, we can head out. Let me make sure my alarm is reset. Grets, we can talk in here."

She went inside her apartment. Greta eyeballed Sadie as she followed. Well, sure. The secret identity was a huge deal. She didn't blame Greta for being nervous.

Sadie walked back to her place and took an extra minute to dump out their experimental beverages and rinse the dishes. She didn't have to leave for work quite yet and figured the friends needed a bit of time.

When could she introduce Joan to her friends other than Amit and Nyah? Would they agree on the gym job as a cover? Would they have to postpone plans because Joan might have to thwart evil?

She swiped on ruby-red lipstick, then grabbed her keys and phone. The vindictive pigeon lounged on her balcony in a sliver of sunlight. "Sure, now you show up," she told the sky rat. "Now that Joan's not here to scare you off."

She was halfway to Joan's apartment when the door swung open. Joan looked half worried, half irritated. Greta held back a smile, eyes bright like she'd been laughing hard enough to cry.

"All set?" Joan said, a touch too chipper. "Mark's on his way over. He can drive you to work."

"All of us," Greta said. "I want to talk to Sadie, too. This is *way* better than I could have imagined."

After an awkwardly quiet elevator ride, they hit the lobby. Joan put her sunglasses on and murmured to Sadie, "Sorry about this."

"I want to get to know your people," Sadie assured her.

A sporty blue car screeched to a stop in front of the building. Greta opened the passenger side door to usher Joan and Sadie into the tiny backseat. In the driver's seat, Mark was wearing sunglasses similar to his sister's.

"Hey, Cute Neighbor Sadie," he said. "I didn't know you'd be joining us."

"We're dropping her off at work," said Joan.

"It's a coffeehouse, right?" Greta peered over her shoulder. "Why don't we all go and have a snack and chat?"

One of Mark's pale eyebrows raised above his shades. "Is Sadie involved in our little chat?"

"No." Joan set a hand on Sadie's arm, almost protectively.

"I have to talk to you two about some things." Greta trained her hard-to-read expression on Sadie. "But first, Sadie, tell me all about you."

They entered Vector City Coffee to the usual lunchtime hustle and bustle. Sadie still wasn't sure whether Greta was vetting her for trustworthiness or being friendly. Her direct manner made it seem like the former, but that could just be Greta's style.

Joan shared a chin nod with Nyah. Then she waved at Amit, who pretended not to notice.

"Hey, Amit," Joan said. "How's it going?"

He grunted in response. It was so cute how she was trying to win him over.

Everything inside Sadie wanted to kiss her and tell her tonight couldn't come fast enough. Professionalism sadly won out as she went behind the counter to grab her apron and clock in.

Mark and Greta claimed a table while Joan stood in line. Sadie kept sneaking glances at the table duo whispering and cackling as she took care of customers. Mark settled his sunglasses on top of his head. Joan had already taken hers off. It was bright and sunny outside, so of course people with light eyes would wear protection.

Finally, Joan stood before her. She gestured at the menu board and said to the table duo, "What do you want?"

"That thing I like," Mark said.

"A medium half-caf almond milk latte with three easy pumps of vanilla syrup and very low foam," Greta rattled off. "*Very* low foam."

Sadie punched that in, repeating, "Very low foam."

"Mark wants a large cold brew coffee with as much sugar as you can dump in it," Joan said. "And he'll want food, so a chocolate chip croissant."

"And what would you like, ma'am?" Sadie purred.

"I think I'll stick with the Kick Me Up. Just a small."

"An excellent choice."

Joan handed over a couple of bills.

"Can you get me a muffin or something?" Mark called.

"Already did," his sister replied. "Grets, do you want something to eat?"

Greta shook her head, then studied the pastry case. "A gluten-free vegan banana nut muffin."

"They're so good," Sadie told her. "Super moist, oodles of flavor."

"Anything else?" Joan said, waiting patiently like a mom wrangling her kids.

Mark and Greta said no.

"That's it. For now." Her lips twitched with good humor. That was Joan for you. Taking care of her loved ones and paying her way. No freebies for this Super.

She placed the ten dollars plus change in the tip jar. Joan had such a big heart. It went beyond the promise she'd made to take care of Mark. It was simply who she was.

"OchoStrike," Greta said.

Nyah paused beside their table, glancing at her tattoo. "You know it."

"I'm part of the Five Hive."

"No kidding. Wave on."

Greta's mouth pulled into a leisurely grin. "Wave on."

They wiggled their fingers at each other, then launched into all things *Sea Voyage Five*. Joan slid an amused glance at Sadie. "That'll keep them busy for the next hour."

"Don't you have to talk about something?" Sadie said.

"It's probably nothing."

At least it wasn't about work. Greta seemed to be a regular friend—a "norm."

Sadie set about making their drinks. Amit caught wind of the *Sea Voyage* conversation and joined with the enthusiasm he reserved for gaming. Joan thanked her when she brought the drinks over. Mark was busy swiping on some hook-up app.

What a weirdly wonderful cross-section of her life. Of Vector City.

She couldn't help studying them as she got the pastries. The Five Hive trio huddled around Nyah's phone. Mark and Joan traded beverages and taste-tested one another's drinks. The vibe was relaxed and happy. Easy. Even the indie music skewed more upbeat today.

Warmth pulsed through her chest. This was the atmosphere she wanted to create at Sadie's Café. A place where people could congregate to talk about video games or whatever their passion was. Open mic nights. Poetry readings. Artists cultivating creativity together. It'd been a dream that felt too out of reach, but now…

She could see it now.

Joan met her gaze and smiled over the cup of iced coffee. A drink she was rapidly heating because she'd said liquids were unstable. Starting a new phase of life with her in it would be a thrill ride. A Superhero girlfriend who was just as super in quiet moments like this. Exactly the sort of excitement Sadie had been craving.

Something in Joan's content expression said she was loving the simple normalcy. This could be exactly what she was looking for, too.

CHAPTER 14

Joan grinned at her text chain with Sadie. Lots of winking and kissing emoji-filled messages about tonight. They were pretty tame given that Sadie was at work, but the thoughts they conjured were decidedly more—

A burst of snow hit the side of her face. She wiped the wet flakes off as Mark leaned back in his plastic warehouse chair. "Hi. Remember me, your brother? The one you dragged to HQ only to ignore and draw little doodles with Sadie's initials?"

The fast-food napkins in front of her were covered in big hearts with *JM + SE* written in them. "So we could finally talk to Perry," Joan said.

Perry glanced at them from where he was on his phone in the nearby kitchenette.

"We've been trying to talk to Perry." Mark picked lint off his cerulean-blue shirt. "It'll be a cold day in Hades before he works with the Supers."

"You said the same thing."

"Do you really want to form an alliance with Darlene and Otis?"

"No, but..." Joan tucked her phone in her pocket. "Zee seemed to get that we don't want to be lumped in with Trick any more than they want to be lumped in with the other Supers."

"It doesn't matter. We're guilty by association. And I don't trust anything a Super says."

She normally wouldn't either, but Zee had opened up in a way no Super had ever done. In a way they hadn't really needed to.

"Do we tell Per about what Greta said?" Mark asked.

"It's just gossip. Per hates gossip."

Greta's words from earlier gnawed at the back of her mind. Rumblings among the criminal element that Spark and Ice were acting weak, not supporting their fellow Villains. How distancing from Trick—even though no one could stand him—went against their code. Losing respect in their line of work was never good since nobody would have your back.

Did that really matter anymore? It'd make it easier to get out of the life. Not get grouped together with the other Villains. Be able to hang out freely at Vector City Coffee to marvel at Sadie in her element. She truly had the gift of connecting with people.

Perry nodded and said something into his phone.

"Sounds like we're unloading that ugly painting of some old jugs and fruit sitting on a rickety table," Mark said.

"That ugly painting is worth over two million dollars."

He made a face. "Really?"

"It's a VanderHooven," Joan said. "And our last job. And the only reason we're helping even though Perry took it from a goddamn museum with goddamn Melvin is this buyer trusts me and has the hots for you."

"I know," he mumbled.

She raised her voice. "And we're using the money to open Hot and Cold whether Péricles is involved or not."

Perry waved a hand to quiet her and moved farther away.

Mark sighed. "Péricles doesn't want to leave the life."

Now it was Joan's turn to mumble, "I know."

Her brother ripped little pieces off a napkin. "He could do all the spreadsheets and agendas he wants."

"He'd be in paperwork heaven balancing the books and placing orders and costing out menu items. Putting his fancy college degree to use."

"I think he's hurt," Mark said. "After all he's done for us, it seems like we're turning our backs on him."

"He has to know it's not personal. We've done this before. Only this time, we have a plan."

"And you have a reason to stick it out." He tapped one of the lovey-dovey heart napkins.

Joan moaned and dropped her chin to her chest. "I hope so."

Sadie kept dreaming up ideas for Hot and Cold and was talking more seriously about her café. Her excitement made Joan excited for the future.

A future that could only happen if she told Sadie the freaking truth. But then that wonderful future might never happen.

Mark chucked her shoulder. "I like Sadie, but I have no idea how you're gonna right this ship."

Greta had said as much. Only she'd all but guaranteed it was going to explode horribly in Joan's face.

"You've been really distracted lately."

"I'm all in on the food truck," Joan said.

"I meant with our current employment. Greta wasn't wrong. We should probably—"

"We have to focus on our next steps." Joan nodded to herself. "We're making this food truck happen."

"Because it'll help you with Sadie?"

"Because it's what you've wanted for a long time."

Mark rolled his eyes. "There you go, being all big sister."

"Making up for sisterly guilt," she muttered.

"Guilt for what?"

Buried shame rumbled to the surface, and for once, she didn't stuff it back. "Don't you resent me for everything that went down? With school, with Mom and Dad...?"

Mark just stared at her. "Are you serious?"

"I was the one who caused the most damage. Who did the worst of—"

"Joanie. Jesus, no. I was just as destructive as you. Maybe more. Remember the basement floods—plural?"

"Yeah, but—"

"No buts." He shook his head. "I've never resented you for a millisecond. You're the reason I'm a somewhat functional adult."

"Okay," Joan murmured.

"My abandonment issues and inability to form attachments aren't from you. They're from dear old Mom and Dad."

"You're stuck with me, bud."

"I know." Mark's blue eyes glimmered. "You're very clingy."

She punched his arm, then rubbed it. "I really want this food truck to get us on a better path. Right some wrongs. It'll be easier to go legit now than when you tried culinary school."

"I sometimes wish I'd tried harder. It just sucked having people tell me what to do. And not being able to tell them why I never once had a hot dish."

"That's why we have to be our own bosses," Joan said.

"Amen."

"A-women."

They snort-laughed and fist-bumped.

Some of the weight she'd been carrying lessened. It was good to know Mark didn't hold a grudge.

Perry ended his call. "You're meeting the buyer at eight. Cash deal. What are you whining about?"

Joan shared a look with Mark. "When was the last time you put together profit and loss projections for a proposal?" she said.

"Is this about the food truck again? We have more important things on our plate."

"On our plate, haha," said Mark.

"Tonight is important." Perry walked over. "I took that painting as a good faith gesture. I'm playing along."

"Wait, what?"

"Trick might trust me enough to let me know his plan. Then we can stop him."

Oh. Wait. "Why didn't you tell us?" Joan said.

"Because you ran off in a huff the other night and Mark was too busy making fun of Trick's new cape."

"It looks fucking ridiculous!" Mark cried.

"I used it as a cover for me being sick of you two. Trick believes I'm trying to break away from *you*. That's why I left town."

It couldn't be that simple. "So you didn't want to steal a VanderHooven?" Joan said.

"I absolutely wanted to. He was the last Flemish master on my list."

Hope fluttered in her chest. "Then you've taken everything you've ever wanted to. You can retire."

Perry glowed the way he did after a big score. "That's just the Flemish masters."

Shit. They weren't gonna change his mind unless *he* wanted to make changes. Even if he cut back on his thieving ways, he'd never create an alliance with the Supers.

"Can we get back to the real problem at hand?" Mark said. "Joanie still hasn't told her special lady she's not Catch."

"*Mark.*" Joan glared at him. Damn her brother for telling Per the other night.

A low groan rolled out of Perry as he sat. "I can't believe you didn't set the record straight from the start."

"Yeah, well, you weren't there."

Mark elbowed her a few times. "This is a *deep* crush. It goes *way, way* deep inside."

"Gross, but yes." Joan didn't fight the smile tugging at her lips. "I've told her things I've never told anyone. How it sucks not being able to drink a cold drink unless I down it really fast. And how I melt shit. I actually told her I melt shit."

Perry groaned louder.

"Buuuut you didn't tell her that's because your insides are a big pool of fire," Mark said.

"I can't or she'll never want to see me again."

"That's not good," Perry said. "You're putting yourself at risk giving her so much information. You've known this woman for what, a week?"

"A couple of weeks."

"That's plenty of time." Mark leaned toward her. "Perry's straight. He doesn't understand gay math."

"Sadie gets me," Joan insisted. "I get her. She's open and honest and a total sweetheart."

"Or a very good actor who's trying to get something from you," said Perry.

She rolled her eyes. "This is why I don't tell you things. I finally meet a nice girl, and you think she's a plant for the Supers. Dude, she thinks I'm Catch."

"So she says."

"Because I've been leading her to believe it. And it's awful." Before he could further rebuke her, Joan said, "I saved a dog in front of her. Oh, Mark, the dog looked just like Sprinkles."

Mark set a hand on his heart. "Aww, Sprinkles."

"I'm trying to have her see Villains aren't all bad before I tell her the truth."

"The only way you can prove yourself is to show her things like that. Prove you're not an evil pile of shit."

Joan met Perry's displeased expression. "She's really great. You'd like her. I want you to meet her if you promise to be on your best behavior."

"She's the real deal," Mark said. "There's a sweet honesty about her. There's no faking how much she wants to dive into Joanie's tight-ass pants."

"She has a clear vision for her life. It feels really good to support each other's dreams."

"She's already helping with the food truck planning."

"Wait." Joan flattened her palms on the tabletop. The solution was so obvious. "I can help her start her café. I've got the money. She wouldn't have to pay me back. I could get her started on her dream, and we can get started on the food truck, and after I prove to her I've changed, I can explain how I used to be Spark, but—"

"Joanie." Perry shook his head. "You will always be Spark. Even if you're not wearing the spandex and stealing cars—"

"One car, one time!"

"That doesn't mean you're not going to have the abilities that make you Spark. It's who you are. You can't wish it away because you want to."

He was right, damn it. But also, "I can make changes. I won't use fire for bad things anymore."

Perry raised his eyebrows. "What are you going to do when the real Catch is still out there? How will you explain that?"

"I'll…" *Shit.* "…cross that bridge when I come to it. I'll tell her soon. I really will."

"I just don't want to see you disappointed again."

"Sadie likes *me*," Joan said. "She likes boring Joanie. That's what we have to focus on. I'm still the same person."

The hidden side door cracked open. A putrid odor wafted over the table. Mark wrinkled his nose and said, "Ah, jeez. The hench-asses."

Joan peered over her shoulder. "What are you doing here, Irving?"

Irving fizzled out of invisibility. He wasn't in his Hide gear, but jeans and a long-sleeved T-shirt. "Who's Sadie?" he asked.

"Your mom," she maturely answered.

"My mom's name is Norma."

Mark snorted and cradled his head in his hands.

"What *are* you doing here?" Perry said.

Irving shuffled his feet. "Trick wants to keep track of the painting you took from the haul. You said you had a buyer for it?"

"Yeah. We're doing the handoff tonight."

"And then none of you ask me or Mark for anything else," Joan said.

"Tonight." Irving gave a thumbs-up. "Good. Get it moved quickly."

Mark pointed both index fingers at Perry. "We're doing this for you, Per. Because we love you and we're eternally grateful to you."

"And so we can have a nest egg to start the next chapter of our lives," Joan added.

Perry adjusted his glasses, not saying anything to keep up appearances in front of the hench-douche.

Ethel scurried in through the side door like a rodent. She was even dressed in shades of brown that matched her dull hair. "Trick wants to make sure you—" She stopped when she spied Irving. "I wanted to ask them."

"I got here first," he said.

"That's not fair. I had to park the van."

Joan gave Mark a chin nod, conveying it was time to suit up and get ready for the handoff. Mark scooted his chair back and said, "You can both tell Melvin—"

"Trick," Ethel said.

"—we're taking care of the ugly painting tonight. And then it's goodbye, so long, smell ya later."

Irving crossed his arms. "Trick's still willing to let you be a part of his big plan."

"This is your last chance to join him," Ethel droned.

"I'd rather eat week-old uncooked lutefisk," Mark said.

"I'd rather eat week-old uncooked lutefisk that's been sitting in a car with all the windows rolled up during a heatwave," Joan said.

"Damn, that's a good one."

Mark draped an arm across her shoulders. She did the same and squeezed. They walked toward the little changing room that housed their gear.

"Do you think those two have ever boned?" Mark muttered.

"I literally never want to imagine that," Joan said.

He snickered and glanced behind them. "Are you coming with us, Per?"

Perry followed them inside the room. He shut the door securely. "Be careful tonight," he murmured. "I don't trust those two. They're up to something."

"We never trust them." Joan leaned against the counter where they kept an array of ropes and grappling hooks.

"Don't give them any information about the drop. Get in and out as quickly as possible. Change out of your gear right after it. Try not to be seen. And for god's sake, don't run into any of the Supers tonight."

"Relax," Mark said, inspecting one of his black gloves. "Joanie's gonna sprint home to Sadie. My dance card could easily be filled, and then my—"

"Don't," Joan groaned.

Perry blew a strong puff of air from his mouth, knocking the glove out of Mark's hands. "Will you two listen for once in your lives? Be fucking careful."

Jeez. Perry didn't swear very often, and almost never dropped an f-bomb. He must not have had his afternoon nap. "Fine," Joan said.

"Okay." Mark picked his glove off the concrete floor.

"Text me when you're home," Perry said. "Let me know if *anything* seems off."

"Aren't you coming with us?"

He looked at the door. "I'm gonna stick close to those two tonight. Let Mel keep thinking I'm not with you."

Joan nodded. "Smart. Let us know if you need us."

Perry reached for his charcoal-gray bodysuit. "Just stay focused."

"Focus is my middle name," Mark said. "Ooh, a penny!"

"You be careful too, Per," Joan said. "You're all Mark and I have, you know."

"Lucky me," Perry groused.

CHAPTER 15

As expected, there was no trouble with the buyer or the painting. Mark had taken the cash to divvy it up while Joan went home and waited for word from Sadie. Her blood simmered eagerly. She couldn't wait to offer Sadie the chance to pursue her dream. To tell her they could both go for what they wanted.

She flicked sparks of excited energy (okay, horny energy) from her fingertips. Perry hadn't reported any Melvin activity, so tonight was going to be all about celebrating.

The second she got the text confirming Sadie was home from work, Joan bounded out of her apartment.

Sadie glanced up from her phone halfway down the hall. "Were you standing by your door waiting for me to text you?"

"Yep," Joan admitted.

She met up with Sadie and wrapped her in her arms. Joan kissed her soundly, then asked, "How was the rest of your workday?"

"Fine."

"Cool." She kissed Sadie again, loving the soft feel of her, the sweet taste of her. "I have so much to tell you. I can't stand it."

"I can tell," Sadie giggled. "Can you at least wait until we get inside my place?"

"Barely."

Joan picked her up and carry-dragged Sadie to her door. She was so excited, and excited in ways that would cause Mark to make all kinds of crass jokes. Her internal fire was stoked high despite the large fireball she'd conjured and extinguished in the shower.

She set Sadie down so the gorgeous redhead could unlock her door. She was wearing the green-striped scoop-neck shirt and electric blue pants she'd had on earlier. The top emphasized her phenomenal chest, while the pants did wonders for her ass.

Joan pushed Sadie's hair to the side and nuzzled her neck. "You're so beautiful," she murmured, sliding her hands across Sadie's stomach.

"Joanie Maloney," Sadie breathed, leaning into the embrace. "How do you expect me to get this door open?"

She chuckled and kissed the pulse point throbbing on Sadie's neck. Then she snagged the key and fit it into the lock.

They waddled inside together. Sadie flicked the bright kitchen lights on. She turned and wrapped her arms around Joan's neck. "How about we close that door?"

Joan kicked the door closed, tossed Sadie's keys, and then kissed her.

"My goodness," Sadie teased with a big grin. "What is this thing you have to tell me?"

"First of all, hi." They shared a kiss. "It's nice to see you."

Sadie nipped her bottom lip. "Nice to see you, too."

She pulled Joan farther into the living space. Joan kissed her and slid her hands up and down Sadie's back. Sadie dug her fingers into Joan's loose hair. Her thigh popped against Joan and pressed against the low area *very* interested in having Sadie's thigh there.

A groan rumbled in Joan's throat, and she had to pull back. "Let me get this out before I can't form words."

Sadie smoothed her hands down Joan's sides. "Talk fast. I've been thinking about this all day."

Heat surged through her bloodstream. "That's not helping," Joan moaned.

Sadie laughed and took a tiny step back, keeping her hands on Joan's hips. "What is it?"

Joan held her by the hips as well. After another kiss, she said, "I want to help you open Sadie's Café."

Sadie's thin eyebrows scrunched in slight confusion. "You what?"

"I want to give you the money to start it up. Not a loan. I have plenty of savings."

"I can't take your money."

"You could consider it a loan if you really want to." Joan grinned and added, "One you never have to pay back."

Sadie took a full step back, letting go of Joan. "That is so thoughtful, but I can't accept that kind of money from you."

"Then consider me an investor. I want to invest in it."

Her smile grew less disbelieving, more enthusiastic. "Are you serious?"

"Completely serious." Joan grasped her hands and kissed them. "Let me help you achieve your dream. I'll help with the insurance costs, too. Whatever you need."

"I mean…" Sadie blinked several times. "We could talk about you investing or loaning me *some* start-up funds."

"Sure. Whatever you feel comfortable with. Just know that I have the money and want to do this for you."

"Joan, I…" She started to speak several times, then paused. Then laughed. "I don't know what to say."

"Say yes," Joan said, rubbing her thumbs over Sadie's knuckles.

"Okay. Yes."

They laughed and hugged tightly. "But wait," Joan said, breaking the embrace. "There's more."

"What more?"

"Mark and I are gonna buy a food truck. We're going to open Hot and Cold. We're doing all this together."

"Wait, wait, whoa." Sadie held up her hands. "You just said you want to invest in my café. How can you have the money to do both?"

"It wouldn't be all my money for Hot and Cold. It's also Mark's. And hopefully Perry's. We're still working on Perry."

"Okay, but you're... You..."

Joan brushed Sadie's hair back. "I know you think I can't do that and my current job. I'm giving that up. I don't want to do it anymore."

"But you do so much good," Sadie said.

"I want a normal life. Making food with Mark, and coffee with you. I..."

I want to start a life that has you in it.

Sadie gazed down at the carpet for several long moments. When she looked up, she squinted at Joan's face. "Are you sure? Have you given it enough thought?"

"So much thought," Joan assured her. "Mark and I have been trying to get out—I mean, get this going—for a long time."

"You'd really give up that life for..."

"The chance to do an honest day's work and come home to you? Yes. Absolutely."

Sadie just stood and stared at her.

Panic flared up. What if Sadie was only with her because she wanted to be with Catch? What if Food Truck Joanie wasn't who she wanted?

"Yes," Sadie finally whispered.

"Yes?" Joan took a tentative step toward her.

"Yes."

She took another step until their noses nearly touched. "Is it okay? Is it what you want?"

Sadie rested her fingers on Joan's white-and-red shirt. "I want it all. Yes to everything."

Sparks ignited under her skin. She smiled at the huge grin stretching across Sadie's beautiful face. They laughed, and kissed, and held one another.

Sadie cupped Joan's jaw and drew her in for a deep kiss. Joan took Sadie's face in her hands as fireworks exploded from her heart and traveled through her body.

"Joanie," Sadie sighed.

Joanie. That was who she wanted. Not Catch. Not anyone but her Joanie. "That's me," Joan murmured.

Desire flashed and melded with her fire, causing it to bubble. Ooh, shit. She kissed down Sadie's neck, breathing in some cooling air.

Sadie tickled under her shirt and up her spine. Joan bit at the hollow of Sadie's neck and dug her fingers into Sadie's hips.

"I'm good on talking for now," Sadie breathed.

Joan hummed against her throat. "We can...talk...about the specifics...*ungh*...later." Her knees nearly gave out as Sadie slid her hand down Joan's breast.

"Mmm. Much later." She lightly squeezed through the stretchy material on Joan's sports bra.

Joan tugged Sadie's hips until their bodies touched. She *wanted* Sadie so, so desperately. Sadie's mouth, her tongue, her hands everywhere. Just the thought made her fire rise from deep inside. Way too much fire.

She tried to step away, only Sadie came with her. Sadie started toward the bedroom, pulling at Joan. Kissing with a hunger that spoke of her own needs. Fisting Joan's shirt in her hands greedily. Possessively.

Fire sat on her fingertips, in her eyelids, in every pore and strand of hair. *Shit.* This had never happened before.

Joan broke the kiss, making Sadie moan in protest. She gently removed Sadie's hands. "Let me wash up really quick."

"If you insist." Sadie kissed her cheek. "I should wash up, too."

She headed for the bathroom. Joan halted her. "I...have to...as well..." she stammered, then whispered, "Pee."

"Oh." Sadie giggled. "Sure. Do what you need to do. I'll use the kitchen sink."

"Thanks."

Sadie sprinted toward the kitchen. "Hurry!"

Joan whipped the bathroom door closed. She hastened to the sink and wrenched the cold water on. Shoved her hands under the steady stream and studied her reflection in the mirror. Her eyes shimmered orange and angry with impending release. "Come on, Joan. Get it together."

She splashed water on her face. Three times. Small fireballs shot from her eyes into the stream coming from the faucet. Ugh, it was so gross when fire came out of her eyeballs. At least the build-up would be gone.

She sank one arm into the icy water, then the other. Shook the droplets off, along with a few sparks. Her eyes were returning to baseline.

"Better." Joan nodded at her reflection.

Her heartbeat pounded, and the throbbing in her clit was like *Only Sadie can take care of this, pal.*

So much emotion. Too much. She really, really, *really* liked Sadie. Was falling fast and headfirst for her.

The fire started building again. "Shiiiiit," she gritted through clenched teeth.

She concentrated on generating a sharp sliver of near-white flame between her hands. She really did have to tell Sadie the truth. Just not tonight. Not when neither her brain nor body were functioning properly.

All her focus poured into the flame. She kept it flickering until she couldn't hold it any longer and shoved it underwater. A cloud of steam rose up, fogging the mirror. Great. Hopefully Sadie would be too preoccupied to notice it was like an oven in her bathroom.

But it worked. Joan was normal-level horny now. She dried off while taking deep breaths. This was good. Everything was contained and under control.

"Time to start your future," she told herself.

A future without Spark, without Catch. Just Sadie and Joan.

CHAPTER 16

Sadie pulled her pale pink bra from the bottom of her shirt. While she was very much looking forward to Joan taking bras off her for many days and nights to come, tonight was about getting naked as quickly as possible. The super woman wanted to be with her. Wanted to help her achieve her dreams. Wanted Sadie to be a part of her life. They needed to get to it ASAP.

The bathroom door cracked open just as she flung the bra into her bedroom. Joan watched it sail, then walked over to where Sadie stood impatiently.

"Starting without me?" Joan teased.

Her low tone sent sensual vibrations through Sadie's belly. She skimmed her fingers up Joan's arms. "Just moving things along."

"Much appreciated."

They joined in a kiss that rapidly grew from soft and sweet to frantic and needy. Joan slid her hands beneath the hem of Sadie's shirt and caressed her skin. Sadie did the same. Joan was so warm. She always tended to run warm, but this was unusually hot. Maybe all the Supers ran this hot.

Joan exhaled heat into her mouth. It felt kind of weird, but not unpleasant. Sadie broke from the kiss to trail her lips across Joan's cheek toward her earlobe.

Joan gripped Sadie's ass and sent a wave of heat through her, like she'd just sat on a heating pad. "You're really hot," Sadie said.

"You're so hot, baby," Joan murmured. She sought Sadie's mouth and kissed her with scorching lips.

"No. Joan." She pulled her hands away from Joan's radiator of a torso. "You're *really* hot. Like temperature hot."

"That's normal for me." Joan kissed her. "I run a little hot."

"Are you absorbing my energy?"

"I told you I don't do that."

A thread of worry cut through her desire. Joan could control herself, but this was unexpected and slightly awkward. Wouldn't sex with a Superhero be fantastic, especially one with Joan's abilities?

Maybe she was overreacting. Sleeping with Joan wasn't going to be like sleeping with an average person. Good, bad, or somewhere in between, it was going to be a whole new experience.

"Then it must be these pesky clothes," Sadie said. She reached for the top button on Joan's shirt. "We should get them out of the way."

"Definitely."

She undid two buttons, glancing up to smile at Joan before undoing the one covering her athletic bra.

Then she noticed Joan's eyes.

Her irises glowed a ferocious shade of crimson. Flickering with…

Fire.

Full-blown fear shot through her body. She stepped back on shaky legs. "Joan." The word came out on a breath. "What's happening with your eyes?"

Joan blinked and shook her head. "Nothing," she muttered. "*Shit.* Nothing."

She ran a hand through her hair. Flashes of light sparked off her fingers.

Why was she shooting off energy? She only did that if she

absorbed something. If she wasn't taking it in, she had to be generating it.

Generating…fire?

"Joan." This time, it came out as a frightened cry. "What is going on?"

Joan opened her mouth, hesitated, then closed it. She dropped her arms to her sides.

Everything became terribly, shockingly clear.

Joan was not Catch.

Sadie held her palms out. "Ohhhh my god."

"Sadie, I…"

"What's going on? Who are you?"

"Sadie…" Joan reached out a hand.

"No." Sadie moved away from her. "Who are you? You're not Catch. I don't know who you are. Is your name even Joan?"

"Yes." Her forehead wrinkled. "I need you to hear this, okay? Please. This isn't how I wanted you to find out."

Joan took a small step toward her, which made Sadie take three in the other direction.

"Almost everything I've told you is true. My name really is Joan Malone. I really did grow up in a small town and get kicked out by my parents."

"Who are you?" Sadie demanded.

Joan shoved her hands in her pockets, then pulled them out when her pants began to smoke. What the hell? "I've been trying to tell you. I didn't know how. I like you so much and didn't want things to change. You…"

Angry tears coated Sadie's eyes. "Tell me," she whispered.

"I'm Spark."

"You're Spark." Her stomach sank like a jagged rock. "You're *Spark*? Are you kidding me? A Supervillain?"

"Yes."

"You're a *Supervillain*? You made me think you're a Hero, but you're a…" A snort shot through her nose, and she flailed her arms wildly. "You're the Villain who shoots fire! You made me think you got into a fight with…with…*you!* You told me you were Catch!"

"I never actually said I was Catch," Joan said quietly.

"You never said you *weren't.* You led me on. Oh my god." She grabbed both sides of her head. *"Oh my god!* I almost had sex with a Supervillain!"

"I'm so sorry," Joan said. "I never meant for it to go on this long."

"Prove it." Every shred of sanity had unraveled. "Make some fire."

"Sadie—"

"Do it. I need to see it."

Joan hung her head, then brought her hands together. A smoldering ball of fire appeared between them, licking and shimmering before she waved her hands and it extinguished.

Holy shit. Joan really was Spark.

Sadie's gut clenched. Hurt, confusion, anger, a little fear, twisted inside her like a devious snake.

"Spark has long dark hair," she said.

"It's a wig."

A sneaky disguise. A lie. Joan had been lying to her. Lying the entire time they'd known each other. About the gym. About her abilities. About *everything.*

Sadie hugged herself as she shivered from too much adrenaline. "Who are all these people you keep talking about? Perry, Uncle Mel? And Mark and Greta? Are they Villains, too? Is Mark even your brother?"

"Yes, he is. Mark is Ice. He also has a wig attached to his facemask."

Sadie snorted and tossed her hair. "Another lie."

That explained Mark's startlingly blue eyes. She'd known there was something about them.

"So Greta must be Volt."

"No." Joan shook her head. "Greta's not a… She's a damn good thief."

"Oh, great. She was at my workplace."

"I wanted to tell you," she said. "I really did. Perry is Breeze. He took in me and Mark when our parents kicked us out. He loves meetings and agendas. He's not a bad guy. The three of us aren't really that bad."

Sadie wound up to retort, but Joan continued, "That thing I said about needing to survive was why I had to turn to villainy. Mark and I were kids. Everyone in the city was terrified of us. We couldn't survive on our own."

"You melt things when you get emotional," Sadie spat.

"Yeah." Joan took a half step toward her. "I'm telling you because I really do want to be honest with you. I'm risking my safety, and the safety of those I care about, by revealing our true identities. But I want you to know."

She looked shamefaced. Utterly sorry and guilty.

Good. She should.

"Do they know you've been lying to me?" Sadie said. "Today, when we were with Mark and Greta. Were you all laughing at me behind my back?"

"No, not at all. They told me this would backfire. They said I should've told you I wasn't Catch."

"But not that you're actually Spark."

"I tried to tell you yesterday," Joan said. "But, I don't know. I didn't want to admit to something so… And you were so happy. You have such a high opinion of the Supers. I wasn't sure you'd believe me."

A tiny glimmer of sympathy flickered in Sadie's heart. Everyone was afraid of the Supervillains. It couldn't have been easy to—

No. Joan was not going to get let off the hook for this. For lying and thieving and—

"The money." Sadie shook her head. This was so unbelievable and surreal. "Were you gonna give me dirty stolen money to open my café? That's horrible."

Shrugging her hands, Joan said, "Okay, yes, it's stolen money.

But we only take from big corporations. We never rob local busi-nesses like Vector City Café."

"No, you just destroy them."

"I *did* pay for the window repair. We do stuff like that all the time. Mark and I genuinely feel bad when people have to clean up after Super activity."

She really wanted to be angry, but that caught her attention. "So, you were the one who made that deposit?"

"Yes." Sincerity shined on Joan's face. "The Supers never pay for their damage. They're kind of assholes. I'm always cleaning up after their messes."

"With money you've stolen from said businesses," Sadie pointed out.

"It's an imperfect system. But again, we only take from corpo-rate fat cats."

"And you want to give it all up and use your ill-gotten gains to open a coffeehouse and food truck? Or was that a lie, too?"

"No," Joan insisted. "I want to go legit. I want everything we talked about. The only way I can do it is with that money. I don't have a financial footprint, or credit cards."

"Then how did you rent an apartment?" Sadie said.

"Paid double the security deposit plus a year's worth of rent in cash."

"Stolen cash," she grumbled.

"Well, it's easier to rob a bank than get a loan, am I right?"

Sadie gripped her biceps and tilted her head in disbelief. "Are you actually making a joke out of this?"

"No, but you know how hard it is to get approved for a bank loan."

"Did you stop to think that's because people like you make it impossible to insure a business?"

"Not until you pointed that out to me." Joan scratched at her scalp. "I'm sorry. I didn't know. You've opened my eyes to—"

"You were going to involve me in illegal, fraudulent activity,"

Sadie said. "What if that money was traced to me? I could go to jail. I could lose everything."

"I…" Joan ground her palms against her eyes and groaned loudly. "Fuck, I am so sorry. I royally screwed this up. I just wanted us to be happy."

"You did screw up. Badly."

Sadie walked to the couch and sank onto the edge. Turned on the lamp beside it so she wasn't in the dark. Joan had kept her in the dark for too long.

She dropped her elbows to her thighs and cradled her head in her hands. It felt like a thousand pounds, it was so filled with pulsating emotions.

Joan cleared her throat. "Look, I'm not going to pretend like not coming clean was right. But having you involved in Super activity is dangerous. There are some real bad bad guys. This Melvin situation has been a giant pain. I don't want you anywhere near it."

"Because you're one of the good bad guys," Sadie chortled.

"I know it's hard to believe, but yes. We're trying to stop him and those who think like him. Then I'm leaving all that behind."

"You're hanging up your Spark wig?"

"Yes."

She studied Joan's earnest expression. She seemed sincere. Joan always seemed sincere. But that was Catch Joan, not Supervillain Spark Joan.

"If you had told me the truth," Sadie thought aloud, "or even warned me to expect…well, I don't know what. Maybe it wouldn't be…"

"Would you have wanted to be with me if you knew I was Spark?" Joan gestured at the wide distance between them as if to punctuate that fact.

"I don't know," Sadie said again.

"You really wanted me to be a Superhero." Her tone was filled with sadness.

"Joan, I'm not even that upset that you're not Catch. I'm mad that you lied to me. You led me to believe you were someone you're not."

"I want to make this right," Joan said. "I know I betrayed your trust, but I'm still the same person."

Sadie scoffed at that. "I don't even know you."

"Yes, you do. I'm still me. I'm still the Joanie who loves cooking for you. Who wants to open a food truck with Mark."

Joan started toward the couch, making Sadie stiffen. She seemed to pick up on that and stopped.

"You got to know the real me. You *know* the real me." A shadow crossed over her face. "Shit. You said you felt safe with me. Now you're scared to let me near you."

"I'm freaked out," Sadie told her. "I wasn't expecting you to turn into a furnace."

"I would never hurt you." Joan placed both hands on her chest. "I swear."

Her intense earnestness hurt worse than any lie. "But you did. Not physically. I really trusted you."

"I'm sorry."

The tears returned in full force, strong enough for Sadie to sniffle them back. "I'd like you to leave," she said.

"Can we please talk some more? I can explain—"

"You've done enough explaining. And if it's because you're worried I'll expose you, I won't." She waved her hands. "I'd rather forget this ever happened."

A tear slid down Joan's cheek, which quickly fizzled and evaporated.

Sadie's heart ached for her. For what they could've had if…

She met Joan's eyes and wordlessly communicated her thoughts.

What we could've had if you weren't Spark.

"Okay," Joan whispered, then cleared her throat. Another tear slipped out and sizzled. "I respect what you want. If you do want to talk—"

"I have nothing more to say to you," Sadie said, which wasn't true at all. She had so many questions. So much she wanted to know. But what good would it do? Joan wasn't who she'd said she was. Even if she hadn't said the words, she'd led Sadie to believe a lie. Like a true Villain.

Joan simply nodded. She turned and headed for the door.

She paused with her hand on the doorknob. "I wish I could be the good person you thought I was," she murmured.

It hit Sadie square in her soul.

The moment the door closed, a torrent of tears poured from her eyes. She buried her face in her hands and sobbed. Despite the lies, the hurt, the betrayal, the stealing and life of crime, that was the worst part of all this.

Deep down, she knew Joan *was* that good person.

CHAPTER 17

Joan pulled the fleece blanket tighter under her chin. She never really needed one unless she was sick. Or curled up on the couch in a pathetic ball of heartache, wanting to disappear under the comforting material.

A bright ray of late morning sunshine beamed across her face. She moaned in misery. Mark squeezed her feet, then rubbed her legs. He was still wearing his club clothes: a dark, skintight T-shirt and pants. His styled blond hair had morphed into bedhead.

Joan moaned again, then managed to say, "Thank you for coming over."

"I've got you, sis."

Thanks to cosmic twin intuition, Mark had shown up last night less than an hour after Joan collapsed on her bed, crying and having the tears evaporate, and then crying more because she couldn't even cry properly.

All because she was Spark, the deceitful Villain who'd tried to start a future with a good, honest person with stolen funds and lies.

"Besides." Mark jiggled her thigh. "You've nursed me through a lot of bad times."

"And you're really annoying when you're super whiny."

"And you're irritatingly grumpy." He rested his arm across the back of the couch. "Which I will overlook today."

Joan's heart ached in a way that hadn't happened since their parents kicked them out. Maybe it had never hurt like this. She felt like complete and total shit.

"I should've told her," she said for the eighty-third time.

"Yes, but hindsight and all that."

She groaned and pulled the blanket over her head.

"No, no." Mark tugged it down. "We're not doing that. If you'd told her, it would've ended sooner. She wouldn't have handled the news much better if she'd found out a different way."

"I hate that I lied to her. She's so sweet and thoughtful and trusting, and assholes have taken advantage of her. Now I'm just another asshole because she really trusted me."

She plucked at the fleece blanket and continued, "I should've known she would never go for Spark, even if I said I was giving it up. She had no reason to believe me, anyway."

Mark slurped the rest of his iced coffee. "Do you want one?" he asked, dancing the plastic cup in front of her.

"No."

"Ice cream?"

"No."

"A big vat of wine you can lie in face-first and drink away your sorrows?"

"Maybe." She shut her eyes, then opened them, because every time she closed her eyes, she saw Sadie sitting on her couch, scared and in pain and not wanting Joan anywhere near her.

Mark stood, saying, "Well, I'm gonna get another one. This is good. You finally cracked the cold brew coffee recipe."

"Sadie made it," Joan grumbled miserably.

"Oh. Shit." He considered the cup. "She does make damn good coffee."

Joan tossed the blanket over her head.

Creaking and shuffling came from the spare bedroom, followed by the door opening.

"Hey, Per," Mark said. Of course Perry would break in rather than use the door.

"Your security system is shit, Joanie," he said.

"Nah, you're just the Man," said Mark.

"We have a problem."

The blanket got yanked off Joan's head, bathing her in unwelcome sunlight again.

"What's this about?" Perry asked.

"Go away," Joan mumbled.

"We have a situation."

"*We* have a situation." Mark gestured with his cup at Joan. "Sadie found out Joanie's true identity and didn't take it well."

"Really?" Perry's expression softened slightly. "Crap. Come here."

He sat beside Joan and held his arms out. She squeezed hers gratefully around him, fresh tears forming but drying up just as fast.

"Sorry. It sounded like you really liked her."

"I really did," Joan snuffled. "I still do. And don't worry. She's not gonna rat me out. At least I don't think so."

"Okay." He patted her back, then eased out of the hug. "You can tell me about it later. We have to deal with something else. It's bad."

That snapped her to attention. They got off the couch, Mark joining them.

"I found out why Melvin was so interested in us selling the VanderHooven." Perry pulled his phone from his suit jacket pocket. He unlocked the screen, then showed them a news article.

String of art heists perpetrated by Breeze, Ice, Spark

"Shit," Mark said.

"He's framing us for a bunch of recent break-ins and that museum job. Even me."

"Asshole," Joan said.

"It's clear from the article he brainwashed a bunch of so-called witnesses to say they saw us at all these places."

Mark shrugged. "Our names will be mud, but the Supers know we weren't there. We haven't been spotted at—"

"They don't care," Perry said. "They'll use any excuse to nab us. If they bring us in, they'll look like heroes."

"Race told me their priority is stopping Trick," Joan reminded them. "This is small potatoes."

Perry shook his head. "Public image is never small potatoes to the Supers. It'd look like they let this slide. Flight gave a quote saying they'll see justice is done."

"*They'll see justice is done,*" Mark said in a sarcastic baby voice.

Joan held up a hand. "I'll talk to Zee. We can reach a deal to—"

"We still don't know what Mel's planning," Perry said. "Other than screwing us over."

"I'm with Joanie," Mark said. "As much as it pains me to say so, we need to form an alliance with the Supers."

Joan nodded. *And then maybe I won't be a bad guy in Sadie's eyes.*

Perry pushed his glasses back. "You can't go to the Supers with no information. I wouldn't trust them even if we did."

An incoming video call popped up on Perry's screen. Fuckin' Melvin.

His pasty nerd face and slicked-back hair appeared. He was in his Trick ensemble from the neck down. "Oh, good," he said. "You're all together."

"What the hell, you douche?" Mark said.

"Framing us?" Perry said.

Melvin didn't bother hiding his amusement. "There's been a terrible misunderstanding. I'd be happy to clear it up and say you had nothing to do with those thefts. All you have to do is join me."

Joan could only shake her head. He was such an asshat.

"Seriously, dude," Mark said. "Why is it so important for us to join you?"

"Strength in numbers."

"And you can't control us."

"I don't want to control you." Melvin grinned. "Siding with me means you can do whatever, whenever. The ultimate freedom for us all."

Perry screwed his face up. "That kind of attention would bring Supers from all over the world. We'd be the most wanted Villain collective in history."

"Wouldn't that be exciting?"

"No," Mark and Perry chorused.

Melvin turned his cocky smirk toward Joan. "Why are you so quiet? You're usually the one with all the answers."

"You suck, Melvin," she told him.

"That's it?"

"I've already said I'm done."

He studied her for a long moment, then looked back at Perry and Mark. "All right. You've made your choice." He squinted hard at them. "Have it your way."

The call ended.

"Oh my god, he loves drama," Mark drawled.

"What should we do, Per?" Joan asked.

Perry put his phone away. "I hate to say wait and see, but I do think we have to wait, and be ready for anything."

Mark set his now frozen-over cup on the coffee table. "Once his plan is revealed, all dramatic-Supervillain-style where he explains every step, then we can go to the Supers and—"

"Wait." Joan grasped his shoulder. "If he had a grand master plan to take over the city, he'd be gloating about it to anyone who'd listen. We haven't heard a peep from anyone. Nothing."

"Maybe he finally learned tact," Perry said.

"Maybe he doesn't have a plan," Mark laughed, then sobered. He locked onto Joan's gaze with wide eyes.

Clarity smacked her upside the head. "He doesn't have a

plan. He needs us because he needs *us* to come up with it. Think about it. He's not an evil genius. Ethel and Irving just agree with everything he says. We're the ones who come up with the good ideas. It was Mark who thought it'd be funny to do things like have us be seen across town while the real crime was taking place."

"Yeah." Mark bobbed his head. "And Perry does all the schematics and flow charts or whatever. Sorry, Per, you know I never pay attention."

Perry waved an unconcerned hand. "You're right. He has no idea what he's doing."

"The only reason he's gotten this far is mind control. And even then, it's more like, 'Hey, I'll make everyone think I'm big and muscular and handsome.'"

Joan squeezed both of Mark's shoulders. "We really don't have to do anything but lay low. We just have to stay out of trouble."

"And we don't have to go to the Supers," Perry added. "Thank god."

They shared more nods and agreements. Part of her was glad they'd figured it out and wouldn't have to form irritating alliances. But another part kind of wanted to do something that would get back to Sadie. The headline would read *Spark aligns with Superheroes and proves she's one of the good guys.*

It was probably too little too late, but better than nothing.

"Then we'll lay cautiously low." Perry shrugged out of his jacket. "Are we having the heartbreak special of Chinese food and cheap beer?"

Mark snagged his phone off the coffee table. "On it."

Joan slumped onto the couch. "It's ten in the morning."

"Oh, yeah." He set his phone down. "I'll order it in an hour."

Perry sat next to Joan, covering her lap with the blanket. His preferred method of supporting her and Mark was exacting revenge on those who'd wronged them, so she said, "Don't retaliate against Sadie. She's not to blame."

"I can't blow the plants off her balcony?"

"She doesn't have plants on her balcony because of a vindictive pigeon."

Mark joined them on the couch. "Maybe in time, after we open Hot and Cold, you can show her you've changed. That we've all changed."

Perry gave him a look, but Joan didn't have the energy to work on him. Besides, what he'd said last night was true. "I'm always gonna be the scary woman who shoots fire," she said.

"Maybe you could be the woman who heats up sandwiches with that fire," Mark said. "Who, I don't know, helps firefighters with controlled burns, or—"

"And I'll still be the woman who didn't come clean. How can she trust me?" Joan slouched deeper into the cushions. "I can't blame her. I was fooling myself that it could work, 'cause I just... I really like her."

They sat quietly for a minute. Perry swiveled his head to look at both of them. "You know what I don't understand about you two?"

Mark opened his mouth to give a smartass reply, then decided against it.

"You've tried to act like average people for years. Why would you want to be like everyone else? We're remarkable, and that's good. Don't hide who you are, you dorks." Perry mussed up Joan and Mark's hair, making them both groan and shove him off.

"It's not about being like everyone else," Joan said. "It's not wanting to freak people out. Just have them be a little more understanding. Not vilify some of us while putting others on a pedestal."

"I mean, the general thievery doesn't help our case," Mark said. "But yeah, the Supers aren't much better than us."

"Sanctioned larceny and destruction," Perry grumbled.

Joan closed her eyes, steeling herself for the image of Sadie's sad, beautiful face. Hopefully, she'd heard all Joan had said about their quasi-benevolent villainy. At least it would help dull the ache if Sadie understood they weren't trying to hurt anyone.

There was a good chance they'd see each other again. What would it be like? Would Sadie ignore her? Want to talk? Rip her a new one again? Whatever it was, Joan would respect her wishes. Finally take responsibility.

"Are you sure it's too early for Chinese food and cheap beer?" Mark said.

"No," Joan said, and pulled the blanket up so she could hide under it.

CHAPTER 18

The clock on the wall behind Sadie had inched all of nine minutes since the last time she'd checked. It was official. This was the slowest Sunday in recorded history. Possibly because she'd spent the past however-many hours in misery before forcing herself to get up and shower and go to work.

Her sweet Joanie Maloney wasn't so sweet. Sadie had gone for the bad girl again. Only this time, a whole new level of bad. Supervillain bad.

She sighed deeply and crumpled against the pastry case. Even their music today reflected her mood—maudlin folksy songs about heartache.

It all made complete sense, and yet didn't. So many of the stories Joan had told her fit the bill for Spark: destroyed parts of her hometown, couldn't hold a real job (what with all the melting), her found work family, problems with the Supers...

But someone who broke into banks and stole things wouldn't be giddy about making plans for a food truck, right? *A food truck,* of all things. A food truck named—hello!—Hot and Cold.

And she wouldn't be so invested in Sadie's dreams. Sure, Joan could throw some money at a café, but it really seemed like she wanted to be a part of it. That she genuinely believed in Sadie.

And Sadie really had felt safe with Joan. Taken care of. She'd been startled by seeing fire in Joan's eyes, but who wouldn't be if they weren't expecting it?

You got to know the real me. You know the real me.

Yes and no. She knew Joan, but there was a whole unfamiliar side of her. Sadie had spent a large chunk of yesterday watching videos of Spark. The body shape, the lips, the *eyes*… They were all Joan. Even bits and pieces of things she'd yelled at the Supers had been in Joan's husky voice.

And then it'd been videos of Catch. Shorter, slightly curvier Catch. With a curt way of speaking about justice. Joan never talked like that.

Then Sadie had rested against her apartment door, half hoping to hear activity from Joan's place. Not that she could hear much over her own sobbing and hiccups and heavy moans coming from the depths of her soul.

Still, she had to begrudgingly admit she maybe possibly should have watched Catch videos with a more critical eye after meeting Joan. It was so obvious now they were not one and the same. She'd made a huge assumption—which Joan absolutely should've corrected—going from *My new neighbor has nice eyes* to *She's a Superhero* in sixty seconds flat.

And of course Joan would say negative things about the Supers. Of course she'd claim they never helped citizens after battles.

Though Lunk had crashed through Vector City Coffee only to make a halfhearted apology and run off. Joan had never wavered from insisting she'd been the one who paid for the repairs.

Okay, so maybe the Supers had been a bit more destructive than… But that didn't mean they… And it didn't mean the Villains were better than…

Her eyes clouded over with fresh tears. She straightened and drew in a deep breath. Work would distract her.

Amit came from the back carrying plastic sleeves of paper

cups. He took one look at her and said, "You know I don't like to pry."

"Ha."

"You've been out of it all day. Everything okay?"

His concern pressed the tears closer to release. "I screwed up again," Sadie said.

"Uh-oh." Amit set the cups on the counter.

"Joan."

"What about Joan?"

"She..." Sadie cleared her throat and waved at her eyes. "She wasn't who I thought she was."

"What did she do?"

"She lied to me about her job."

Amit raised an eyebrow. "And...?"

"And what?"

"There's usually more."

"Her job's a really big part of who she is," Sadie said. "She led me to think she did something else."

"Ah. That sucks."

He went quiet after that. Amit never went quiet. "What?" Sadie said.

"Nothing," he said. "I kinda thought she might be different."

"Nope. A big liar, like the rest of them."

"It's just..."

Sadie crossed her arms. "Don't tell me you want to defend her."

"No," Amit said. "I knew she was hiding something. It just seemed like she had a good reason."

"Seriously?"

"It's a government job, isn't it? Some top-secret thing?"

Wooo, how to answer that? "Top-secret, yes."

"Something she couldn't tell you due to security or clearance?"

"Well, maybe safety, but that—"

"I could be way off base." Amit ripped at the plastic covering one of the stacks of cups. "She does give off a military vibe. Watchful and wary. Doesn't trust a lot of people."

She trusted me.

"She made an effort to talk to me," he added. "I could tell she was trying to win me over."

"You like her because she was nice to you?"

Amit hesitated, then gave her a look bordering on sad. "You seemed happy together. Like you got each other. I've never seen someone dig on you as much as you dug on them."

Sadie sighed again, heart pulsing grief with every beat.

"Her friends were nice."

"You talked about gaming for a solid half hour with them," Sadie pointed out.

"Yeah, so I can confirm they were nice. And you hung out with them. Joan let you meet her—"

"No," she stated. "She lied to me. End of story."

"Okay. You're right. Lying is bad."

His subtext hung thick in the air. *Unless she had a good reason.*

Sadie slumped against the counter and dug her chipped red nails into the other plastic sleeve of cups. Objectively, she understood why Joan hadn't told her she was Spark. And even why she'd let Sadie keep thinking she was Catch. But it still hurt. Even if Joan had simply told her she wasn't Catch, that would've been okay. It wasn't like Sadie expected a Super to reveal their identity. But leading her on was just unfair.

Her intuition had been trying to tell her to question Joan. For once, that nagging voice had been spot on.

Joan tried to tell you.

A hot flush climbed up the back of her neck. Joan *had* been trying to tell her something over the past few days. And Sadie being Sadie, she'd plowed right over her.

The plowing always got her in trouble.

Settling the stack of cups next to the espresso machine, she said, "So you really think Joan's lie was justifiable?"

"I'm not saying that," Amit said. "I'm just sorry it didn't work out. You were cute together."

"You never say anything is cute."

"Which should tell you how cute you were."

Sadie kicked at a lower cabinet with the toe of her sneaker. Damn it, they *were* cute together. Their relaxing mornings and walks to work holding hands had been perfect. Could they still have those? Could she have a sustainable, honest relationship with Joan?

You still think of her as Joan. Not Catch. Not Spark.

Ugh.

"Can I take my break?" Sadie said. "I need some fresh air."

"Sure." Amit nodded at the mostly empty coffeehouse. "We're not swamped."

She ambled to the supply room in the back, checking her phone. Not that Joan would—or should—call or text. But still…

Once out of the alley, she breathed in the warm afternoon air. It sucked not being able to talk to her friends and family about everything. They'd only give her the usual *"Again?"* Plus, it wasn't like she could tell them the whole story. *"I assumed my new neighbor was a Superhero, but no, she's actually Spark."*

She should've known Joan was too good to be true. She just didn't want to believe Joan wasn't who she'd made her out to be.

A small group of people congregated around the convenience store on the corner. One of the walls was missing a big chunk. As a tall man stepped to the side, Flight and Lunk became visible in front of a pile of bricks and broken glass.

Flight's red cape fluttered in the breeze. "If you go on the SuperWatch app, you can file a claim for reimbursement," he said to the Middle Eastern man and woman beside him.

A short young white guy in a suit held up his tablet for Flight to read something. He looked familiar. Wait—he'd ran past her recently when she was walking home from work.

"Mr. Flight," the young guy said. "We have the meet-and-greet with the garden club in thirty minutes."

The woman storeowner gestured at the rubble. "What are we going to do about this?"

Lunk scooped up armfuls of bricks. "I can put these back."

He set them in the hole in the building, piling the debris atop a busted produce shelf. Apples and oranges rolled and squished out onto the sidewalk.

Flight motioned to the young guy. "Ward can take your information. We do want to assure you we successfully thwarted the robbery."

The repairs would probably cost more than what would've been taken from the cash register, since most people paid by credit card.

Lunk took a step toward Ward. He must be a sidekick. "Is there going to be food at the plant thing?"

"Finger sandwiches and such," Ward said.

"But I'm really hungry."

"You did tell them no dairy, right?" Flight said to the sidekick.

Ward's mouth hung open. "Uhh…" He consulted his tablet.

"You know I can't have dairy. Now we'll have to eat before we go, just in case."

"I'm sorry, sir. I'm pretty sure I told them, but…"

Flight turned to the storeowners. "Could we get two sandwiches? Turkey or roast beef. *No cheese.*"

"Can I get three?" Lunk flexed his bulging arm muscles. "I eat a lot."

"And large diet colas. We would appreciate it." Flight flashed a winning smile. "Thank you, citizens."

The woman made a faint semblance of a smile. She muttered to the man as they entered the store. The man shrugged like *What else can we do?*

Two employees began picking up the fruit and throwing it away. What an unfortunate waste. Lunk signed an autograph and posed for a photo with a giggling middle-aged white lady.

Flight pulled Ward aside. "You can't forget about the dairy. It destroys my stomach. That's not something we want to happen while I'm in the air."

"Yes, sir," Ward said, typing on his tablet.

Sadie headed back to work. The whole situation sat badly in her gut, apparently like how dairy sat with Flight. The Supers were acting like gratitude was expected. That they should get free food and drinks as thanks for damaging the store. Lost product, lost business and repair costs, yet they had no problem asking for handouts.

Joan always paid for everything. It was the right thing to do. Why could a Villain see that but not the Supers?

Had she really been wearing blinders so tightly that she couldn't see what others saw? Maybe Joan's viewpoint had some merit.

Shoot. The most honorable person she'd been interested in was a benevolent Supervillain.

The past few days felt like one long, fuzzy workday. Sadie had stayed late Sunday, gone in early Monday, and was now walking to VCC on her day off to cover for Nyah for a few hours while she took her aunt to the doctor.

She squinted at the early afternoon sunlight cresting over the buildings. It was shaping up to be a hot day and she hadn't been sleeping, so the grump level was high. Maybe when she got home, she could chill at the rooftop pool. She highly doubted Joan would... But then again...

Ugh, why had she chased someone who lived so close? She didn't even want to get her mail anymore.

The start of a Vultures baseball game played on TV inside a sports bar. Joan was a loyal fan even though the team hadn't had a decent season in years.

Ugghhhh. Joan was everywhere.

By habit, she checked her phone for any SuperWatch notifications. Dreaded seeing anything involving Spark. Or Ice or Breeze, for that matter. There had been a lot of talk about them doing art heists. Was that what Joan had been up to? What Greta had needed to talk about?

Was all of Joan's very nice home décor stolen? If she ever did talk to Joan again, she'd ask if the artists had been properly compensated. Not paying creatives for their work was the real crime.

An incoming call from Mom popped up. *Not todaaaayyyyyy.*

"Hey Mom, I'm just about to work. Can I—"

"Why are you working?" Mom said. "It's your day off."

"Just filling in for a little bit."

"What's wrong? You usually throw yourself into your job when you have a breakup."

Leave it to her mother to remember that little factoid. "I'm just helping Nyah out," Sadie said.

"I wish you'd spend *less* time at that deathtrap."

She chose to let that go and pay attention to crossing the street.

"Well, anyway, your dad wanted me to call and tell you he heard they're hiring at Allegria Insurance."

"Mom," Sadie snickered. "Allegria Tower is still under construction because it got damaged by Super activity. I'd be trading one deathtrap for another."

Mom chose to let *that* go.

The skyscraper had been smashed into by Breeze, who was actually some guy named Perry who liked to have meetings. How was Sadie supposed to deal with knowing the people behind the masks?

"I know you don't want a boring office job," Mom said. "But I'm sure they have a marketing or advertising department. You could still be creative and have decent benefits."

Sadie started to say she had benefits at VCC, but she was tired of deflecting and rationalizing every tiny thing. "I've been thinking about opening a café," she said instead. "The one I've talked about for years. I think I'm actually going to do it."

"You can have fun making your coffee drinks—"

"Not be a barista, though I do love doing that. I want to run my own coffee shop. One of my neighbors encouraged me to go for it."

"Who was that?" Mom asked warily.

"Just a new neighbor. Joan." Saying her name made her chest tighten. "She was talking about opening a food truck, so we were tossing around ideas. She was the one I was having brunch with last week. She made the food, I made the drinks."

It was like putting Joan's name back in her mouth had opened the floodgates. Sadie mashed her lips together to stop the rush of words before her mother put two and two together.

"Does she have experience with such a thing?" Mom said.

"*I* have tons of experience. I'm qualified."

The thought stopped her in her tracks. "I'm really qualified for this," Sadie murmured to herself.

"You have a college degree," Mom said.

Why did her family keep mentioning some damn piece of paper Sadie'd received over a decade ago? She marched into the flow of sidewalk traffic. "Mom, I love you, but I need you to listen. *I like what I do.* I want to open a café. That's my dream. And even if I don't do that, I don't want to work in a corporate environment. Especially not an insurance company."

"I know, honey. It's just…"

"I don't have the greatest track record and haven't given you many reasons to trust me. But this is who I am. I go into things with my heart on my sleeve."

Like falling for a secret Supervillain.

Mom was quiet for several moments. "You're a lot like your dad when we first met. He had those wild ideas about starting a greenhouse. Or no, it was a farming co-op. The greenhouse came later."

"Dad likes gardening as a hobby. He's told me he didn't want the enjoyment he gets from it to be a source of stress. Like how I do little craft projects for fun."

"I'm just saying he realized what he needed to do to support a family. Maybe when you meet the right person, you'll change your mind."

"Maybe I will," Sadie said. *Or maybe that person will encourage my dreams. Like Joan.*

Somehow, her body was able to produce yet another wave of tears.

She turned down the alley leading to VCC. "I'm at work. Tell Dad I'm glad he didn't give up his love of gardening. Maybe I'll take the train out this weekend to see you."

"We'd love that," Mom said. "Other than going to Jazz on the Square with the Ditmeyers tonight, we've got nothing going on."

Sadie said something about having a good time before they hung up. She couldn't go into work all weepy again.

A SuperWatch notification appeared.

New Report: Trick is the mastermind behind the recent uptick in criminal activity. Hide and Volt are working alongside him. Multiple sources have reported Breeze, Ice and Spark deny being involved.

Her heart leapt into her throat. Was that because they were busy working on plans for Hot and Cold? Could they... Could Sadie...

Joan's mournful expression filled her head. *I wish I could be the good person you thought I was.*

Dang it, Joan really had been fairly honest (minus the One Big Lie). She'd saved a dog's life. She was a good person, and it stung to think she didn't believe that about herself. The world had told her her entire life she was to be feared, that she was bad and not to be trusted. That would do a number on anyone.

"Oh, Joan," she whispered.

This felt so different than all the other times she'd discovered someone had been using her. Because that was the difference— Joan never asked her for anything. Only offered and supported.

For someone who could've easily manipulated Sadie, she'd done anything but.

If it weren't for Joan, Sadie's Café would seem far, far away. Though doing it without her might not be as fun. But it *could* be done. Joan had shown her that. Joan had shown her a lot of things were possible.

Joan Malone was pretty incredible and needed to know that.

Hope twirled in her chest as she pulled up their text chain. They had *a lot* to talk about and work through, but it was worth giving it a try. Giving Joan a try. No more holding back on questioning things. Joan needed to give her the whole truth.

A sudden, sharp urge to drop her phone overwhelmed her. She blinked to try to clear the thought, but it pulsed strong, steady, relentless. Her phone slipped from her fingers.

Another wave told her to empty her pockets. Then to turn around.

She moved as though being guided by an unseen force. A foul, acrid odor assaulted her nose. Someone grabbed her from behind and covered her mouth. Panic spiked through her.

She tried to yell and fight, but whoever it was held her tight. A woman in black and yellow stepped out from behind the dumpster and shot a bolt of lightning over Sadie's head.

"Don't even think about screaming," she said.

Volt. And Sadie couldn't see who was holding her. *Hide.*

Oh, no. Oh, shit. Was this because of—

That wave of unbidden thought came again, instructing her to go with them. She walked out of the alley toward a black SUV. Everything inside her shouted to pull away and run, but she couldn't. She was no longer in control.

CHAPTER 19

Joan's phone buzzed with an incoming text. Her heart skipped a beat as she sat up straight at the table in the warehouse lair. Maybe it was Sadie.

No, just Greta. Nice to hear from her, but still.

> Got the word out you're not with M. You're welcome. Hang out when you're done moping

That wasn't happening anytime soon. Joan was turning moping into an art form.

Mark hunt-and-peck typed on his laptop. Menu ideas for Hot and Cold. What they were busying themselves with while laying low. It was no fun without Sadie's enthusiasm and encouragement and her big brown eyes and beautiful smile and her low-cut shirts and—

Another text popped up.

Her heart stopped.

A photo filled the screen. Sadie zip-tied to a tall metal pole on a flat rooftop, mouth covered with duct tape, eyes red and raw and filled with fear.

Words appeared below it. Not from her—from fucking Melvin.

I have something you want. Give me what I want.

"That fucker," she ground out.

Mark looked up.

"Melvin has Sadie," Joan said, her voice shaking with anger.

He swore under his breath and peered at her phone screen. "He didn't have a bargaining chip, so he…"

Fiery rage surged through her. She stood so forcefully, her chair flipped. "He picked the wrong person to fuck with."

Nobody messed with the people she cared about. Especially not the woman who'd captured her heart. She stalked toward their changing room, Mark on her heels.

"We're going to the Supers." Joan raked a hand through her hair. "Damn it, why didn't we already do that?"

Mark didn't say anything. Probably 'cause he could feel the fury radiating off her. Sadie was in danger, and terrified. Exactly what Joan had been worried about. She should've been more proactive about this Melvin thing.

This was all her fault.

"He better not hurt one hair on her head," Joan growled.

"Hey, buddy." Mark tugged her arm. "Let's go in our civvies. If we bust in as Spark and Ice, they won't listen to a word we say."

"I'm fucking pissed. And scared for Sadie's safety."

"I know. That's why we have to go in without guns blazing. We'll bring our outfits. I'll drive, okay?"

"Shit." Joan instructed her phone to call Perry as they hurried to gather their gear. It went to voicemail. "Fucking Melvin kidnapped Sadie. We're on our way to make a deal with the Supers. Meet us there. Or I'll let you know where Mel's keeping her. Stay close to your phone."

It didn't matter what Perry wanted. Sadie needed them. Needed Joan to step up.

She went to reply to Melvin's text. She wanted to ask if Sadie was okay. To talk to her. To reassure her everything would be all right and they were coming for her. That she was sorry for every-thing and would do whatever it took to make things right.

Her internal fire blazed with a roiling inferno of emotion. Melvin didn't need to hear any of that. Asshole only needed to know one thing.

I will end you for this.

The Vector City Superhero headquarters was a modern concrete structure with imposing columns at the front. Like it dared evil-doers to fuck around and find out.

Joan shot up several fireballs to be seen through the high windows along one side. Mark sent a few large chunks of ice. One bumped the glass and broke into pieces.

She checked her phone again for anything from Perry (prob-ably too busy afternoon napping) or Melvin (definitely too busy being an asshole).

Someone raced onto the sidewalk in a red jumpsuit. Wait—was this Zee? She'd never seen them unmasked. They had flat features set in warm undertones, full lips and tousled straight black hair.

"What are you doing?" they said.

"We're ready to make a deal," Joan said.

"We know what Trick's up to," Mark added.

Zee studied them for a long moment. "You're not here to cause trouble, right? If I let you in—"

"He's taken someone hostage," Joan said. "He wants us to join him and kidnapped someone I care about. A civilian. The people you're supposed to be protecting."

"All right." Zee nodded. "I'm vouching for you. If you do anything—"

"We don't want to be here any more than you want us here," Mark said. "We have to stop Melvin once and for all."

Zee didn't say another word. Just led them to a nondescript entrance around the back. They settled their hand on an electronic pad, which opened a small section of the concrete wall.

It was surprisingly bright and airy inside. Light colors on the walls, an Art Deco-style crystal chandelier. The spacious lobby was filled with plush furnishings.

"What the hell?" Mark muttered, taking it all in. "This puts our janky warehouse to shame."

New Sidekick hustled down the wide marble staircase. "You don't have any meetings scheduled today," he said, looking up and down from a tablet. "Are these citizens in need of help? I just saw some fire and ice."

Zee glanced at the twin sources of fire and ice. "They're here to help with something."

"Welcome." New Sidekick gave them a polite smile. "I'm Ward. Can I get you something to drink? Mineral water? Fair trade organic coffee?"

Sidekick Ward walked over to a beverage station. Zee shook their head and said, "This is time-sensitive. I need you to look for signs of activity from Trick."

"Yes, Mx. Race."

Zee walked ahead of them up the stairs. The quartet reached a richly carpeted landing. Joan snorted at the paintings—actual *paintings*—of each Super along the wall. "That's a bit much."

Zee made a vague shrug. Farther down both sides of the hallway hung paintings of former Supers from the past hundred plus years, retired or dead. The one of Amazing Woman, young and perky and blonde with a 1960s flair, looked like it'd been torn at some point.

Ward headed to a partially open door to the right. "Whom shall I say is here to see the Supers?"

"Spark and Ice," Mark said.

The sidekick's eyes bulged behind his glasses. "Wait, what?"

"I'll go in first," Zee said.

"By all means." Mark did a broad arm gesture.

Joan's pulse kicked up another notch. This better not backfire. Sadie needed her. Getting detained would waste precious time.

She followed Zee into a large, well-lit room. The other three Supers lounged on couches and armchairs, also in casual wear. Flight read a book while Catch and Lunk played on their phones. It was a bit jarring to see them so relaxed.

"I'm terribly sorry," Ward said from the doorway. "Spark and Ice somehow got in."

The Supers quickly jumped to their feet. Joan conjured a fireball by habit.

Darlene fisted her hands. "What are they doing here?"

Zee held their arms between Mark and Joan and an approaching Lunk. "I said to give them a chance. Let's listen to what they have to say."

Flight soared above them, his bald ebony head shining against a nearby light. "You're not welcome here," he boomed in his mighty voice.

"Yeah, no shit," Joan said. She kept her focus on Catch, who looked every bit as prissy as she'd imagined with her pinched face and brown hair slicked into a high ponytail.

"We know what Trick is up to," Mark said. He shot a spray of snow at Lunk. "Did you miss me, sweetie?"

Kade looked like a big, confused, curly-haired palomino.

"Stop," Zee said. They held a hand up to Flight. "You, too. All of you."

Darlene fixed her intense gaze on Joan. Joan gave it right back.

"No powers," Zee said. "Everyone."

Shit. Joan had to be the one to make a good faith gesture. She stepped back and waved out her fire.

Zee gave Flight a look. Flight—Otis—glided slowly to the laminate floor.

Darlene crossed her arms. "Why should we trust you? We believe in justice. You don't believe in anything."

I believe in Sadie.

"We don't want anything to do with you, either," Joan said. "But Trick needs to be stopped."

"What is his grand plan?" Otis asked, crossing his arms.

Kade looked at his cohorts, then crossed his bulky arms, too.

"He doesn't have one," Joan said.

The Supers erupted in disbelief.

"He wants me and Mark to come up with something. He can't think of anything, so he needs us to do it for him. He tried to get us to join him. When that failed, he kidnapped someone close to me."

"Do you honestly expect us to believe that?" Darlene said.

"It's the truth," said Joan.

"If he kidnapped someone close to you, that person is obviously a criminal."

Angry flames flared from both palms. Catch lunged at her, but Zee stepped between them and speed-waved Joan's flames out.

Joan pointed at Catch. "Fuck you, Darlene. She's a harmless norm who's in danger."

"Anyone who consorts with the likes of you has no integrity."

"*Look.*" She pulled her phone from her jeans pocket and brought up the photo from Melvin.

Darlene was only marginally interested. Zee took a look, thin eyebrows drawing close in concern. "Who is that?" they asked.

"Her name is Sadie Eagan. She works at a coffee shop. We're… She's my neighbor."

"They're more than neighbors," Mark said, "but it's a bit complicated at the moment."

"She's a good person who doesn't deserve any of this." Joan held the phone out for Otis and Kade. "We have to save her."

Otis eyed her warily. "If we allow you to work with us, what will you give us in return?"

Joan shared a *What the fuck?* look with Mark. "If we work *together*, we take down Trick, Hide and Volt for good," she said.

"You have our word we'll put aside our differences," Mark said.

Darlene snorted. "What good is the word of a Villain?"

Joan turned to Zee. They'd already had this argument. The only way forward was to trust each other.

"I'm not comfortable working with those two," Darlene continued.

"Let's hear them out," Zee said.

"We believe in *justice*." She punctuated the word with a fist to her opposite palm. "We stand for *justice*." She did the fist hammer again. "If we let them go, *justice* will not prevail."

"Oh my god," Joan groaned. "I can't believe Sadie thought I was you."

Darlene's face scrunched in confusion. "What?"

"Who's Sadie?" Kade said.

"Your mom," Mark and Joan chorused.

Otis floated in front of them. "We can work together to defeat a common enemy. But you have to give us something in exchange for—"

"Mark and I are out," Joan said. "We're done with villainy. We're retiring."

Darlene snorted again. "You can't just retire. You belong in prison."

"If we help you, we walk away. For good."

"No."

"Then we can continue making your lives a living hell," Mark said. "*Or* we can go live quiet, normal lives and give you three fewer bad guys to keep track of."

"Breeze is in for this as well?" Otis made a big deal out of looking around the room. "I don't see him here."

"Sure, yeah, of course he's in." Mark waved a hand like that was guaranteed.

"He's doing stuff back at our HQ," Joan said.

Otis made a face, and Darlene was winding up to rebuff everything, and Kade was probably still trying to figure out who Sadie was. Damn it, they were wasting time.

"This is what we always wanted," Joan told them. "The life we could've had if you'd given us a little support back in the day. Do your jobs and give us that fucking support now."

Zee tilted their head at their fellow Supers, eyebrows raised like *She has a point.*

Darlene wandered in a tight, stick-up-her-ass circle. "How does this grand plan Trick has been preparing not exist? All we've been hearing is how he's going to take over the city."

"The dude does mind control," Joan reminded her. "He's got the norms worked up into thinking something big is coming. But he can't come up with anything. We're the ones with all the great ideas."

Mark leaned close and said, "Maybe not the best place to bring that up, sis."

"You know he's full of shit." Joan looked at the Supers. "He controls people. That's what makes him dangerous. He's been framing us for things we didn't do. I swear to you, Mark and Perry and I want him put away."

"Irving and Ethel, too," Mark said. "They suck."

Otis did his *Look at me, I'm a Superhero* arm-crossing again. "And then you'll leave villainy? Perry, too?"

Joan gave him a firm nod. "Yes. Gladly."

Anxious energy blazed through her bloodstream. If they said no, she'd go all gangbusters and rescue Sadie herself. Even if it meant *a lot* of destruction.

Zee seemed to pick up on her vibe. "I vote yes," they said.

"I vote yes," Otis said.

Kade looked between them. "I vote yes, too," he said.

"Thanks, sugar." Mark winked at him.

"Huh?"

Everyone turned to Darlene. Her nostrils flared, and she clearly wanted to do anything but agree. Her gaze settled on Joan.

"His hostage," Joan said quietly. "Sadie. I'm way into her. She makes me want to stay on the straight and narrow."

"Aww," Kade said.

Zee cracked a tiny grin.

"Do it for love, Darlene," Mark said.

Darlene pursed her lips. "I'm doing it for justice. I vote yes."

A tiny thread of relief cooled some of Joan's rage. "Let's find where Sadie's being held and get her and take those assholes down."

Otis held up a finger. "We need to coordinate a plan of attack."

"That wasn't a fully thought-out plan?"

"Made sense to me," Mark said.

"Ward?" Otis addressed the sidekick.

Consulting his tablet, Ward said, "There have been multiple reports of activity on the roof at Thirty South Mansfield. Trick and Volt, which suggests Hide is there as well."

"To the control center!" Kade announced.

Darlene made a beeline out of the room, Ward hurrying after. The other Supers surrounded the Villains down the hallway. Any other day, it would've been unnerving.

Mark bumped Joan's shoulder with his own. "We'll bring her home."

"We will," Joan vowed. Sadie would never forgive her after this, but right now, only her safety mattered.

They walked into a darkened room filled with monitors showing live feeds from all across the city. One big touchscreen had SuperWatch on it.

"You guys seriously use SuperWatch?" Mark snickered.

"It's the best way to get the word on the street," said Zee.

Ward typed on the expansive keyboard. Otis sidled up to Joan. "What exactly is Perry doing?"

Joan checked her phone. Still no word. She couldn't think of a good excuse, so she admitted, "I think he's taking a nap. Which he'll need if he's gonna help us."

"How did you get him to agree to this?"

Uh, I didn't? "Trick's giving him a bad name. He wants it cleared so he can pursue legit business ventures."

"An art gallery," Otis said, almost like he'd remembered something.

"Yeah." Joan turned to face him. "How did you know that?"

One of the monitors zoomed in on a rooftop with Trick pacing and swishing his fugly purple cape. Ethel marched dutifully behind him. He had a few armed guards because of course the coward did.

The Supers gathered around the screen, Mark and Joan following. The camera panned and caught Sadie tied to a tall pole, squirming and trying to get free.

An orange haze blurred Joan's vision. She had to shut her eyes before fire shot out. That didn't erase the horrible image from her mind's eye.

"Is that her?" Zee asked.

Joan opened her eyes. The haze was still there. "That's her."

Darlene cleared her throat. Joan made a fist, ready to pop off at her.

The Super nodded at Joan's hand and said, "I have a plan."

CHAPTER 20

Sadie watched the three men with big guns guarding her on the skyscraper roof. Several more were gathered around Trick. The Villain was large and imposing, with chiseled features and a ripped physique. Hide and Volt circled around him, growing more and more fidgety.

She twisted her hands behind her back, grimacing through the thick tape across her mouth. The plastic zip-tie had her pinned against the metal pole warmed by the late-day sun.

"Where are they?" Hide said.

"They'll be here," Trick said. He glanced at Sadie.

A wave of confusion washed over her. Mind control? Why else had she followed him up here? It was like her brain and body were two separate entities, 'cause her body wanted to get the hell out of there.

What did Trick want with her? In moments of lucidity, she'd heard *Joan* and *Mark*, but everything was fuzzy.

A roar sounded through the sky. Sadie blinked, trying to clear her mind, and saw a figure in black shooting two long streams of fire. They landed in a crouch, dark hair falling over both shoulders.

Spark.

Spark stood, searching the area. The armed guards moved closer to Sadie.

"About time you showed up," Trick said.

"Melvin, you shitbag!" Spark shouted.

Melvin?

She looked at Sadie. "Are you okay? Did he hurt you?"

Sadie shook her head. That voice. So familiar.

It was Joan.

Shock surged through her. *Joan.*

Joan stalked toward Trick, but Volt and Hide stepped between them. "If you touched one hair on her head…"

"She's fine," Trick said. "Glad this got your attention."

Another figure shooting icy snow flew onto the roof. *Ice.* He gestured at Sadie and said, "You okay, hon?"

Wait, that was Mark. Sadie nodded, squeaking unintelligible words through the duct tape.

"You're a real piece of guano, Melvin."

"It's Trick," Volt said.

Joan looked strong and confident and a little intimidating in her Spark outfit. She stared down Trick, who apparently was… Uncle Mel?

A third figure shot onto the roof in solid gray. *Breeze.*

"Really, dude?" Mark said.

Breeze shrugged. "It was a good nap."

"Did you get our texts?"

"Yep."

Trick rubbed his gloved hands together. "Now that we're all here, we can start taking over the city."

"How are we going to do that, Melvin?" Breeze said.

"It's *Trick*, damn it. And I'm open to your suggestions. To go along with my ideas."

"Riiiight," Mark drawled.

"We have tons of ideas," Joan said. She planted her hands on her hips. "In fact, we brought some friends to help with them."

Movement came from everywhere. Flight sailed through the

air, and Lunk charged ahead, and Catch…ran toward Joan? Everything was a bit muddled.

Blurry action surrounded the guards near Sadie. They crumpled into a pile. Race stopped running and swiftly disarmed the rifles.

Joan shot fire into Catch's hands. They turned in tandem to thrust fireballs at Volt. Volt retaliated with bolts of electricity.

Lunk knocked out the rest of the guards in quick order. Hide disappeared, but Mark shot snow all around until Hide's silhouette appeared. Flight swooped down and grabbed him.

Breeze blew strong wind at Volt, sending her electric bolts high in the sky. The fireballs pushed her over.

Trick-Melvin sprinted toward Sadie. She screamed as loud as she could through the tape. Joan turned and flung her hand in their direction. A roaring flame shot up in front of Trick.

"I've got this," Catch said. "Go."

Joan stomped over, fiery hands at her sides. Her eyes burned red and orange and hot. Her whole body glowed with ire.

"Get up!" Trick yelled at the unarmed men lying on the roof. "Defend me at all costs!"

They stood like creepy zombies. Race zigzagged around them, hog-tying them with heavy neon rope. The guards wiggled and wobbled like crabs.

Trick backed up, sneering at Joan. "Working with the Supers? Really, Joanie? After everything we've been through?"

"You fucked up big time," Joan growled. "That woman means more to me than you'll ever know."

"Enough to forget your loyalties? Our code?"

"I don't owe you a thing." She veered toward Sadie. "Shitheads like you have kept me in this life far too long."

"Perry kept you in this life," Trick scoffed.

"And now it's time for all of us to get out. Only you'll be locked up for a very, very long time."

Joan paused in front of Sadie. Her familiar lips, the worry in her amber eyes. "Hey, sweetheart," she said.

She shot a fireball at Trick's feet, causing him to jump.

"I'm really sorry for everything. I should've been honest from the start."

She shot another fireball at his ass. He howled.

"I know I don't deserve a second chance," Joan said. "Especially not after you've seen all this."

A sharp flame blazed from her palm. It slammed into Trick's chest, knocking him over.

"But I really, really like you. And I think we could work through some stuff. If you want to try."

Sadie's heart swelled. Joan was rescuing her. She was working with the Supers. She was…

…the reason Sadie was in this mess. Trick had used her as bait. She tried to say, "I got kidnapped because of you," but that was not what came out.

"What?" Joan said.

Mark hastened over. "I got this."

He touched a finger to the duct tape. It froze and crumbled off Sadie's mouth. She drew in a deep breath. The air tasted of smoke and cold and electricity.

Trick started to get up. Joan lasered her eyes at him. A tall inferno encircled him.

"Isn't he going to get burned?" Sadie asked.

"Nah," Joan said. "Our suits are resistant to stuff like that."

Race stood with them for a few moments, then gestured at the fire circle. "Are you done playing with him?"

Joan's eyes narrowed. "He's all yours."

Breeze walked over and blew a big gust of wind to extinguish the flames. Race wasted no time wrapping Trick in full-body ropes.

Sadie shook her head, which felt like her own again. At some point, Trick had changed. He was much shorter, and his face wasn't remotely chiseled, and he looked more like a Melvin. Were those fake muscles built into his suit?

The *whomp-whomp-whomp* of an approaching helicopter sounded nearby. Could be the police, could be the press.

Flight scooped him up and flew off, Trick's wails echoing farther and farther away.

"Good riddance, piece of shit," Joan said.

"Make sure he's contained in a way that blocks him from doing mind control," Breeze said to Race.

"We do know how to properly secure Villains," Race said. That made Breeze rapidly retreat.

Across the roof, an unconscious Hide and Volt were being tied up by Catch. All the guards had already been bound.

Joan pulled her facemask off, revealing wild, sweaty hair and eyebrows knit in concern. She extended a tentative hand and gently brushed Sadie's hair back. The tender gesture was pure Joanie, not at all Spark.

"So that was Uncle Mel?" Sadie said.

"Yeah."

"He kind of sucks."

"Yeah."

"This happened because of you," Sadie said. "Because of my connection to you."

Joan closed her eyes. "I'm so sorry."

"That was why you didn't want me involved with this part of your life."

"I put you in danger," she murmured.

"Well, I've never wanted an ordinary life." Sadie mustered up a smirk. "Meeting you has made it very interesting."

Lunk lumbered over. "Let's set you free," he said to Sadie. He pulled the zip-tie between his hands until the plastic broke. "There you go, little lady."

She rubbed at the raw skin on her wrists. Her shoulders and arms ached from being pulled taut behind her back.

Lunk stood expectantly, fists on hips, waiting for her to fawn over him. Sadie reached for Joan instead, who drew her into her arms. Joan rested her cheek against Sadie's forehead. It was warmer than usual, but nothing Sadie couldn't handle. Being in Joan's protective embrace was *everything*.

"Stand back, stud," Mark said to Lunk.

He waved his hand. A thick ice arch formed to cover Joan and Sadie, affording them some privacy as the helicopter hovered overhead.

Poking his head beneath it, he said, "Hey, it's me, Mark."

"I know," Sadie said. "It's nice to see you again."

Mark winked at her.

Under the other side of the arch, Breeze leaned in. "Hi, Sadie. I'm Perry. I've heard a lot about you."

"Nice to meet you," Sadie said to the masked man. "I've heard a lot about you, too."

Breeze-Perry shared a look with Mark and Joan. Then his gaze shifted behind them.

Race cocked a hip, amusement dancing on their lips. "We did it," they said.

"We sure did," said Mark.

Joan tilted her head to see Race. "Thanks for trusting us. This wouldn't have happened without you."

"You're right," Race said. Then they nodded. "Thank you for trusting *us*. Uphold your end of the deal."

Mark and Joan agreed to whatever that meant. Sadie nestled closer to Joan's bodysuit.

"You too, Perry." Race did the *I'm watching you* two-finger gesture. Perry appeared to be confused by that.

The Superhero headed to where Catch watched over the guards. Lunk looked back and forth, then trudged in the same direction.

"Hate to see you go," Mark said, "but I love to watch you walk away."

Lunk turned around. "Huh?"

Mark shook his head. "The lights are on in his beautiful head, but no one's home." He squeezed Sadie's shoulder, then went to join Lunk. "Hey, big guy. Thank your sidekick for us. He's not half bad."

Perry stepped beneath the ice arch. "What did Race mean about your end of the deal?" he asked Joan.

"We'll have to talk," she said. "Later."

His mouth set in a grim line. "Get Sadie home safely."

"I will." She pressed Sadie tighter.

He strode to the ledge and hopped over. Not something you saw every day. But today was filled with things Sadie didn't see every day. Like the woman she knew as Joan Malone glowing with waves of fire. It was honestly kind of…hot.

A second helicopter hovered on the opposite side of the roof. Sadie adjusted her position so Joan couldn't be seen. Several water droplets hit the top of her head. The ice arch was melting from Joan's body heat and the sun.

Joan pulled back just enough to look at Sadie. Her eyes shined amber and genuine. "I'm so sorry for everything. Can you ever forgive me?"

"I was about to text you," Sadie said.

"What?"

"Right before I got taken. I was just about to text you. You *did* try to tell me the truth. I wasn't listening. Or hearing what I wanted to hear, I guess."

Joan shook her head. "Don't take any responsibility for this."

"I need to own up to my part," Sadie said. "I assumed you were someone and ignored my intuition when things felt off. But I was right about one thing."

Joan raised her eyebrows.

"You *are* a good person. What you did today proves that."

A small smile tugged at her mouth.

Linking her fingers low on Joan's back, Sadie said, "We have to work on honesty. And I need to speak up when something doesn't seem right. But I'll listen, too. I want you to tell me your whole story."

"I will," Joan said.

Someone cleared their throat loudly.

Catch stood with her arms crossed firmly over her chest. Joan stiffened, dropping one hand to form a first.

"Justice was served today," Catch stated.

"Yeah," Joan said, wariness in her voice.

"It's not the full outcome I want, but I will give you the benefit of the doubt. But make no mistake." Catch pointed her index finger. "We'll be watching you."

Joan rolled her eyes and made a halfhearted noise in agreement. Water from the ice arch dripped onto her head.

Catch nodded at Sadie. "Not to worry, citizen of Vector City. Justice has prevailed."

A laugh bubbled up in her throat. "I'm not worried at all," Sadie said, swaying in Joan's arms.

Joan grinned at her.

The Super turned on her navy-blue heel and marched off. The too-straight posture, the way she talked in clipped tones, her lack of humor…

"I can't believe I thought you were her," Sadie said.

Joan snorted and dropped her forehead to Sadie's. "I mean…"

"But I always knew you were good." She rested a hand on Joan's chest, over her black-and-red Spark outfit. "You don't have to be a Superhero to do good."

"Maybe I'm neither good nor bad, but a little of both."

Sadie smiled widely. "Aren't we all?"

CHAPTER 21

Joan held Sadie's hand securely as they exited the elevator onto the seventh floor. Home at last.

She'd barely let go in the past few hours. Or at least hadn't wanted to while Sadie gave her statement to the police at the hospital and had a quick exam to make sure she was okay. After changing into her street clothes, Joan had been there as a "supportive friend."

It was kind of funny and a bit terrifying to have been so close to the cops as Sadie made it known Spark, Ice and Breeze had been integral in capturing the very bad guys. She'd explained that she didn't know why Trick had taken her. Wrong place, wrong time.

Sadie caught her staring and squeezed Joan's hand. "I'm fine. Just a little sore."

"I hate that you got hurt," Joan murmured.

"I'll feel better after I wash up and put on comfy clothes."

They paused outside Sadie's door. Amit had come by the hospital to check in and give Sadie her keys and phone, as well as some food. He'd told her to take the next few days off. He'd also told Joan to take care of her, which had been unexpected but very welcome. He reminded her a lot of Perry with his gruff way of showing he cared.

"Can you come in with me?" Sadie said. "I don't want to be alone."

"Of course. You shouldn't be by yourself. You went through a pretty traumatic event."

"I guess one good thing is that I was under mind control most of the time, so I don't remember much. It's more like a dream I had, in bits and pieces."

Joan nodded. Sadie had said as much in her statement.

Sadie hesitated, key poised at the lock. Then she turned to Joan. "Can I stay at your place tonight? I'd feel safer if I was with you. And you have all those alarms and stuff."

"Absolutely. Stay as long as you want. I'll have the arnica gel at the ready."

Sadie swayed a little. Joan scooped her into a tight hug. She honestly couldn't believe Sadie felt safe with her after seeing her in all her flame-throwing glory. But Sadie didn't seem bothered. She knew the good, the bad and the fiery and still wanted to be with Joan.

She was *everything*.

"Okay," Sadie said, and drew back. "Let me get a few things and we'll hunker down."

She gathered her bathroom essentials before rummaging around her bedroom. She emerged with her hair down, in a faded City School of Design T-shirt and short, girly flannel boxers.

"You're getting full-on Comfy Sadie," she laughed.

"Comfy Sadie is cute," Joan said. Comfy Sadie also didn't appear to be wearing a bra.

She handed Joan her cosmetics travel bag, then grabbed her phone and keys off the kitchen counter. "I'll call my parents tomorrow. I don't have the energy to tell the story again tonight."

Thank god Sadie's parents were out so they wouldn't tune in to the nightly news. She'd asked not to be identified by the press, which would hopefully delay their inevitable freakout.

Guilt twinged Joan's chest. If it hadn't been for her, Sadie would have never been in harm's way. What if being together meant more danger ahead?

Sadie gave her a small smile. The twinge grew in warmth and pressure.

What if being together was the best way to protect her?

They headed over to Joan's apartment. She disarmed the alarm when they entered, then swiftly reactivated it. "Let me do a quick sweep," she said.

"Only if you want to," Sadie said.

"I very much want to."

Joan checked the sliding glass doors, all the windows, every room, looking and listening for anything suspicious. Everything was as she'd left it that morning, including the empty Chinese food containers and beer bottles sitting on the kitchen island from the weekend.

Sadie leaned against it. "This looks like the set for a sad heartbreak montage in a rom-com."

"That's basically what it was."

She stretched forward to give Joan a soft kiss. "Not tonight."

"Not tonight," Joan repeated, mostly so she didn't blurt out *Hopefully never again.*

"Can I ask you something?" Sadie said.

"Anything."

She looked in the direction of the living room. "Is all of that stolen? The paintings and expensive trinkets?"

Taking in a steadying breath, Joan said, "Some of it. A few things were gifts. I bought some things."

"I don't like the idea of the artists not getting paid."

"I don't, either. Everything was originally bought and paid for. I wouldn't take anything from an artist. That's shitty."

"You should give the creators some money for their troubles," Sadie said. "If they're still alive. It can't feel good to know your work got stolen."

"You're right. I should. I mean, I appreciate and enjoy it all."

"That would be a nice gesture."

The way Sadie looked at her—*I like you, but do better*—anyone would agree to whatever she wanted. "Okay. I'll do that," Joan said.

"Good." Sadie released a huge yawn. "Whew. I'm exhausted."

"Me, too. Generating as much fire as I did takes a lot out of me."

"I can only imagine." Toying with a button on Joan's chambray-blue shirt, Sadie said, "How are you feeling about everything that went down? You had some old friends arrested. That couldn't have been easy."

"I don't care," Joan said. "They hurt you. They deserve everything they get. I'm more concerned about you."

"I keep telling you I'm okay."

They stared at each other, silently acknowledging neither was being all that forthcoming.

"We need to be more honest about how we're feeling," Sadie said.

Joan hesitated for a long beat. She wasn't used to *feelings* talks. "I don't think it's sunk in yet. It probably will in a day or two."

"I'll be here for you when it does."

"Thank you. I'll have to process it with Mark. We've gone through everything together. I can't process things without him."

Sadie nodded.

"But I want you there," Joan quickly added. "I didn't mean for it to sound like—"

"It didn't, but thanks for clarifying." Sadie stared down at her baggy T-shirt. "I haven't processed what happened, either. It might be hard going back to work."

"I'll drive you to and from the café. Every day. I'll hang out there and work on plans for the food truck if you need me to."

She glanced up and smiled at Joan. "My sweet Joanie Maloney."

Joan yawned, fatigue settling around her like a thick fog. Sadie yawned too, and they both laughed.

"Why don't you get comfy and we'll relax?" Sadie tugged on Joan's shirt. "We can talk more after a good night's snuggle."

Snuggling sounded like the very best soothing balm. Joan pressed a kiss to Sadie's temple. Sadie studied her face.

"What?" Joan said.

"You look worried. What's wrong?"

She met Sadie's beautiful brown eyes. "I was scared this might never happen again. That we wouldn't…"

"Don't worry." Sadie kissed her cheek. "We will."

"Thank you for giving me a second chance."

"Don't blow it."

"I won't."

They shared a grin. It was such a relief to not have to hide anymore.

Joan started for her bedroom. She paused, spying the keypad on her office door. Sadie needed to know everything. Had to be let into the world she was now a part of.

"I want to show you something," Joan said.

She typed in the code and opened the door. Flipped on the overhead light she rarely used, preferring the room be kept dimly lit.

Sadie stepped cautiously inside. It didn't look intimidating—just a table with two large computer monitors and a locked metal trunk in the corner. Joan went to the closet to reveal her large safe and pile of extra Spark gear. Gloves, boots, an unused wig that was even more annoying than her current one.

"That's the First National Bank of Malone," she said, gesturing to the safe. "Sorry, that's a terrible joke Mark started years ago. I know it's not funny."

Sadie averted her gaze. "Don't open it. I don't want to see what's in there."

She gingerly picked up the wig. She eyed it, then plopped it on her head. Her curled red bangs poked out from the front. Smirking, she snagged one glove, then another, then put them on. She held up her fists and did a karate kick.

"I'm a badass Supervillain," she growled, kicking her other leg.

"You're too sweet to be a Villain."

"That's my superpower. I disarm people with my kindness." She punched the air a few times. Right now, her bouncy untethered breasts were an extremely disarming superpower.

Sadie noticed the wear and tear on the gloves. She held the palms up and appraised them. "Does it hurt when you create fire?" she asked quietly.

"No, it never does."

"Can your Spark suit really absorb most hits?"

"Mostly."

Her lips curved into a smile. "How does it feel to fly?"

"Pretty cool. I can take you sometime."

"Maybe."

It was surreal talking about this. Seeing Sadie in Spark accessories. Even Greta never put them on.

"What was Race talking about?" Sadie said. "What deal did you make with the Supers?"

"If we helped them, me and Mark and Perry can get out of the life. As long as we don't do anything to give them cause for concern, they'll leave us be."

"You really were serious about wanting to do that."

"Every word."

After a few moments, Sadie said, "How was it working with the Supers? That had to be weird."

"It was weird. But good? I don't know. There's a lot of bad blood there."

"They were willing to work with you. And you were willing to put aside your differences..."

"For you," Joan murmured.

"Really?" Sadie's eyes shone with the appreciation Joan thought she'd never see again.

"We all wanted to stop Trick. But I was there for you."

Sadie beamed a glorious smile. "My hero."

Joan had been called many things in her life. *Hero* had never been one of them.

Her heart pulsed with warmth and...pride? Was this what virtuous pride felt like?

Pulling the wig off, Sadie said, "It feels kinda wrong wearing this."

She tossed it and the gloves back into the closet. Joan closed the door. That was enough for an already very long day.

"All right." Sadie waved at the open doorway. "Go get changed, hot stuff."

"Oh, so it's gonna be Spark jokes from now on?" Joan teased.

"I think I've earned the right to all the jokes."

"You can do whatever you want to me, Sadie Eagan."

Sadie pinched her ass on the way by. "I absolutely will, Joan Malone."

CHAPTER 22

Sunlight streamed through the bedroom curtains. Joan rolled over, feeling the fading heat on the sage-green sheets where Sadie had been. At some point after falling asleep on the couch last night, they'd stumbled to bed and drifted off in each other's arms.

Familiar sounds came from the kitchen. Her heartbeat drummed in anticipation. She couldn't wait to kiss Sadie good morning. To kiss Sadie every morning they were together. Which would hopefully be many, many mornings to come.

She tossed the covers back and snuck into the bathroom to take care of business. She splashed some water on her face and rinsed her mouth out for a certain degree of freshness.

Sadie looked perfectly at home in the kitchen, scooping coffee grounds into the filter for pour-over coffee. "Good morning," she said brightly.

Everything seemed bright this morning. "Hi," Joan said.

She wrapped her arms around Sadie from behind, loving how they fit together. Joan kissed her cheek a few times, then nuzzled her ear.

Sadie hummed in pleasure and set the small bowl of coffee grounds down. "Did you get some sleep?"

"Yeah. I hope I didn't drool or snore."

"If you did, I was too comatose to notice." She giggled. "This wasn't how you envisioned spending the night with me, was it?"

"Not exactly. How are you feeling?"

Sadie touched one of her bruised wrists. "My shoulders are sore, but not too bad."

"A long massage and arnica gel treatments are heading your way."

"Awesome." She turned and wound her arms around Joan's neck. "It was nice to wake up to you."

Joan settled her hands on Sadie's hips. "It was nice cuddling all night with you."

It was more than nice. It was *right*.

Sadie tilted her head, inviting Joan to kiss her. An offer she couldn't refuse.

Their first few kisses were sweet and playful. Then Sadie sighed with so much contentment, Joan's internal match lit. She gently prodded Sadie's mouth open with her tongue, tasting minty toothpaste.

Sadie dug her fingers in Joan's hair, bringing her closer. Desire zoomed to the heaviness growing between her legs. Sadie's thigh grazed that spot, pulling a moan out of Joan. She bunched the cotton of Sadie's shirt, wanting to get at the soft skin beneath.

"Oh my god," Sadie breathed, nibbling a trail across Joan's jaw. "I've got weeks' worth of horniness built up."

"We should take care of that," Joan murmured.

Sadie nipped her earlobe, causing a low quake to rumble around Joan's abdomen. "We *should* take care of that."

"Here?" She slipped her fingers under Sadie's T-shirt to the elastic waistband of her flannel boxers.

"Bedroom," Sadie said. "I want to take my time kissing every inch of you."

Joan's inner fire swelled from the image of Sadie doing just that. *Shit*. This again.

Sadie slid her hands down, thumbs caressing the sides of Joan's breasts. It made her knees quiver.

She gripped Joan's black tank top and pulled her out of the kitchen. Well, shit. They had to work on honesty, so Joan paused, setting a hand on Sadie's. "We should talk about…"

"Right. Yes. The…" Sadie made a whooshing sound and twirled her free hand. "Fire thing."

"I don't want what happened last time to happen again." *I don't want to scare you.*

"Does that usually happen?"

"Never," Joan said. "I think it's…"

Sadie blinked, waiting for her to finish that thought.

"I think it's because I like you so much."

"You do, huh?" she murmured.

"If you want complete honesty…" Pulse pounding, Joan said, "I've never felt this way about anyone."

Sadie released a little gasp. "Me, too."

Joan kissed her because she had to. Because she was head over heels for this wonderful, understanding woman. Because there was more than fire racing through her veins.

"Hmm," Sadie hummed. "Can you, like, direct it somewhere specific? A certain place in your body to keep it contained?"

Joan raised an eyebrow.

"Not *there*." Sadie gestured with her chin at Joan's light-blue pajama bottoms. "Unless that's a good spot."

"It might be a good spot. For both of us."

"Really?"

"I can direct heat where it'll be most effective," Joan promised.

"Mmm, nice. Or what about…" Sadie glanced up through her lashes. "Your heart? Unless that's a bad place to store a bunch of fire. I'm not an expert."

"Any spot is as good as another," Joan said. "Although…" She tugged Sadie closer. "Some are better than others."

"Try your heart," Sadie whispered against her lips.

"Okay." Joan brushed her nose over Sadie's. "Let me know if anything feels too hot or off or uncomfortable and you need me to stop."

They shared several languid kisses that only stoked the fire. Sadie giggled, then said, "This is the oddest safe sex talk I've ever had."

Joan chuckled and heated in a different way—from slight embarrassment.

"I last saw my doctor a few months ago. Everything was fine. I haven't slept with anyone since then."

"I..." Joan cringed. "...can't go to the doctor. At least not a proper doctor."

Nodding, Sadie said, "Your lab results would be rather interesting."

"I haven't been with anyone in a while. I think everything's okay."

"Let's hope so." She tickled the skin beneath Joan's top. "I want you so damn much, it's become a taco emergency."

Joan laughed loudly, her breath hitching at the end from how much she wanted this, too. "I'm here to take care of your emergencies."

"And I'll thoroughly fuss over you. Shit, why are we still talking? Get my clothes off."

Laughter bubbled with her heat as she let Sadie drag her into the bedroom. Sadie didn't seem to be bluffing to cover any fear or concern. But this desire was so sharp, so intense. What if Joan couldn't contain it?

Try your heart.

Sadie sat them on the edge of the bed. Sunlight caught on her red hair, her luminous skin. The whole room was bathed in welcoming light.

Joan drew in a deep breath. She sent the swirling fire to her torso, then directed it toward her heart. It concentrated down, throbbing with each heartbeat.

Sadie cupped the sides of her face, drawing her in for a lingering kiss. She leaned back and smiled, so beautiful it should've been illegal.

Joan tangled her hands in Sadie's thick hair, sharing kiss after kiss. Sadie tugged at the bottom of Joan's tank top, saying, "We don't need this anymore."

Joan raised her arms to be freed. "Nope."

She gave Sadie a moment to stare at her small breasts with keen hunger before pulling on Sadie's T-shirt. Her breasts were lovely and full, little white stretch marks shimmering in the sun, rosy nipples awaiting attention.

Sadie wasted no time trailing her fingers across Joan's nipples, sending tiny jolts through her chest. Her thumb grazed one tip, then circled it more deliberately.

Joan palmed Sadie's left breast, kneading it, lifting it slightly for better access. A rainbow arched across one of her ribs. "Secret tattoo," she noted with glee.

"That's one," Sadie breathed. She leaned in to press her lips against Joan's pounding pulse point.

Sadie kissed and licked and nibbled down to Joan's chest. Her heart stuttered as Sadie's mouth took over for her hands. She toyed with Joan's hardened nipple with her tongue, her teeth, teasing and tasting. Then she claimed the other breast.

A moan vibrated in Joan's throat. She wanted to taste every bit of Sadie. She gently tweaked her nipples, rolling them between her fingers, until Sadie groaned.

Sadie pulled back and scooted up to the pillows. Reaching for Joan, she said, "Get over here."

Joan lay down beside her—well, half on her, since Sadie grasped the back of her neck and made no bones about wanting Joan to kiss her breasts. Joan lightly flicked the tip of one pert nipple, gradually increasing the pressure, the length of each lick. Taking this slow and easy would hopefully keep the fire at bay.

Sadie dug her nails into Joan's hair. Slid her legs against Joan's. "So good," she rasped. "More."

Joan softly bit her nipple, causing Sadie to shudder. "More?"

"Mm-hmm."

She moved to Sadie's other breast. "More here?"

"Yeah."

She kissed the tender skin and fine lines. Teased the tip with her tongue. Sadie squirmed to get contact at the apex of her thighs. She was at an awkward angle and struggled to rub against Joan's thigh. Joan skimmed a hand down Sadie's smooth stomach until her fingers found the wet spot on her boxers.

"More here?" Joan murmured, stroking the flannel.

Sadie moaned eagerly, fisting Joan's hair in her hands. "A lot more there."

She rubbed there for a short time before her own arousal shot through her body, shifting the carefully contained fire. *Shit.* She popped Sadie's breast from her mouth and gripped the sides of her shorts.

"You okay?" Sadie said. Her eyes were bright and her cheeks flushed, and damn, she looked absolutely perfect, but also a little concerned.

"I just need a second," Joan said. She took in a steadying breath.

Keep it in your heart.

"Everything's really good," Sadie said. She brushed Joan's hair back. "You're not hurting me. You feel amazing. And taste amazing."

"*You* taste amazing." Joan backed that up by kissing the salty skin between Sadie's gorgeous breasts.

"Kiss me," Sadie said, tugging Joan's shoulders upward.

Joan complied, soothed by the reassurance in Sadie's kisses. She drifted her fingers to the waistband of Sadie's boxers. Sadie hummed her approval and shifted so she was flat on her back.

Joan tickled down one leg and snaked her hand up and under the flannel. She was greeted by Sadie's heat. Her small patch of hair. And how open and wet she was for attention. She slid her fingers through the slick folds, savoring the feel of Sadie's most intimate places.

"*Ungh,* much more there," Sadie groaned. "You don't have to be so gentle."

Joan laughed a little, slight embarrassment creeping in again.

"I'll tell you if something doesn't feel good, but I'll probably just point you to where I need you."

She laughed again. No surprise Sadie would be as candid in the bedroom as she was everywhere else.

Joan made little circles, seeking the spot that made Sadie twitch and jerk. She kept her thumb there and moved two fingers down to her opening. When she tucked them inside, Sadie bit Joan's lower lip.

"Oh, shit," she gasped, wrapping her arms around Joan. "I'm not gonna last long."

The way she ground her hips against Joan's hand, Joan wasn't gonna last long, either. She licked inside Sadie's hungry mouth. Increased the rhythm, the pressure, the circling and tapping.

Sadie released a startled cry and came hard. Joan stayed with the rapid tempo as much as she could, trying not to lose the spot that was making Sadie shudder and shake. A pool of wetness surrounded her hand. Fuck, she needed to taste that.

She glided down Sadie's body, pausing to suck one nipple as she continued fingering her. Then the other nipple. She looked up from kissing a path down Sadie's stomach. Damn, she looked so gorgeous, so wanting, her chest rising and falling.

Sadie shivered and bobbed her head. Her eyes telegraphed one singular command: *Keep going.*

Joan kissed to the elastic waistband. She hated having to stop touching Sadie long enough to yank her boxers off. She flung them off the bed, taking in Sadie's light-brown landing strip, her beautiful pink labia...

Her second secret tattoo of several small, round-petaled flowers on one side of her lower abs.

Joan kissed it, bringing her hands to pull Sadie's thighs farther apart. Normally she'd tease and finger her some more, but she wanted Sadie to come again. And she wanted that on her tongue when it happened.

She pressed her mouth against Sadie's mound, breathing in her essence, licking up the center. Sadie swore and grabbed a handful of Joan's hair. She tucked a leg around Joan, shifting to give her greater access.

Joan's heartbeat pounded wildly. Sadie tasted so fucking perfect. Deliciously savory. The way she was looking down at Joan, watching her, was perfect, too. She wanted this moment to last forever and be over at the same time so she could do it again and again and again.

She slid two fingers back inside and matched the rhythm of her tongue. Sadie seized Joan's other hand and drew it up to her breast. She laced their fingers and guided them over her nipple, panting and moaning.

Heat squiggled up her throat. Right. She could direct it. She'd promised Sadie as much.

She focused the heat into her mouth, just enough to warm her tongue.

A strangled cry flew out of Sadie. She gripped Joan's hair like it was the only thing keeping her alive.

Her body bucked wildly. Joan applied a tiny bit more heat to her tongue. She nearly lost herself making Sadie come so hard, she could barely make a sound. She released Joan's head to grasp the comforter and ride out the remainder of her orgasm.

Sadie's legs flopped to the sides. Her back returned to the bed. Her chest heaved, causing her damp breast to slip from their joined hands. Joan didn't lift her head or stop caressing her on the inside until the very last of the delectable shudders and shivers had ceased.

Sadie dropped a loose hand on Joan's shoulder. She stared at Joan like she couldn't quite believe what had just happened but was happy it had.

Joan removed herself slowly. She kissed the inside of one thigh, then the other. Sadie guided her up until Joan lay against her. She wrapped an arm around Sadie's belly that Sadie gripped with both hands.

A sated smile stretched across her face. "Holy shit," she said, laughing. "I don't know what you did, but whatever it was, never stop."

"I told you I could direct heat where it was most needed." Joan grinned, rather proud of herself.

"*Je-sus.*" Sadie kissed her several deep, grateful times. "I've never felt anything like that in my life."

"Plenty more where that came from," Joan promised.

Sadie blinked at the haze covering her eyes. She readjusted to face Joan, running a hand down her cheek. "Tell me what you want, baby."

Joan gazed into those coffee-brown eyes. She wanted *a lot* of things with Sadie, for Sadie, from Sadie. But there was one thing she needed right now. The pounding in her heart wasn't lust, wasn't a need for release. It pulsed with a deep need for connection.

"You." She tucked her hand around Sadie's waist. "I want you to hold me. I want to feel connected to you."

"That will *not* be a problem," Sadie said. She rolled on top of Joan and sat up. "I can't create literal sparks, but I'll come close."

"I hope I don't create literal sparks, either."

"Keep doing what you're doing with all that."

Keep the fire in your heart.

Sadie skimmed both hands down Joan's breasts, then her stomach. "What are these still doing here?" she teased, tugging on Joan's sleep pants.

"Getting in the way," Joan said. "Please relocate them."

"With pleasure."

Sadie inched them down, taking in every bit of skin as it was exposed. Once she dropped them on the floor, she stared at Joan.

"Your body," she whispered, almost reverently. "God, Joan, you're perfect." She ran her fingers across Joan's abs. "What do you have, a twelve pack? And these *thighs.*"

Her touch moved down one thigh, making Joan shiver. At least she thought it was a shiver. She'd never shivered before.

Sadie dragged her hand up the inside of Joan's thigh, her

pinky skipping over the outer edge of Joan's trimmed dark hair. She shivered harder, marveling at the electric sensation.

Sadie climbed on top, stretching and purring like a sexy, turned-on cat. "I'm obsessed with your body. I can't wait to spend the day exploring it."

"We've got all day," Joan assured her.

"And I intend to use it."

Sadie lowered and kissed her, gliding a leg between Joan's. She didn't make contact with the throbbing center of need, making Joan whimper and rise to meet it. Her wetness slid against Sadie's thigh. The friction made Joan sigh into her mouth.

"Can I touch you?" Sadie asked.

"God, yes," Joan begged against her lips.

Sadie kissed her, then dipped her fingers into Joan's mouth. The unexpected move caused a thrill to dance through her. Sadie used those fingers to tease one of Joan's nipples on the way down. She sucked on Joan's neck, swirling her tongue, using her teeth. It all felt so, so good. The anticipation was delicious torture.

Her hand finally made contact, fingers tickling through Joan's swollen folds. She pressed into them, wanting this so badly.

"Joanie," Sadie exhaled.

Joan could only whimper again. She reveled in Sadie's exploration, her discovery of sensitive spots, driving Joan to moan when the contact made her quiver. She looped her arms around Sadie, wanting more connection. She slid Sadie to the side, wrapping around her.

"Keep doing that," Joan said. "I just need to hold you."

Sadie repositioned her hand. The heel of her palm rubbed high while her fingers dipped low. Joan squeezed an arm and leg around her, kissing her with all the emotions spiraling through her. Their breasts rubbed together, causing the tingles there to travel south.

"Hang on," Sadie muttered. "This isn't working."

She maneuvered her bottom arm until she had both hands

available. One continued teasing Joan on the outside. Then the solid pressure of fingers filled her. A jolt of pleasure rocked Joan's body, making her suck in air.

Sadie's fingers curled, working and tapping as Joan moaned and clenched against them. "Is this good?" Sadie panted. "Harder? Lighter?"

"Faster," Joan gritted against her mouth. She ground her clit into Sadie's hand, wanting to come so fucking badly.

Her orgasm built, and Sadie tongued her mouth deeply and pleasured her thoroughly with her hands, and they were so close, so connected physically, and…

The fire melded into one singular sensation.

Love.

She loved Sadie.

"Come for me, baby," Sadie said.

The plea sent Joan over the edge. She cried out, clutching Sadie, shuddering as the release consumed her. She loved Sadie. Loved her so much. She wanted to stay wrapped in her arms for a lifetime, kissing her as heat escaped and warmed the inside of their mouths.

It was so overpowering, tears coated her eyes. She rode through the orgasm, shaking and shivering. Sadie relaxed her hands but continued gently playing with Joan, kissing her tenderly.

When it was definitely over, Sadie slid her hand across Joan's hip. She leaned back slightly and grinned. Opened her mouth to say something. Then her face morphed into alarm.

"Joan." She reached up to touch her cheek. "Honey. You're crying. What's wrong?"

Joan shook her head. "Nothing," she said with a watery smile. "I'm really happy."

Sadie sat up and wiped at the tears flowing from Joan's eyes. Even though they were evaporating. "Is everything okay? Did I hurt you?"

"No, sweetheart." Joan rested a hand on Sadie's thigh. "I've never… And I just… And I…"

Sadie stared at her, eyes wide and worried.

Joan squeezed her thigh. "I love you. And I've never been in love. Not like this. It overwhelmed me, is all."

She'd never felt more exposed. Vulnerable. Putting her whole heart—her whole true self—out there for another person.

Sadie cupped Joan's face in her hands. "I love you, too," she murmured, leaning in to kiss. "Never like this before."

Relief flowed through Joan's veins. She pulled Sadie to her, kissing with all the joy and promise they shared. Loving Sadie was the way to harness her fire and put it to good use.

Sadie kissed across one cheek, then the other. "No more tears. Not with me."

"Thank you," Joan whispered.

They hugged tightly, then nestled in for a proper snuggle in the warm sunlight. Joan ran her fingers across Sadie's rainbow tattoo. "I can get a tattoo now," she realized.

"Hmm?"

"Mark and I never got any tattoos. They're identifying marks." She let the silence speak the rest.

"You're free to do whatever you want now," Sadie said, skimming a hand up Joan's arm.

Free. Free to love Sadie. Free to pursue new dreams.

Free to be Joan, not Spark.

"I love you, Sadie Eagan," she murmured, a little thrill twirling through her.

"I love you, Joanie Maloney." Sadie smiled brilliantly. She kissed the tip of Joan's nose. "Do you need to take care of any excess fire or anything?"

"Nope. I'm good."

"You were able to contain it?"

"Turns out falling in love and focusing it in my heart does the trick."

Sadie nuzzled her nose. "I'm glad you discovered that. And doubly glad you discovered it with me."

Joan kissed her, running a hand over Sadie's rather perfect rear end. "Me, too."

CHAPTER 23

The heavy metal garage door rolled open. Sadie still wasn't quite sure if she was nervous or excited as Joan drove her black sedan into the Villains' secret lair. She took in the blank cement-block walls, the emptiness, the lack of…anything.

As far as secret lairs went, she'd been expecting more.

"I told you it wasn't much," Joan said, shutting off the ignition.

"Hiding in plain sight." That was something Sadie had been learning about Joan's life. Joan didn't like to draw attention to herself, preferring to be in the shadows.

Sadie was in those shadows now. Or rather, was involved in bringing Joan out of them.

Raising her eyebrows, Joan said, "Are you ready for this?"

Sadie gave her thigh a reassuring squeeze. "You bet. We're in this together."

They exited the car to meet with Mark and Perry. She couldn't bear not touching Joan, so she laced their fingers.

They'd spent the past two days cocooned in Joan's apartment, minimally clothed, talking a lot, learning one another's bodies a *whole* lot. She loved discovering what made Joan feel good. Sex with her was better than anyone could possibly imagine. Oh boy, was it incredible. Bone-meltingly incredible.

But Joan also really enjoyed cuddling, being connected. Which made sense, considering she hadn't had much affection in her life.

Not anymore.

Mark was seated at a long table, reading a text chain on his phone. He glanced up and broke into a smile that resembled his sister's. "Hey, Sadie. Welcome to where the magic happens."

"Thanks. It's strange to be here."

"How are you doing?"

"Much better." She gazed appreciatively at Joan. "Joanie nursed me back to health."

"I'll bet she did," he drawled.

The table held a disorganized mish-mash of fast-food napkins that had been written on. Ohhh, one had her and Joan's initials inside a big red heart. "Aww, babe," Sadie cooed, picking it up.

Joan drew their joined hands to her mouth and kissed Sadie's knuckles.

Mark retched and said, "We'll have none of that here. This is a serious place of business."

"Setting ground rules for Hot and Cold?" Joan said.

A new text on Mark's phone distracted him, causing him to grimace.

A handsome Latino man stepped out of a small washroom in glasses and a deep blue dress shirt and dark slacks. Wait, was this Perry? The gruff longtime Villain? He looked like a sexy TV doctor. Not at all what she'd imagined.

Joan tilted her head. Sadie blinked and opted not to tell the woman she loved that the guy who raised her was pretty darn hot. "Hi...Perry?"

Perry gave her a solid nod. "Are you feeling all right?"

"Mostly healed, thanks."

"Let's get to it."

He sat across the table from Mark. Joan moved to sit beside her brother, then paused as her arm stretched from being attached at the end to Sadie. "Sorry," she said. "I usually sit here."

"Then sit there," Sadie said. She squeezed Joan's fingers.

Joan seemed reluctant to let go—a shared sentiment. But it would be good for them to focus on the conversation instead of how amazing it felt to touch one another. All over. Again and again.

She slid the sweet napkin into her coral-hued skirt pocket and walked around to occupy a chair next to Perry. Giving him a small smile, she asked, "Is there an agenda today?"

"No agenda," Perry said.

"Topic of conversation…" Mark wiggled his phone. "How we're gonna handle the fallout from our little betrayal."

"How bad is it?"

"I've received a steady stream of insults from our criminal contacts. You should see the creative use of curse words. It's actually quite impressive."

He leaned over to show Joan his screen. Concern creased her forehead, though slight amusement toyed at her lips.

"I've gotten the same," said Perry. "From Villains in other cities, too. We didn't just break the code. We did it with the help of the Supers."

"Gossip travels fast in our world," Mark told Sadie. "Nobody wants to be on the wrong side of the wrong side of the law."

Joan had said this would likely be the result. She'd acted like it didn't matter, but villainy had been her life for so long. Even Greta had texted a *WTF?* and hadn't responded to any of Joan's replies. That had to hurt.

Sadie cleared her throat. "Is it okay if I say something?"

"Of course," Joan said. "You're a part of this."

"To give you a different perspective… I mean, I can give you the viewpoint of what the norms are thinking and saying."

Mark bobbed his head encouragingly.

"It's been all over the news that you three—well, your alter-egos—helped the Supers. There are a lot of theories about why, but the overall opinion is that you did a good thing."

"I've also heard people say we wanted to take out our biggest competition," Mark said. "So we played the Supers to get the others out of our way."

"No one ever wants to paint us in a favorable light," Joan said.

"I saw that, too," Sadie said. "But the emphasis has been on all of you working together. And that time will tell what your next move will be." She glanced at one napkin with a simple drawing of a food truck and *HOT and COLD and AWESOME!* written on it. "I think no more activity will send the message that you did it for the right reasons."

Joan met her gaze, the tenderness in her eyes saying she'd done it for the most important reason of all: love.

Perry set a clenched hand on the table. "Who cares what the public thinks? We've lost all credibility with the people who know us."

"We're blacklisted," Joan said. "None of our contacts will want anything to do with us."

"We have to open a food truck now," Mark said. His tone held little joy. It was still their choice, only they had no alternative now.

"At least I won't have to lie about my job anymore," Joan said quietly.

Sadie gave her an understanding, close-mouthed smile.

Perry fidgeted in his rigid plastic chair. He appeared to be uncomfortable, or like he was holding back.

"What's on your mind, Per?" Joan said. "I know you're not thrilled to have—"

"You think? Why would I be thrilled to have my name connected to the Supers? Why would I want every contact I carefully curated for years to disappear overnight because of something you did without my consent?"

Joan and Mark looked at each other.

"No, Joanie, I'm not thrilled that I was dragged into a situation by some random texts while napping. You gave me no time to respond or think about it. You jumped in headfirst without thinking about the consequences. As always."

"Tell us how you really feel," Mark grumbled.

"We needed to act fast to save Sadie," said Joan.

Perry banged his fist on the table. "How many times do I have to tell you? Don't ever trust a Super. It never turns out well."

"Dude, why are you so anti-Super?" Mark said. "Joanie and I have a boatload of reasons. You've never told us what yours are."

Joan's expression said she knew Perry was keeping secrets. "Otis said something the other day. He knew you wanted to work at an art gallery. How?"

Perry gave her a look. "What, you think you're the only ones who got treated like crap by those assholes?"

"Ooh." Mark raised his eyebrows at Sadie. "Perry never swears. It must be good."

Sadie found herself tilting forward with interest.

The only one not interested was Perry. He hemmed and hawed as the seconds ticked by.

"Do you know those guys better than you've let on?" Joan asked. "Like, do you know their real names because they told you?"

"Not exactly," Perry muttered.

"Then what?"

More seconds passed. Finally, he said, "The one time I trusted one of them, it didn't end well."

They waited for him to continue. Perry leaned back and crossed his arms.

"You can't leave us hanging like that," Mark said.

Perry stared him down—the kind of stare that would've freaked Sadie out if it'd been directed at her.

Mark huffed. "You are literally the worst storyteller."

Perry didn't budge.

"You're free now, Per," Joan said. "You can work legitimately in the art world if you want."

"That bridge was burned a long time ago," he said.

"Then you can help with Hot and Cold," Mark said. "Do you know the paperwork involved with starting a business?"

"There's a lot," Sadie chimed in. "More than you think."

"I don't know anything about running a restaurant," Perry said.

Sadie smiled at him. "I do. And I'm going to help."

The handsomely irritated man considered her. "I didn't want any of this, Sadie. These two have been pestering me for weeks about this damn food truck. Once they set their minds to something, they'll grind and grind and wear you down until they get it."

Mark sat up, brightening. "Is that an enthusiastic yes?"

"Come on, Per," Joan said. "We want to do this with you."

Perry held out a hand at them. "You see? Relentless."

Sadie giggled. "They're pretty annoying kids, aren't they?"

"You have no idea." He looked at Joan and Mark. "If this gets you off my back, fine. We'll shift our focus."

The twins whooped and jumped up. They ran over to throw their arms around Perry. "Thank you thank you thank you," they chorused.

Perry acted resigned and exasperated, but the faintest hint of a smile flashed across his mouth. Like a good father figure, he was going along with what his kids wanted. Their happiness mattered a lot to him. You had to respect him for that.

"That's enough." Perry patted their arms before pushing them off. "We still have to talk about what the Supers expect us to do."

"Stop doing crime," Mark said.

"Do we have to turn things over to them? Return stuff we took?"

Joan shrugged. "Whatever it is, we have to do it."

She stepped to Sadie and rubbed her back. Leaning down, she murmured, "It's all happening, sweetheart."

Pure happiness danced throughout her body. "I can't wait to get started."

"I don't know why we'd have to return things," Perry said. "The agreement is for us to walk away."

Mark smiled at his sister. "That's why, Per."

Perry glanced over, then seemed to comprehend that Joan was going to do whatever it took to get the life she wanted. And deserved.

"Did you know, Sadie…" Mark's grin turned wicked. "Our very own Péricles Barbosa has an MBA, which for a long time I thought meant Master of Butt Air. Turns out it has something to do with business."

"Master of Butt Air?" Sadie laughed.

Joan slid an arm around her shoulders. "He is that. But he's also pretty book smart. I think with what each of us brings to the table… The hot." She nodded at each of them in turn. "The cold, the business acumen, and the people skills, we have the perfect recipe for success."

"Perfect recipe," Perry muttered. "I see what you did there."

"Let's not dwell on the bullshit." Mark started spreading out the note-covered napkins. "Yeah, we'll have to deal with some transitional crap, but one thing we never do is dwell."

"I've dwelled many times on why I brought you two into my life."

Joan and Mark took that in stride. Sarcasm was their familial love language. More extreme than her own family's dynamic, but at least these three were open with one another. Sadie still hadn't told her parents about being abducted, and quite honestly, might never. They would be relentlessly overprotective for the rest of her days.

"Let's clean this place up." Joan dropped a kiss on top of Sadie's head. "Make it presentable for…well… Just make it presentable."

For the Supers, perhaps? Or to sell it? Maybe cleaning it up meant—

Wait. When she had questions, she had to vocalize them. "Do

you mean actually *clean* it, or remove things you don't wany anyone to find?"

"Both." Joan took a step back. Her cue she didn't want to say more.

"Let's start with the kitchenette." Mark made his way to that makeshift area.

Joan held her hand out, which Sadie clasped. Whatever she wasn't proud of, or didn't want Sadie to find, they'd work through it. She'd already demonstrated wanting to do better by giving money to the living artists whose pieces graced her home with the message *"I very much enjoy your work. –Spark"*

Joan was hoping to transfer money in her illicit ways until the Supers stopped her. It was, after all, for good. With not so good money.

Whew, the moral conundrum was a lot.

Sadie took in the sad little sink, the old countertops, the fridge that sounded like it was about to take off into space. "You're not planning on cooking here, are you?"

"God no," Joan said. "We can use Mark's kitchen. It's gourmet."

"You know how Joanie and Perry love art?" Mark grinned. "I love kitchen."

A handwritten sign taped above the sink caught his attention.

Keep Our Lair Beautiful! Wash your damn dishes. That means <u>you</u> Irving.

Irving was Hide. Which meant all of the Supervillains used to meet here. Which meant Trick, Hide and Volt's stuff had to be among the things they wanted to clean out.

Mark ripped the sign off the cement wall. "One thing we never do is dwell."

EPILOGUE

Three months later

Sadie smiled at the trio of customers as she handed their orders out the service window on the food truck. "Thanks so much for coming to our grand opening. Please let us know how you like your sandwiches."

Joan's familiar warmth brushed against her as she held a wrapped sandwich out the window. "One Irish Spring."

"Thank you," the businessman said as he took it. "The names of your dishes are catchy."

Joan gave Sadie the adoring grin she loved. "They were all this beautiful lady's idea."

"Variations on warm and chilly things," Sadie said.

"Let us know if you have any critiques. We just opened, so we're looking for feedback."

The man thanked them both, pulling at the white deli paper.

Mouthwatering scents of freshly cooked ham and crisp veggies filled the truck. Sadie took a big gulp of water, then leaned out and checked the sky over Friendship Park. A rare overcast day in Vector City. No rain in the forecast that afternoon, so hopefully customers wouldn't stay away. She had to hit the sidewalk to drum up business.

"Doing great, Team Hot and Cold," Joan said as she stood at the flat-top grill.

"We're looking good, too," Mark added from where he was dropping ingredients for his green chutney into the blender.

Their vertical-striped aprons went with the rest of Hot and Cold's theme of pinks and pale blues. One of the many decisions they'd made over the past few months. Lots of trial and error and taste testing of sandwiches. Lots of design ideas for the truck.

Joan held her palm over the caramelized onions atop a thick slice of sourdough bread and three-cheese blend. She gave it an easy blast of fire to melt it into yummy gooey-ness.

The rear door opened, and Perry climbed inside. "Hey, Per," Joan said.

"Péricles!" Mark called.

Sadie greeted him as well. Perry scooted behind her with a file folder tucked under his arm. He pointed to the licenses taped to the service window. "Good visibility on those. How's it been going?"

"Pretty good," Mark said. "People seem to like the food so far."

"I've only gotten positive feedback," Sadie said. "My friend Amit stopped by earlier and said it was one of the best BLTs he's ever had. And he's my former boss, so I can attest that he doesn't give compliments lightly."

"Good." Perry flipped through his papers. He'd jumped into budgets and timelines like a champ and had kept them on task. He'd be a real asset for future investments and projects. Sadie and Joan were hopeful it was occupying him enough not to miss his former way of making a living. He really did enjoy all the office work nobody else wanted to do.

"Are your parents coming today?" he asked.

"Maybe," Sadie said. "They hate driving into the city."

Joan spatula-ed the November Rain off the flat-top. "They're still not keen on supporting the woman who caused their daughter to quit her stable job and follow a wild whim."

"They don't know you well enough. Yet." She smiled at Joan. "But they will."

Because Joan wasn't going anywhere.

"Let me meet them," Mark said. "Parents love me."

"Mark does way better with parents," Joan said.

"Mark's not the person I love." Sadie blew him a kiss. "Though I do love you, Markie."

"Back at 'cha, Sades," he said with a wink.

She'd grown to love Joan's twin like her own brother with his hilariously crude sense of humor. And grown used to his stopping by at all hours to hang out. It was clear Mark and Joan were so close because they were lonely. Their old friends—not that they'd really been friends—had disappeared. Greta had only recently started talking to Joan again.

"Nyah's coming tomorrow," Sadie said. "And a bunch of my friends are planning on it this weekend. So we'll get some good customers to provide honest input."

Joan passed the sandwich out the window, then did a double-take. Her hand flexed.

Sadie followed her line of sight. Zee stood beneath a nearby tree, hands in their wide-leg trouser pockets.

"Really?" Joan muttered. "Today?"

"What?" Mark left the prep counter to join them. He fisted both hands. "Our pal's making sure we're staying on the up-and-up."

"We should go talk to them. They could be checking to make sure everything's up to code or whatever."

"Or that we're not flash-frying difficult customers," Mark said.

"Or maybe to congratulate you," Sadie pointed out. Those two could be so dramatic.

"I'll watch the window," Perry said, even though he'd pinned himself against the sinks.

"Come on." Sadie waved for him to join them. "I'm sure Zee wants to say hi."

He stared at the nearby panini press.

Realization dawned across Joan's face. "Perry! You still haven't turned in all your shit to the Supers?"

"Per," Mark said. "You promised."

"I'm working on it," Perry said.

Their deal with the Supers ended up being conditional upon the three of them turning in their Villain gear and computers and only using the warehouse to park the food truck. Mark and Joan had done their part months ago. It hadn't been easy, but it was a necessary concession to wipe the slate clean.

"Damn it," Mark said. "You could mess this whole agreement up."

"*I'm working on it,*" Perry gritted between his teeth.

"Why don't you work on profit and loss statements?" Joan said. She tossed a cleaning rag at him.

"I am."

Mark and Joan shook their heads and hopped out the back. Sadie gave him a look that said *Try harder* and stepped onto the curb. She'd learned Perry did things when he was good and ready.

Every time she saw the exterior of the truck, happiness welled in her chest. The bold colors, the sharp magenta-and-azure logo she'd designed, the Progress Pride flags and rainbows painted here and there. She was so proud of their hard work, and glad to support the woman she loved.

Zee ambled away from the small crowd at the line of food trucks. They shared a hello with Sadie. "I like the new hair," she said.

"Thanks." Zee ran a hand over their shaggy raven-black 'do.

The two of them never acknowledged Sadie knew Zee was

Race, and that was why they randomly showed up to have short, awkward conversations with the former Villains. She liked Zee, and got the sense the Super liked her.

"Checking on us again?" Mark said.

"Just here for lunch," Zee said. "I heard your sandwiches aren't half bad."

"They're great," Sadie said. "Our hot sandwiches are toasted and topped with cold toppings to give them a little extra crunch. A local bakery supplies us with the sourdough bread. You can have the option of vegetarian, vegan or gluten-free, too. We use a panini press for those so there's no cross-contamination."

"We'd be happy to sell you a sandwich," Mark said. "At full price."

Joan snorted, and even Zee looked slightly amused. "Of course," they said. Their gaze settled on the sky-blue food truck. "Perry didn't want to chat with me?"

"He's watching the truck," said Mark.

"Funny how he never seems to be available when I'm around."

"So weird," Joan said, making an exaggerated shrug.

Sadie gently pushed one of her arms down. "We have the necessary paperwork in order if you want to take a look."

Zee's smirk deepened. "Food truck permits are a bit low on my priority list."

"We've done everything right thanks to Sadie," Joan said, squeezing Sadie against her. "We really couldn't have done this without her."

They shared a smile that spoke of the gratitude and love and respect they had for each other. Because man oh man, her love for Joanie Maloney grew more every day.

"She knows all about branding and customer service," Mark said. "And licenses and shit like that."

Joan grinned at her. "It's good practice. Sadie's going to open a coffeehouse. She makes *the best* coffee drinks."

"Once Hot and Cold is stable," Sadie amended.

Leaning slightly toward Zee, Joan said, "She's doing it with her own money."

"That's good," Zee said.

"It's important to me," Sadie said. She understood how Hot and Cold had to be funded, but Sadie's Café needed to be legit from the get-go.

"We're finding lots of ways to save money," Joan said. Her grin widened. "We moved in together last month. What would've been her rent money goes straight into savings."

"And we're growing vegetables on the balcony since this jerk pigeon didn't follow me from my old place."

"We'll be using them in our recipes," Joan added.

Sadie struggled mightily not to kiss her. "We're figuring everything out."

Joan's way of helping with the start-up of Sadie's Café was to keep paying all the utilities for the apartment that was formerly just hers but was now filled with Sadie's patterned throw pillows and clothes. Their shared office (sans a keypad on the door) was cheerful and comfy thanks to Sadie's furniture. Its closet now housed Joan's impressive sneaker collection. And besides, it just made sense, with Sadie basically living there since Trick and his associates had been locked up. They hated spending a single night not tangled together.

It was also good to be there when Joan had bad dreams so she could hold her, reassure her everything was okay. Joan claimed the dreams were just weird visions of people she knew staring at her, but there had to be something deeper at play. Communication was still a work in progress.

"If you need assistance with getting a loan or insurance…" Zee's smirk reappeared. "I have some friends who might be able to put in a good word for you."

"That would be amazing," Sadie said. A recommendation from a Super would definitely help.

Zee nodded at Joan and Mark. "You've managed to keep these two in line. It's the least we could do."

"Hey, we're trying," Mark said.

"We're doing a damn good job," said Joan. Sadie gave her a side hug in support.

"You've been behaving," Zee said. "From what I can tell. But I'll still be watching."

"Creepy," Mark mumbled.

"Give me a reason not to."

He cocked an eyebrow at Zee. "You couldn't look away if you tried."

The Superhero took it in stride. "I would love to occupy my time in better ways."

Sadie subtly tapped Joan's hip. Joan did the same. What was going on with those two?

"I imagine you have oodles of free time now that the city's been rid of Supervillains," Mark said.

"That doesn't mean there aren't things that need to be addressed," Zee said.

It seemed so quiet in Vector City these days. Almost too quiet. People were still wondering if and when Spark, Ice and Breeze were going to resurface.

Mark waved at the food truck. "Do you want a sandwich or not?"

"Excellent customer service," Zee drawled.

The two of them started for Hot and Cold. Sadie gestured with her chin. "What do you think that's about?"

Joan studied her brother making a pretend annoyed expression. "He does like to tease the Supers."

"But he's like, *teasing*. And look at Zee. I think they like it."

Zee's amusement was evident. They even tilted a little toward Mark as they verbally sparred.

"Huh." Joan's brows met in the middle. "They do flirt more than either of them will admit." She laughed and added, "I don't know if he could actually go for a Super, no matter how hot they are."

"I went for a very hot Super," Sadie said, patting Joan's butt.

"Emphasis on *hot*." A whisper of heat seeped off her into Sadie's side.

"You are *very* good at using that talent to its full extent. Particularly with your mouth."

Sparks flickered in Joan's amazing amber eyes. She leaned in and gave Sadie a perfect kiss. "God, I love you," she murmured.

"Love you, too." Sadie rested a hand on Joan's chest. "I'm so proud of you. And Mark."

"'Cause you're stuck with him."

"You Malone twins are a package deal."

Joan looped her arms around Sadie. "So are we."

She looked into those eyes filled with love, and yes, a few horny sparks. But also truth and honesty. Pure Joan Malone.

Sadie nestled her arms around Joan and agreed, "So are we."

That's not the end of Joan and Sadie's story.

Things are a little too quiet in Vector City. And do you really think a former Villain can just walk away? And what's up with Perry and the Supers?

More adventures await in FANNING THE FLAMES, Book 2 in the Vector City Supers trilogy.

If you enjoyed SECRET SPARK, I would be forever grateful if you could leave a quick review. Reviews are invaluable to help authors gain visibility and readers connect with new books. Win-win!

. . .

To stay up to date on the latest with my books and events and the wild journey that is publishing, please visit my website to sign up for my monthly newsletter. You'll also get access to exclusive free bonus content available only to newsletter subscribers: www.kellyfarmerauthor.com

Thanks!
Kelly

ACKNOWLEDGMENTS

This book was truly a labor of love. My first venture into indie publishing has been a lot of fun, and I absolutely could not have done it without the help of so many wonderful and generous friends.

First and foremost, all my thanks to Shannyn Schroeder. Talking with you calmed my fears about going indie. Thank you for answering *all* of my texts and questions, and for beta reading. I don't know what I would do without you!

Mackenzie Walton was, as always, a dream editor. I so appreciate your enthusiasm for this world of heroes and villains and your knowledge of comics.

Steve Buccellato gave me the exact cover I'd been dreaming of for this book. I love how it perfectly captures Joan and Sadie's bright and colorful love story.

Julie Cassidy, thank you for the copyedits and attempts at explaining what I keep doing wrong with hyphens and commas. Sorry I still don't get them.

Chandra Blumberg, Beccan James and Kelly Smith, many, many thanks for your insightful beta reads. And also hugs to Rachelle Paige Campbell, Bryn Donovan and Pamala Knight for your excitement and encouragement.

A lot of authors stepped up to give support and resources about the world of indie publishing. Huge thanks to Jeanne Oates Estridge, Rachel Lacey, Kerry Lockhart, and Mary Oldham. And also everyone who's so giving of their time and experiences in the Wide for the Win Facebook group.

I'm super-duper grateful for the several awesome critiques given at Chicago-North Romance Writers meetings. You all rock!

Shout-out to R.L. Merrill for inviting me into the Happily Ever After Collective, and Avery Flynn for organizing it so I could write the silly little novella this book grew out of.

Bottom-of-my-heart appreciation to The Super Readers (my awesome ARC review crew!) and reviewers who were like, "Sure, I'll read this wacky supervillain book!" I can't tell you how much it means to me that you took the time to share in the ridiculous fun of this story.

As always, my deepest thanks go to you, awesome reader. My hope with every book is to bring joy to your life and give you a happy escape for a few hours.

Secret Spark is at its core a story about what it means to be extraordinary in a world that wants people to conform. If you've ever been told not to stand out, or to do things the way everyone else does, or not to embrace who you truly are, find that spark inside of you and shine!

ALSO BY KELLY FARMER

The Out on the Ice Series:

Out on the Ice (Book 1)

Unexpected Goals (Book 2)

Calling the Shots (Book 3)

It's a Fabulous Life

ABOUT THE AUTHOR

Kelly Farmer (she/her) has been writing romance novels since junior high. While the stories have changed, one theme remains the same: everyone deserves to have a happy ending. She is the bestselling author of queer contemporary romances with snarky humor and lots of heart.

When not writing, she enjoys being outside in nature, quoting from eighties movies, listening to all kinds of music, and petting every dog she comes in contact with. All of these show up in her books. Kelly lives in the Chicago area, where she swears every winter is her last one there.

To connect with Kelly, talk about current TV binges, and subscribe to her newsletter for access to free bonus stories, head over to:

www.kellyfarmerauthor.com

www.ingramcontent.com/pod-product-compliance
Lightning Source LLC
Chambersburg PA
CBHW011852300726
48970CB00009B/2756